Shell Game

A Cadillac Holland Mystery

INDIES UNITED PUBLISHING HOUSE, LLC
P.O. BOX 3071
QUINCY, IL 62305-3071

www.indiesunited.net

Special Thanks

This story was conceived over cocktails with friends who have called Lexington, Missouri home for many years. Adding this book to the catalog of Cadillac Holland Mysteries has allowed me to delve into Cadillac's history and personality, and I hope loyal readers will appreciate learning more of what makes him tick.

Thanks go out to Joann and Mark Ritter for directing me to locals who could make sure the Lexington I have described is as accurate and contemporary as possible.

Special thanks to Carol Levy for her gracious hospitality, and for providing the use of her short-term rental during our visit and as lodging for Cadillac during his fictional stay in Lexington.

Thanks also to Sue Webster and Monte Lauderdale at Wentworth Military Academy Museum, who were generous with their time to help me be sure the details about life as a cadet are as precise as a uniform's creases.

I apologize in advance that my character's time at Wentworth was not as pleasant as most of its graduates enjoyed.

Prologue

Cultural theft has been a problem for as long as there have been things to steal. The tombs of Egypt's pharaohs were supposedly emptied by the same workers who built them.

What constitutes the theft of an antiquity has come into sharper focus as the countries which were too long the primary targets of cultural theft have begun taking steps to identify and reclaim their cultural treasures plundered by conquering armies, archaeologists, organized bands of thieves, and run of the mill tourists.

The British Museum currently has many times more Egyptian artifacts in its collection than the Grand Egyptian Museum in Cairo, Egypt owns. There is an old joke that the only reason the Pyramids of Giza are not in the British Museum is that they were too large to move.

Recent investigations have exposed Sotheby's Auction House's link to the pillaging of temples in Cambodia, and the owners of the craft store chain Hobby Lobby were forced to return thousands of artifacts stolen from southern Iraq. The quantity and dollar value of antiquities in private collections is incalculable.

American art experts and museum curators braved the battlegrounds of World War II to secure endangered landmarks and repatriated thousands of artworks Hitler's generals stole for their own collections. No efforts were made to embed such teams with the Coalition troops who captured Baghdad in 1991, and the result was the wholesale stripping of the Iraqi National Museum's antiquities during the initial weeks of disorder which followed the capital's fall.

Iraq is considered the cradle of civilization by most archaeologists and historians. Multiple cultures rose and fell on its shifting sands long before the city states of the Greeks and the rise of the Roman empire. The historical value of its artifacts far exceeds their dollar value. The Iraqi National Museum's staff had the foresight to hide as much of the museum's inventory as possible once the fall of Baghdad became a foregone conclusion in 2003. The museum's subsequent pillaging was spearheaded by thieves the museum staff believes had planned their raid long in advance. Specific artifacts were targeted, and most of the replica pieces were left behind, despite not being marked as such. Items from the museum's collection continue to surface and are returned thanks to the efforts of an international team of law enforcement officers and antiquities experts.

The radical caliphates which have sprung up in the Middle East over the past thirty years have chosen to make the destruction of national heritage sites a priority, while quietly financing their jihads by selling the antiquities they steal from those sites on the black market.

UNESCO has claimed that antiquities trafficking, apart from the theft of paintings and other objects, may involve as much as ten billion dollars a year in illegal sales and purchases. The FBI formed its own Art Crime Team in 2004, and its agents have recovered over twenty thousand individual pieces of stolen art worth over $900 million dollars during their first twenty years in existence. The Department of Homeland Security added its own division to interdict the trafficking of stolen art and antiquities in 2007. The federal agents of their Cultural Property, Art, and Antiquities Program began receiving specialized training from the United States Department of State's Cultural Heritage Center and the Smithsonian Institute in 2009. HSI's agents follow credible leads alongside international, federal, and local law enforcement to pursue and recover cultural artifacts and return them to their nation of origin.

Dedicated To

Gregg Barrows, USN (Ret.)

1957 – 2023

And In Appreciation of Other Friends Who Served

David Campbell, USMC

Ginger Lux, USNR

Erica Lanter–Stewart, USA

Bill Tatum, USA

Monday

June 21ˢᵗ, 2010

A true friend is someone who is there for you when they'd rather be anywhere else.

-Len Wein

One

Daniel Logan, Attorney-at-Law, planted a pair of .22 caliber bullets behind my left ear late one night in June of 2010. This was in retaliation for my exposing his connection to a Russian mobster named Dudiyn Alekhin, and for thwarting the Russian gangster's well-thought-out plan to become the Don Corleone of New Orleans. Alekhin placed this unassuming attorney in New Orleans immediately after Hurricane Katrina had done its own damage to my hometown. The disruption the storm brought to the criminal justice system allowed Logan to find and exploit weaknesses in the court system and in the laws themselves. Logan spent the first five years of the city's post-storm recovery defending a precisely chosen sort of criminal. All of them committed the exact sort of crimes Dudiyn Alekhin had in mind to advance the resurgent New Orleans underworld. A titanium plate in my skull saved my life and drove home to the attorney and his client that not only was I not going to be easily removed, but that I would continue to stymie them at every turn. The plate that saved my life this time was only there because my skull had been cracked open in a previous attempt on my life nearly six years earlier. I tell you this not so you can be impressed by my luck, or to offer comfort for the way life and death seem to be playing a game of hot potato with my soul.

I share these details mostly because not dying meant I entered the hellish bureaucracy of the Louisiana State Police's human resources department rather than the actual Hades that surely awaits me. I could not return to duty until I convinced the same state psychologist who objected to my initial hiring that I was not suffering debilitating flashbacks or harboring severe anxieties from having been shot yet again. Doctor Jorgens had been justifiably concerned with the VA's PTSD diagnosis in the military records submitted with my application to join the Louisiana State Police. It took the intervention of a politically connected uncle to secure my place in their ranks. Uncle Felix had also arranged for me to leave the academy as an Inspector 2 thanks to my background in military intelligence.

Logan's assassination attempt had inflicted nothing more than a flesh wound, but I phrased my responses to Doctor Jorgens's questions about my reaction to the attack to at least sound as if I took the attack seriously. The state police cannot afford to employ a detective who is cavalier about life and death. Dr. Jorgens was satisfied that I was successfully dealing with being shot while also emotionally juggling my almost-fiancé leaving town because *she* could not handle the latest attempt on my life.

The doctor cleared me to begin two weeks of desk duty before returning to active duty. Being sidelined came at an inconvenient time. The Chief of Detectives was about to retire, so I went on vacation for the two weeks rather than face whatever administrative tasks he might find for me to do until his replacement took office.

Hopefully this explains why I was wide awake at two o'clock on a Monday morning holding a half-empty plastic cup imprinted with "Huge Ass Beer" and watching a street hustler shuffle a trio of red cups on an old TV tray. He was pocketing five bucks at a time from anyone dumb or drunk enough to think they were going to beat a short con's game that pre-dates Cleopatra. Roux, my seventy-five-pound pit bull and unofficial K-9 partner, was mesmerized by the hustler's hand speed.

The trick in this game was to keep up a patter that distracted the mark while he shuffled the trio of cups. He allowed his marks to 'win' enough times that they started placing large bets. The hustler's movements became subtly different, and he made eye contact just long enough to change the position of the ball from where the mark had been tracking it. I was much less concerned with this hustler's practiced trickery than I was that he might be working with one or more of the Quarter's pickpockets to rob the distracted crowd the hustler had attracted. I was about to flash my badge and let the young man know it was time to move along when my phone rang.

"You have reached me," I said after checking the caller ID. The incoming number displayed as Caller Unknown on the screen. While I had no idea who was calling me at that hour of the night, the caller had to know me because this was my private line.

"Ghost?" a male voice inquired. Now I knew the mystery caller was someone from very far in my past. I have been called 'Cadillac' nearly my entire four years' of posting in New Orleans. The nickname the caller used dated to my days in the 75th Rangers. I had gradually developed my habit of distancing myself from my teammates after burying one too many of them. I earned the nickname Ghost because I was always the first to lose contact with my Army buddies as soon as one of us left our unit.

"Who is this?" I asked. The connection was not very good.

"Brian," the caller said. "Brian Hollis."

Brian Hollis was my high school roommate for three years at Wentworth Military Academy in Lexington, Missouri. We served one tour in the Rangers together. The last time I had seen Brian was after my Army discharge and I was looking for work with the private security outfit he was operating in Iraq at the time.

"Are you in New Orleans?" I asked. Perhaps he was in town on business and was looking for a familiar face to join him for a late-night cocktail.

"No such luck," he said with a hollow chuckle. "I am in serious legal trouble. That's where I am."

"I am not a lawyer," I reminded him. "How much trouble are you in and where are you?"

"Think lawyers, guns, and money. I am being persecuted for doing the right thing." Referencing a Warren Zevon song did not satisfactorily address the first part of my two-part question. "I am on my way to Lexington. I can explain everything better in person. Can you meet me there on Saturday?"

"Probably not," I decided. "Do you have any other friends you can call?"

"Friends got me into this," he answered cryptically.

"Well, good luck," I said and waited for Brian to hang up.

I felt bad for less than a minute about refusing to get involved in his legal woes. I could not forget that I received the skull plate which saved my life doing a job he recommended I take. What he led me to believe was a State Department-sanctioned operation proved to be an illicit conspiracy by a private contractor intent upon influencing the election of the Iraqi Transitional Government. I was not inclined to trust Brian, and his vague answers did not overcome my reluctance to lend a hand to a former brother in arms.

The first colorful tints of Monday morning's sunrise were illuminating the corner of Esplanade and Frenchman Street and the Marigny neighborhood across from the French Quarter by the time Roux and I returned to our apartment above the Italian-Creole bistro on Decatur Street where I have a partner's stake. Brian's call was forgotten by the time I crawled into bed, but that damn song was stuck in my head.

Two

Ralph Easter and I were enjoying cocktails at Strada Ammazarre's L-shaped bar that evening. Ralph works for the State Department, and I do not believe Ralph is his real name. He was responsible for monitoring and blocking Iraq's efforts to extradite Tony Venzo and me to answer for our roles in the illegal operation which nearly ended my life.

I was lavishing free cocktails on Ralph to celebrate his thirty-fifth birthday and I was doing my best to keep a friendly look on my face while the confirmed bachelor provided his unsolicited advice on my love life.

"Face it," Ralph said before sharing another of his philosophies. "People get sucked into a relationship because the sex is like the odor inside a new car. Sooner or later, that new car smell dissipates and leaves you with a beast that needs constant maintenance."

"It's why I prefer cars that challenge me to do my best driving," I said. I should have told him in plain English that the reason Katie and I had worked as a couple was that we were compatible outside of bed. The great sex was just a bonus.

"Now there is a new car I wouldn't mind spinning around the block," Ralph said and adjusted his barstool to watch the woman who had just walked into the restaurant. Our high-backed barstools were at the street end of the bar so I could keep an eye on the door and the dining room beyond the service well. We were tucked into a corner, so most of the regulars and guests did not notice us.

Jason, the happy hour bartender, moved to the center of the bar to take the striking woman's drink order. She was a tall blonde who looked closer to forty than thirty. She wore a knee-length red dress with a halter top and very low back. The garment covered less skin than it exposed. I could literally hear Ralph panting.

She handed Jason a gold Amex card and ordered a bottle of Krug champagne. Jason poured her first flute and twisted the bottle into the ice filled bucket that he set on the bar just to the left of her seat. The bar only keeps six bottles of it in stock at a time. I suspected that she had ordered the Krug to set a price for her company that few men standing along the bar could afford.

She looked around and then leaned forward to ask Jason something. He pivoted and pointed directly at Ralph and me. She gave a small shake of her head but then looked at the two of us again. She downed her flute in one long gulp and continued to stare at us as Jason silently refilled the slender wineglass.

There was a visceral intensity to the woman's expression, but she allowed a thin smile to crack the line of her lipstick as she approached us. I had initially failed to recognize the woman because she was the last female I expected to walk into my bar. This was not going to be any scene from Casablanca.

"Make your escape while you can," I advised Ralph as the blonde beauty closed the distance between us and I finally put a name to her face. He ignored the advice and offered his seat to her. His gentlemanly act allowed him to stand behind her at an angle which allowed him to admire her tanned back and partially exposed breasts. She touched his cheek as she thanked him for his manners and made sure he had a good look at her cleavage before she swiveled the stool to face me.

"Hello, Princess," I greeted Alexis Hollis with her derogatory nickname from our childhood in hopes it might make her reconsider speaking with me. Brian Hollis had lobbied for his kid sister to be our military high school's Queen for three years running, but she had received fewer votes each year she was nominated.

"I didn't recognize you. Have you had plastic surgery?" Alexis may have thought this was an insult in turn.

"I needed some reconstructive surgery a few years back, and my sister saw an opportunity to make me handsome." Tulip had provided the plastic surgeon who reconstructed my face over my rebuilt skull in an Italian hospital with an actor's photograph she had ripped out of a magazine in the hospital's waiting room because she had no recent pictures of me.

"Kudos to your sister." Alexis touched my face before firmly pressing her hand to my arms and chest. "And you work out. Very nice."

"I am going to pass on swapping compliments," I informed her and fell silent. She did not need my validation to know she was even more attractive than she was as a fifteen-year-old harlot who had amused herself by seducing my classmates.

"How are you doing these days?" she asked, to salvage the conversation.

"I am getting by." I leaned far enough back to stop her touching my face.

"I should say so," she laughed. "You own half this place and still find time to play cops and robbers for the state police. I always imagined you were going to be a lifer in the Army."

I had not spoken to Alexis Hollis in over twenty years. There was no rational explanation for how she knew this much about me.

"Plans change," I replied and waited to hear what else she knew.

"You seem to have changed course very well," Alexis said and waved her empty champagne flute. Jason appeared with practiced timing to refill her glass. He pressed three fingers to the stem and barely raised his left eyebrow to let me know her rate of consumption exceeded the bar's usual tolerance. We prefer not to overserve and create problematic guests.

"It's been an interesting transition," I continued to deflect her attempts to act as if we were old friends. "What brings you to town?"

The man sitting to Alexis' left stood up to answer the hostess's call that his table was ready. Ralph jumped into the empty seat rather than make a quiet exit.

"He is never going to tell me how the two of you know one another, so let me ask you," Ralph joined the conversation I was doing my best to end.

"My brother was his roommate at Wentworth," she told him before turning back to me to fill in the lost years I had not asked her to explain. "I got married straight out of high school and divorced six months later. It turns out I am not a one-guy kind of girl. I kept my married name because I like the name Paradis more than Hollis. I majored in Art History at Stephens College and then I earned my doctorate in archaeology from Brown. That was where I developed my passion for Persian history and antiquities. I do provenance research for museums and private collectors, but I have done consulting work for the government, as well. My meal ticket is finding antiquities for private collectors. I am in town to meet with a client, but I would love to pitch you on investing in antiquities. Nobody is making any new ones, so they keep increasing in value, just like real estate.”

“What is providence?” Ralph asked. I thought he was making a joke, but he was so busy gawking at Alexis that he completely misunderstood the word she said.

“Provenance, not providence, silly,” Alexis managed to correct and flirt with Ralph in four words. “Provenance is the certification that a given piece of artwork has followed a legal path of ownership, is not stolen, and is not fake. I sort through receipts and any evidence the owner can produce before I certify an item is authentic and legal to sell or buy.”

The way Alexis rocked her legs was meant to let me know she remained interested in adding me to her long list of conquests. I placed my right hand atop her leg and squeezed until she stopped moving her knee. She pouted again. “I am not a minor anymore, Cooter. We can do all those things you wouldn’t do with me when we were kids, and maybe some things we’ve both learned since then. Come on, we are finally consenting adults.”

“This is me at my most adult and very least consenting, Alexis,” I said and pulled my hand from her leg. “I am flattered that you still want to collect my scalp, but I am never going to sleep with you. You are still my roommate’s kid sister. Speaking of which, have you spoken to Brian lately?”

I hoped Alexis might have more information on Brian’s situation than I had allowed him to share with me before I refused to be pulled into his drama.

“We have not spoken in years,” she informed me. “Our

politics are not on the same page. I have no interest in knowing what his mercenaries are up to and he doesn't want to listen to my rants about the number of antiquities and historical landmarks which have been lost thanks to the wars he fought."

She had answered my question and I saw nothing to be gained by reminding her that Brian and I had fought in the same military conflicts.

"Are you afraid I am too much of a woman for you to handle?" she tried to return the conversation to her own topic. This made my decision to remove myself from the conversation that much easier.

"I am afraid of finding myself in whatever briar patch you are trying to pull me into," I informed her. "Ralph here is more adventurous. Today is his birthday and I am sure he needs a good birthday spanking. Why don't you two enjoy dinner on the house?"

Alexis reached into the purse slung over her right shoulder and pulled out a silver business card holder. She removed one card and silently placed it beside my last Manhattan of the evening. The embossed card bore her married name, Alexis Paradis, and addresses on three continents, along with a phone number for each address. She turned the card over to show me a handwritten phone number.

"My cell number," she explained. "Let's not waste another decade."

"Impressive." I studied the card in my hand, but I was already dismissing her suggestion.

"I am serious," she stressed and took my hand.

"That is what I am afraid of," I deflected one last time.

Alexis smiled but she could not conceal the look of disappointment a child has when a parent substitutes their favorite ice cream with an apple. I left the two of them at the bar and retreated to the kitchen. I took a plate of spaghetti Bolognese from the kitchen's service window and locked myself in my apartment.

Tuesday

June 22, 2010

A real friend is one who walks in when the rest of the world walks out.

-Walter Winchell

Three

Ralph checked in with me the next morning. He had spent the night in Alexis' suite at the Ritz-Carlton and decided to call in sick rather than try to explain why he had missed his morning meetings. He wanted to meet me for lunch to discuss the questions Alexis had peppered him with all night. I felt a bit less paranoid now that someone else shared my concerns that a woman I had not seen in over twenty years was so well informed about my current life.

We agreed to meet at the small booth set in a niche within Napoleon House's bar area when they opened in half an hour. The sunlit barroom promotes the establishment's decades of service as a tavern. Random framed photographs and magazine articles about the place cover remnants of the wallpaper clinging to the former residence's original plaster dating to 1794. The state Supreme Court building fills the next block, and the kitchen was doing a brisk lunch time take-out business with judge's clerks and appellate lawyers. This constant flow of impatient foot traffic provided more privacy than a table on the slower paced patio offered.

Ralph entered through the French doors opening onto St. Louis Street in the same clothes he had worn the night before, minus the necktie. The final bill for his birthday dinner and Alexis's taste in champagne was more than two weeks of his government salary, but it was a small price for me to pay to escape that situation.

We both ordered bowls of gumbo and I added a charcuterie board along with a pair of the bar's signature Pimm's cup cocktails.

"Please do not regale me with any details about last night," I beseeched Ralph once the drinks arrived. He grinned and nodded as he raised the cocktail to his lips.

"That's tasty," Ralph commented as he set the drink atop the wooden tabletop which had been worn smooth by thousands of previous patrons. "There are things you should know about your friend, though."

"Tell me anything that doesn't involve sex," I rephrased my plea. I thought this might shorten the conversation by hours. His hair was matted, and he looked exhausted. He had not bothered to fully button his shirt. His necktie was folded in his shirt pocket. I thought I saw small bite marks on his neck and hairless chest.

"She claims she is here on business, but she refused to tell me the name of her client. All I know is that the guy is an attorney whose client is looking for someone to provide provenance for a sizeable collection of antiquities from somewhere in the Middle East. She seemed a lot more nervous than excited at the prospect. I think she was hoping to rope you into being her bodyguard while she is in town," Ralph briefed me on what little had been spoken between the two of them over dinner. Ralph told me that he informed Alexis that our own connection was that of a restaurant owner and happy hour regular. He was disciplined enough not to divulge any state secrets in a strange woman's bed.

"That is not going to happen," I assured him. "I plan to hide at our place in the Rigolets if she shows up again."

"Don't bother. She is wrapping up her business this afternoon and leaving town," Ralph tried to reassure me.

"Did she give any indication of how she knows so much about me?" I asked him before dipping my spoon into the gumbo the waiter dropped off with our second round of drinks.

"Not really," he said but I sensed this was the first part of his answer and held off changing the topic. "She seemed to know a lot about Tulip as well, and she told me to tell you that Katie was a coward for leaving you like she did. Neither of us told her your girlfriend's name, did we?"

"Not once." I was certain I had not done so.

"She also asked if you were still mad about how some friend of yours set you up in Iraq," Ralph said in a near whisper. "I know neither of us brought up your work before joining the state police.

"Her brother recommended me for Operation Stoplight," I informed him to calm his fears over Alexis possibly knowing the details of that disavowed mission.

"Then I wonder why she referred to him as being your friend rather than admit that they are siblings," Ralph pointed out the linguistic curiosity. "She left me with the feeling that someone else you knew was responsible for what happened to you in Iraq. Any clues to who that might be?"

"I no longer care what happened," I assured him. "At the time, I was too busy worrying that Tony and I were going to wind up on matching gallows to think about who tried to kill us. Now I know that the guy I reported to was behind the ambush meant to keep us from interrogating the prisoner we were transporting. We risked upsetting his apple cart."

"Keep in mind I should not know any details of that operation." Ralph hurriedly reminded me that his security clearance was not high enough to be told details of the covert operation he was responsible for protecting Tony and me from being extradited to be put on trial over.

Avoiding Alexis during the last hours she was in town struck me as being the best way to contain any damage she might cause. "Did you make plans to get together when she comes back to New Orleans?"

"No," Ralph said and chuckled mostly to himself. "I don't think I could survive a second round with her."

"Let's just leave it at that," I said and waved my hands between us. The bartender brought the meat and cheese board at that exact moment and my hand gesture confused him about whether to leave the food or take it back to the kitchen.

I smiled and told him to leave the cutting board and to bring our third round of drinks. Ralph changed the subject so we could enjoy the rest of the meal comparing notes on a couple of new restaurants that had recently opened in the Quarter, because it is a New Orleans custom to discuss both one's previous meal and next meal over any given plate of food.

"I can understand how her appearing out of the blue would rattle you, so I made a couple of phone calls before I came here." Ralph's expression abruptly changed. "I asked around about any large collections of Persian artifacts coming on the market."

"She mentioned that to me last night," I interrupted him.

"Did she mention that someone stole a twenty-foot shipping container of antiquities belonging to the Iraqi National Museum last month? They had been recovered from a dozen locations and loaded into the container in a supposedly secure freight yard, but the thieves still managed to drive off with them," Ralph informed me. This explained his concerned expression. "My contact on this told me to drop my interest in the matter. He says it is a huge political mess that could seriously damage relations between the Iraqis and us. My understanding is that the Iraqis are accusing American companies and individuals of being behind the theft and that there are counteraccusations by those parties of corruption among the Iraqis conducting the investigation into the theft. It would be a very bad thing if Alexis was involved with any of those antiquities, and even worse if you get sucked in."

"It would almost be hard to call it a coincidence if she is not involved, don't you think? She might not know about the theft, but she will surely recognize at least some of the items her new client hands her," I said and sighed. I paused to take a drink before I added my own troubling piece to this puzzle. "Her brother, Brian, reached out to me early yesterday morning and said his friends had landed him in some sort of legal trouble. He asked me to meet him in Lexington, Missouri this weekend. I didn't ask what sort of trouble and I told him flat out that I was not going to meet him. He was working in Iraq the last time we spoke. I really hope his troubles are not related to the theft," I informed Ralph. "Do you think the two of them are in this together?"

"You know them better than I do," Ralph pointed out. "It seems unlikely that their involvement is not related in some way."

"They almost have to be connected." I agreed. I began kicking myself for not letting Brian explain his situation before telling him he was on his own.

"Well, don't change your mind and run off to meet the guy. The Iraqis will suspect that you are in on the theft if you do. They have almost given up on their demands that you and

Tony be extradited over Operation Stoplight. State will let the Iraqis extradite you if it even remotely looks like you are involved in robbing their museum," Ralph sternly warned me. He could tell by my own expression that I was still lost in thought. "Are you even listening to me?"

"I hear you loud and clear," I assured him. He studied my face and frowned.

"Do. Not. Go. There," he said and wagged a finger in my face for emphasis.

"I won't," I promised in hopes he would change the subject.

Brian was my former high school roommate, had served beside me for three years, and had done his best to help me find work when I needed it most. Balancing that against reigniting the fury of the Iraqi government over the operation that Brian had recommended I take part in would lead any other person to make a wiser decision than I was about to make.

Four

Tulip watched as I placed Alexis Paradis's card on her desk. She took notes as I gave her a recap of Brian's telephone call and my encounter with Alexis, and Ralph's thoughts over lunch. She set her pen down and looked up at me.

"Let me get this straight," she sighed as she straightened her posture in the heavy leather chair. "Your high school roommate might be a thief who has gotten into something way over his head and his slut sister showed up at Strada out of the blue and let slip that she is going to help fence the goods you think her brother stole. Does that sum up what you have gotten yourself into this time?"

"It sounds really bad when you say it," I said. I took a seat on her office sofa.

"Did you run their rap sheets? This pair sound like they should have one."

"I can't access the criminal database until I go back on active duty," I explained my failure to do this basic homework.

"It doesn't matter anyway," Tulip said and stood up. She walked to the fridge and poured herself a glass of wine. "You have already made up your mind to dive into the hole these two have dug for themselves."

"I have not promised either of them that I will get involved in anything they are doing," I lamely protested. We both knew I would not be asking for her advice if I were not already determined to do so. I should have tossed Alexis's business card in the trash and gone on with my life, unchallenging as that life promised to be for the next two weeks. "I am concerned that Alexis was able to tell me things about the two of us that she couldn't possibly know without someone with a very high security clearance giving her those details. I think there is a bigger picture than whatever these two have gotten themselves involved in."

"You're going to Missouri. Just admit that much." Tulip continued to study Alexis's card. "Brian Hollis is counting on your being reckless enough to get rolled up in his legal problems. You and I both know you are an adrenaline junkie, and that you are always going to charge to the sound of gunfire, even if it is your own gun doing the firing. You should have died twice so far that I know about, and I think you decided to continue taunting death rather than avoid it after Katie left."

"Fair points," I grumbled and slouched even deeper into the plush Pottery Barn sofa across from the wing-backed chair where she sits to interview prospective clients. She has reached an enviable place among the city's preeminent civil trial attorneys. She can afford to pick and choose her cases. She has never billed me for the hours of legal advice that she has provided in any of my past investigations, but she also eats and drinks for free at Strada Ammazarre, so there is at least some sort of quid pro quo.

"Have you tried calling Brian back?" Tulip clearly thought I had not done so.

"Number is no longer in service. He used a burner phone to call me," I replied.

"I will see what I can find out about Alexis," Tulip said and stood up. She was dressed casually and walking around her office barefoot because this was not a court day. I could tell that she had no afternoon appointments by the glass of chardonnay in her right hand.

"What do you plan to do?" I wondered aloud as Tulip pushed Alexis's card across the coffee table for me to take when I left.

"I am going to pick the bitch apart," she said far more casually than her words indicated. "It would be just like you to have a rebound fling with someone this devious."

"I am not having rebound sex with anyone, Tulip. Feel free to pass that along the next time you speak with Katie," I said a bit sharply. "I am storing my sexual energy for her return."

"At least you chose to do that instead of holding your breath. You'd be dead by now," she eased up. "I have been getting reports that you are still a mess over her leaving town."

"I learned how to grieve for the guys in my platoon that died, but I have never had to grieve over an emotion, and I have no idea how to do so," I shared. "The death of someone else's love for you is a lot different than them actually dying.”

“Sitting in your apartment blasting Warren Zevon and Tom Waits on your stereo and drinking the bistro out of tequila is not a healthy way to grieve anything,” Tulip advised me. I had been asked to turn my music down by Strada’s manager more than once in the last month. My repeatedly blaring Warren Zevon’s song *Reconsider Me* on my stereo had only added to my alcohol-fueled sullenness, and the song carried down the elevator shaft to the kitchen, where it depressed the line cooks and wait staff.

“Like I said, I am having trouble with this,” I offered as a lame rationalization for my behavior.

“Tell me this, then. Would you take Katie back if she walked through the door right now?”

“That’s a moot question. We both know she isn’t coming through the door.” I batted her question aside because I did not like the answer that sprang to mind.

“Well, we both know she is coming home, eventually,” Tulip said. “No woman born here can live anywhere else. I should know.”

“You have never left New Orleans, sis,” I pointed out.

“Exactly,” she declared and walked across the room to refill her wine glass. We paused the conversation long enough for her to sit down again and make herself comfortable. “Katie sold her house to Tony and me because she was positioning herself to make a clean start. She got the house in her divorce settlement and selling it got rid of any memories of her ex-husband and you that it holds. I would not say that attitude bodes well for you. I hate to say it, but it is true.”

“I thought you were in my corner.” I could not argue with her conclusions.

“I am, but you need to step out of your own corners.” Tulip used my own words against me. “Being a detective is never going to make either of you any safer living here. She is not going to stop being the most by-the-book state prosecutor either of us knows, and that will always pose a workplace problem for the two of you no matter what she decides about your personal lives. The worst thing is that you are never going to learn to ignore things like this new puzzle."

"I might have left well enough alone if Alexis had not magically appeared hours after I spoke to Brian," I lamely offered.

"To me that is even more reason to let this drop," my sister tried to warn me.

"Probably true," I conceded. "But aren't you curious why two people I knew in high school both contacted me on the same day?"

"I could say something about your choice of friends, but that does not answer your question," Tulip relented. "When are you leaving?"

"I never said I am going anywhere," I tried to argue about being so transparent.

"You don't have to. Someone asked for your help, so you are going," Tulip sighed in exasperation. She had me there. "You would do yourself a big favor if you followed your own advice. You keep telling the kids at the pizzeria that they are only one wrong friend or wrong drug away from ruining their lives."

"I do not consider Brian to be a bad friend," I could barely argue. "I'll slip out of town tonight. Call me if you find anything I should know about Alexis."

I stood up to leave and Tulip took a sip of her wine before she gave me a disapproving look for having taken this much of her time to ask for advice I clearly intended to ignore.

"You seem to already know you need to avoid Alexis. Do I really need to tell you to not get yourself killed?" Tulip asked.

I shook my head. "That has never worked."

She stood up and gave me an extended hug and a kiss on the cheek. She saved any crying or shouting until I was out of earshot.

Five

Tony was far more accepting of my decision than my sister. He turned the kitchen over to his number two and helped me pack. The chef and I had done things far more dangerous and likely to end badly together in Iraq than what this situation seemed to entail. I sensed he was waiting for me to ask him to mount up one more time. Tulip would have put up a formidable argument against her new fiancé risking his life for something she considered to be unworthy of my own involvement.

I added a suit and tie to the pile of clothes I chose to pack. I added them because the rest of my clothing choices were all tactical wear designed to survive combat. I had two sets of lightweight body armor to wear under the loose-fitting polo shirts sitting beside the stack of multi-pocketed dungarees. My military experience had kicked in and I packed more socks than were probably necessary. You can never have enough dry socks. My wardrobe choices fit into a garment bag and a medium-sized duffel bag.

I carried these bags from my bedroom to my office. I opened the heavy gun safe bolted to the exterior brick wall behind it and handed Tony a Kevlar vest with a ceramic chest plate to pack in the open Pelican rolling case at his feet. I selected an Israeli-made Tavor bullpup carbine and filled a bandolier with high-capacity magazines for the rifle and selected a suppressor for it from among the half a dozen in the safe. Tony silently added these to the case. I anticipated any gunfights would be at close range and this compact rifle was designed for close-quarters combat. The Tavor was chambered for the same thirty-caliber cartridge as the Steyr SSG 08 sniper rifle hidden in the trunk of my Cadillac XLR coupe. One round from either weapon could easily take an opponent out of any fight. The suppressor would fit both weapons. I also removed two boxes of ammunition for the compact Springfield Armory .45 caliber handgun I chose over the full-size ten-millimeter Glock I carry as a service weapon. This smaller pistol uses the same round as the Kriss carbine secured in the trunk with the Steyr. I added a nine-millimeter handgun that would not trace back to me and a double-edged combat knife with a seven-inch blade to my arsenal while Tony grabbed the night vision goggles from the top shelf of the safe without being asked. He tested them and made sure the spare battery pack was in the case.

"This should be a fun weekend." Tony understood what I intended to do by my choice of weapons. Neither he nor Tulip believed my claim that I was making the trip solely to escape the doldrums from being sidelined by the state police. I repeated it anyway, but we all knew that I felt obligated to help someone I had served with, despite subsequent events. A similar bond connects Tony and me, and these bonds always supersede good judgement or other obligations. Tony said it was unnecessary to justify my decision.

"I just need to track Brian down before he digs himself into too deep of a hole," I said despite his absolution.

"You should pack a shovel and not a gun then, right?" Tony asked pointedly. "You can dig a grave with both things, but you can only fill a grave with a shovel."

I was sure that this sounded far cleverer in Tony's native Italian, but the point was made, and his warning was merited.

Roux had been sitting patiently just inside the door to the office the entire time Tony and I packed. He was familiar with this routine and seemed eager to get back to work, as my mandatory leave was being imposed upon him as well. Our hiatus from taking a bite out of crime likely seemed far longer measured in dog years.

"Sorry, dude, not this trip," I apologized and knelt to give him a hug. "Uncle Roger is going to let you stay with him while I am gone."

Traveling with a pit bull posed a logistical problem with only limited benefits. I would have a difficult time finding a hotel that would take him because of his size and the notoriety of his breed. He would need to be walked and fed, which was time I could not spare while racing the situational stopwatch that Brian's plea imposed. Roger was the skilled dog trainer who had provided Roux's K-9 training. He sounded happy at the prospect of a week's paid vacation at our camp in the Rigolets. It overlooks the stretch of water which links two of the large lakes north of the city.

Roux growled unhappily and stalked out of the room. Tony and I exchanged amused looks, but I had no time to soothe Roux's feelings as I picked up the heavy plastic weapons cases and Tony grabbed my luggage as we headed towards the elevator.

Tulip was seated at the breakfast bar separating my kitchen and living room. She stood up and gave me one last hug before she turned her attention to comforting Roux. The petulant dog had jumped onto the barstool next to her and flashed me another frown as I walked past him. She would drive him to Roger after I left. Whatever Tulip told Roger about my trip was going to get back to our mother, because Mother and Roger were enjoying some sort of November/December romance.

"So, you are really doing this," Tulip challenged me. "I wish I understood why. You cannot tell me Brian Hollis is still your friend. You have not mentioned him to me once in the past four years. You are also the least sentimental person I know. There are no photographs of anyone in this apartment. Not even me."

"I know what you look like," I barely argued. I knew better than to tell her that I do not carry photos of anyone on my phone or in my wallet, either.

"Are you sure you are not doing this because of Brian's sister?" Tulip demanded. I shook my head but did not answer her question because I could never convince her how little Alexis mattered to me in deciding to seek out Brian in Missouri. "I am still digging, but your lady friend is not lying about her credentials. She has done a lot of work for museums and auction houses. Some of those clients have sketchy reputations for dealing in stolen antiquities. I called the FBI to ask if she had done any work for them, which they say she has, but they also gave me the line about not commenting on open investigations when I asked about her brother. I get the impression the FBI is aware of the family connection and have gone into damage control mode in case she turns out to be involved."

"I could have told you that much about the FBI. They will always protect their reputation above all else," I said and started for the door before Tulip could gnaw on me again.

The cooks briefly looked up when the elevator doors opened. They saw our expressions and the familiar shape of gun cases and hastily turned their backs until we were past the hot line and on our way to the delivery entrance.

I opened the metal delivery door and was relieved to find one of our valets had parked my Cadillac coupe at the curb with its trunk open. I pressed a twenty-dollar tip in his palm. Tony and I both visually swept the street for anyone who might be interested in my departure. Tony unexpectedly gave me a hug rather than a handshake before returning to the kitchen to resume his civilian life while I headed north with a renewed churning in my warrior's gut. I had thrived on this energy for half my life, across multiple continents and against an impressive array of worthy opponents. Two weeks of sitting on my hands would have driven me insane.

Tulip had identified my defining characteristic. I *am* addicted to the rush I get heading to the sound of firing guns. I was lucky that Dr. Jorgens was nowhere near as insightful as my sister. NOPD would have lost its best detective if she were.

Six

I paused long enough to plug my phone into the Cadillac's auxiliary jack before I pulled away from the restaurant and sorted through my downloaded music play list until I found Warren Zevon's song *Lawyers, Guns, and Money.* I felt the need for theme music.

There was no sense in taking anything but the most direct route to Lexington, Missouri. There was only one place I was likely to be going if anyone followed me out of town. I hoped to trim the fifteen-hour drive with the judicious use of the lights and sirens tucked into the grille of the supercharged Cadillac coupe. I could get away with the ruse of being a State Police Investigator answering a call only until I was outside of my jurisdiction. After that I needed to rely on the tolerance Mississippi's highway patrol has towards fast moving vehicles which are not weaving through traffic. Arkansas would be a bit less forgiving, but the bootheel of Missouri and most of Interstate 70 would offer plenty of opportunities to trim some time.

I averaged ninety miles an hour between the Quarter and Jackson, Mississippi. Traffic was heavy between Jackson and Memphis, and I lost some of the time I had gained because I was repeatedly stuck behind lumbering RVs and truckloads of freshly cut pine trees. I was stopped twice in Arkansas because of the plates on my car, which read COP CAR, and had to produce my badge and an explanation for using such a sporty ride as a patrol car. My standard story is that the Cadillac was confiscated from a drug dealer, and I drive it to remind the city's younger criminals that crime does not pay well or for long. The patrolmen laughed at this explanation and let me proceed, with a warning to behave myself.

I stopped in Blytheville for a bite to eat and then took a short nap in the first rest area in Missouri. It was nearly one o'clock in the morning by the time I approached the fourth exit in Missouri. I am named after the two towns listed on its exit sign thanks to my father's homesickness. His side of our family traces our roots back our great-great-grandfather's arrival in Cooter from Preston, England.

The irony that my girlfriend was staying with her retired cop father in my own father's hometown, a place I have consciously avoided my entire adult life, was not lost on me. I overcame the impulse to surprise Katie with a visit at such a dark hour only because she had made it clear that she had her own timetable for our being reunited.

Seven

The first time I ever made this drive was against my will. My father had enrolled me at Wentworth Military Academy, where his father and grandfather had attended high school, but my father had not, the day after he pulled me out of a Bourbon Street bar at the age of fifteen.

I arrived at Wentworth Military Academy in the middle of the second semester. This is a sure sign that a new cadet had made a huge mistake wherever they came from. I felt a mental vise that I imagined newly incarcerated felons experience the first time their cell door slams shut and they must come to terms with the fact their ability to come and go freely was gone. Fifteen was a late age to adjust to have to adjust to someone else's fiercely dictated schedule, especially a military academy's. It was more than a little humiliating to have to ask for permission to do things I had previously done without parental discussion, even simple things like leaving campus.

Brian Hollis and I made perfect roommates because we were both enrolled after misbehaving once too often. Brian was enrolled at the beginning of his freshman year, after damaging his father's trucking warehouse by getting stoned and trying to teach himself how to drive a forklift. I came in as what the academy called a 'rat' in our sophomore year. Brian patiently coached me through my first year because he had endured being a rat as a freshman and knew the indoctrination I would face.

Peter Yoder and Sean Nicholas roomed across the hall from us. Hank Grainger had a room to himself adjacent to our room because his foreign-born roommate's parents had withdrawn their son shortly after the school year began and room assignments had already been made.

Sean Nicholas was the oldest son of Midwest banking scions. Sean loved to help his fellow cadets make connections that would eventually benefit himself. He used to tell us that his life was mapped out from the day he was born. Sean would graduate from Wentworth, go to Pitt to study finance and then to get his MBA at Wharton before joining his family's bank. He had even picked out the fraternity he would pledge because it was popular among students who went into jobs on Wall Street. I had read that the collapse of the real estate bubble in 2008 had nearly wiped out his family's fortune, which had likely derailed his plans. I never reached out to him when I knew he could have used a friendly shoulder. I was busy with my own problems at the time, but I was always curious how he fared.

Peter Yoder was always hustling something. He traded tutoring for canteen goods that he sold to other cadets at a steep profit anytime the canteen was closed. Peter's father was supposedly in sales, but Peter never told us the name of the company his father worked for or what it was he sold. Rumor had it that he was a drug dealer, but it was more likely that his father was just a licensed pharmacist.

Every good circle of friends needs an oddball, and Hank Grainger more than filled the role as ours. He was an electronics fetishist, one of those guys who built things to specifications that only existed in his own head. Hank was especially bad about recognizing personal boundaries. It was not uncommon for him to barge into our room without knocking just to demonstrate his latest gizmo. Hank applied to MIT, but I never learned whether he was accepted before we graduated.

I was old enough now to recognize that these were all friendships made when my choices for companions were severely limited. I suspected that most of us would never have become friends had we attended a large public high school where we would have known a broader range of students. This was probably why it had been so easy for me to move on without looking back or staying in touch with any of them after we graduated.

There were undoubtedly many life-long friendships made by other cadets in our graduating class, just not by me and these former acquaintances.

This was not enough to make me question my decision to involve myself in Brian Hollis's problem. I could hardly say I wanted to help a life-long friend out of a bind. It was just an excuse for me to get involved in something that promised to challenge my capacity to solve problems.

I could not deny that my life was in turmoil, but had it truly become so much of a mess that I was willing to come to the aid of an antiquities thief?

Wednesday

June 23, 2010

It is a very dangerous thing

to know one's friends.

-Oscar Wilde

Eight

It was mid-morning Wednesday when I exited Interstate 70 to turn north on Missouri Highway 13. I ignored the ominous associations attached to that number and focused on what I needed to accomplish in the next few hours. I had left New Orleans without arranging any accommodations. There was no reason to believe Lexington had built an overabundance of hotel rooms in my absence. I was counting on there being an insufficient demand for any available rooms and began to watch for road signs pointing me towards whatever hotels lay ahead of me.

Being attentive to that made me miss the sheriff's department cruiser until it was behind me with its lights flashing. I turned on my blinker to signal the deputy that I intended to comply at the first opportunity. Whatever his interest was in me, pulling over on the two-lane road's narrow shoulder invited an accident. I pulled off the highway and parked in the gravel parking lot of a sale barn less than a mile farther down the road. There were no estate or livestock auctions going on, so we had the place to ourselves.

I reached into the center console for my registration and Louisiana State Police badge, because I knew the first question was going to be about my license plates. I had foolishly traded speed over subtlety. Now that I thought about it, I was never going to blend into a place as small as Lexington driving a bright red Cadillac convertible tagged as being an out-of-state police car.

"Good morning," the middle-aged but fit deputy said through the narrow slit of my driver's side window. He had to stand back an extra step or two to see me through the small opening. The anxious look on his face seemed to indicate he would have likely kept his distance anyway. "Nice car."

"Thank you, deputy," I casually replied. I handed him the vehicle registration and my detective's identification an dbadge through the window. I could not afford to appear nervous or impatient. A small-town lawman discovering the arsenal in my trunk would be a bad thing.

"Sheriff. Sheriff Franks," he introduced himself to let me know I was not going to shrug him off as easily as I might one of his deputies. "Interesting plates you have on here."

"Yeah, I probably should have driven my station wagon," I readily admitted. "I am on leave and should have left my work car back in New Orleans."

"This is your work car?" he asked with considerable doubt. "I have never heard of a Cadillac police car. You state cops must have a generous budget."

"I had to buy this one," I explained. The story I gave the patrolmen in Arkansas is just the cover story I use to justify my preference for driving high performance automobiles. My first patrol car was a Cadillac sedan NOPD expropriated from a dealership right after Hurricane Katrina. I liked it so much I have been buying my own Cadillacs ever since. "It doesn't like the streets in New Orleans very much."

"So, you are an NOPD officer?" I wondered if he thought he was going to catch me in a lie. He was holding my badge, so he knew I worked for the state police. I was curious why he thought I might lie to a fellow police officer.

"No, sheriff, I am a Louisiana State Police Investigator, as my identification says. I have been working with New Orleans's detectives since 2006. I get a bit of latitude because neither department seems to want me very much," I said with more detail and candor than necessary. I wanted to see if I could get a smile out of the wary lawman.

"I can see why." He cracked the faintest of smiles. "I just needed to check you out after I saw the plates."

I stared him in the eye for a long moment.

"That's not why you stopped me," I argued without being combative.

"No, it's not, but you are free to go," he admitted and turned to walk away.

"Then what was your real reason?" I leaned my head out the window to ask as he continued walking towards his cruiser.

"None of your concern," he said and kept his back turned

towards me.

Like hell it wasn't.

I watched him pull away to chase after another vehicle headed into town. That driver pulled over almost immediately. I noticed nothing strange about the driver or their vehicle as I passed by, other than that it had Kansas license plates. Was the sheriff really stopping every unfamiliar vehicle approaching Lexington? This was no more discreet than using a roadblock, and doing so still required a major commitment of his time and manpower. There were at least two more ways into town, so Sheriff Franks's entire department must have been positioned to screen anyone they could not immediately identify.

I assumed Sheriff Franks was on the lookout for Brian, but this level of interdiction seemed excessive, and the arrival of an out-of-state police detective was certain to raise questions for the sheriff.

Nine

I drove past a pair of motels at the edge of town and then turned around to take another look. The parking lot of the smaller motel next to a small liquor store was full, which struck me as being more than a little odd for the middle of the week. Even the sort of people who stay at a place that rents rooms by the week need to be at work at some point, and this many guests could not all be working nights. I could not see the parking lot of the better of the two motels because its bar and café blocked my view. I saw the rooftops of quite a few cars and multiple people on the second-floor balcony, so it was probably running close to full as well. I did not intend to stay in either motel, but their high occupancy struck me as more than a little strange.

What made me take special notice of these lodgings were the unmarked van parked in the liquor store parking lot adjacent to the first motel, and the black Ford Crown Victoria sedan parked across the street from the entrance to the second motel. I undoubtedly caught the attention of the occupants of both vehicles after doubling back and I was certain they had noticed me after I turned around and passed them a third time.

I can always spot surveillance if I have enough time to watch a given location. The longer surveillance is in place, the more likely a subject will notice their presence. It is also true that a subject will ignore any surveillance after it has been in place long enough to become part of their normal routine. I would need a few hours doing my own surveillance to determine whether the two vehicles belonged to one interest or to separate ones. The black sedan was situated to challenge anyone approaching the motel and to follow anyone leaving it. The van had a good view of both the larger motel and the motel adjacent to the liquor store, but a van is a lousy vehicle for tailing anyone. No amount of signage or distance can keep even a soccer mom driving a van full of kids from looking like she is following you.

The FBI struck me as being the obvious source of the vehicles. The sheriff and state police would have stationed marked patrol cars where they were certain to be seen to give whoever they were watching enough reason to leave town without any of the officers involved needing to directly confront them or necessitating a lot of paperwork. I had a short list of federal agencies in mind. Brian's supposed crime was not likely to draw the attention of the NSA, but the CIA might have taken an interest because his company operated in one of their active backyards, except they are not authorized to operate within the United States. A joint CIA/FBI investigation into something unrelated to any sort of national security threat had laughably low odds of being behind such surveillance.

I made a mental note to steer clear of the motels until I knew for certain who was watching them and why. There was nothing to be gained by making enemies in a second FBI field office, and not giving the local FBI office a reason to share their notes about my activities with the one in New Orleans made a lot of sense. The New Orleans Special Agent in Charge had been reassigned in the wake of a scandal I might have created. My reputation for disrupting things would survive any regime change in that office.

Ten

Lexington was not a big place when I arrived in 1984. It had expanded southward along its main north/south highway in my absence, but not very far and mostly with commercial properties. There was an overabundance of new filling stations, all of which offered gas at prices within pennies of what I paid in New Orleans. I passed a grocery store and a couple of churches I remembered from my short time there. The grocery store bore the same family name and the churches all seemed to still be well attended if the condition of their parking lots was any indication.

Lexington's downtown seemed to remain centered upon its antebellum courthouse. The city fathers have highlighted the cannon ball lodged in one of the building's front columns during the three-day battle at the edge of town in 1861. The small battle site and the nearby Anderson House Museum, a well-preserved antebellum home which served as a hospital for both armies during the battle, still shows its scars from the skirmishes for control of the plantation. All three have long been draws for the town's tourist trade.

I noted how many of the new commercial ventures occupied spaces of businesses I remembered as being something different. Many of the cafes and clothing stores in business that I could recall were now bookstores and real estate offices, and a few new cafes and bars had opened in places I remembered as other businesses. The brief tour reminded me just how long I had been gone, but I was heartened to see the shopping district's weekday foot traffic seemed to be as active as ever.

I headed away from the courthouse towards Wentworth's campus, only a few blocks from downtown. I was glad to see that the Maid-Rite café was still in business. It meant there was at least one familiar place in town to get a good fast meal.

I followed Main Street until I turned left onto Seventeenth Street, and then almost immediately turned right onto the academy's campus at Washington Avenue. The road flanked the shallow escarpment above Wentworth's football field. The brick dorm where I had been housed as a student still towered over the playing field. School had been out of session for several weeks, but the academy's summer camps looked to be as popular as ever judging by the number of young kids on campus. The groundskeepers ignored me as they mowed and trimmed the manicured campus. I passed the Administration Building and parked in front of the red brick house which housed the Alumni Office. I had evaded their newsletters and fund-raising pleas for more than two decades and felt more than a little chagrined to be here asking for their help.

Norma Maring was the Alumni Director when I graduated, and her husband was one of my mathematics instructors. She had served quite a few years in the position at that point, and she was still doing the job twenty-five years later. She certainly looked older than I remembered, her hair having gone gray, but she still seemed sharp as a tack.

"May I help you?" Mrs. Maring asked when she looked up to see who was tapping on her office doorframe.

"Good morning. You probably do not remember me," I said as I stepped into the small office. It had been the home's parlor at one time. "My name is Cooter Holland. I graduated with the class of nineteen-eighty-seven."

"Good Lord, Mister Holland," she beamed as she walked over and shook my hand. She never once acted as though she did not recognize me, though she surely must have drawn a blank on my new face. "I thought the planet had opened up and swallowed you whole."

"Well, it has spit me back out a couple of times," I assured her. She had a hearty laugh and returned to her seat behind a heavy oak desk. I sat down in one of the chairs opposite the desk. This was no time to ignore formalities.

"I heard you joined the Army after college. I must say that came as a surprise, considering how hard you resisted being here that first year," Mrs. Maring said to let me know she had been keeping tabs on me.

"Enlisting was never my intention, but I joined the ROTC while at LSU and I graduated as a Second Lieutenant with a degree in economics. It turned out that my skills at analytics had a place in military intelligence, but sitting behind a desk was not my cup of tea. No offense," I hastily tried to cover my potential faux pas. "I made it through Ranger training just in time for Desert Storm and was selected for the Special Forces after I re-upped. I broke a kneecap during an operation in Afghanistan and wound up back in New Orleans as an investigator for the state police."

"It sounds like your entire life has been nothing but doing everything you swore you would never do," she commented a bit unkindly, but she had a point. I never intended to wear a uniform of any description after I slipped the bonds of Wentworth, and I never considered following my father into law enforcement after what I witnessed of his career firsthand. Yet I had made both career decisions with surprisingly few regrets.

"Another one of those was to never lose touch with my friends." She had provided the perfect segue to explain why I was sitting in her office. "Could you give me the current contact information on Sean Nicholas, Peter Yoder, and Hank Grainger?"

Mrs. Maring narrowed her eyes for an instant. I did my best to act as though my unexpected appearance and sudden interest in re-connecting with my former classmates after being apart for so long was normal behavior.

"Funny thing about you and your friends," she finally spoke. "Brian Hollis asked for your contact information about a week ago and his sister was here just the other day asking me how to find you. Do you remember her?"

"Alexis is a hard person to forget," I allowed. This was the right thing to say if Mrs. Maring's abrupt burst of laughter was any indication.

"From what I have heard, the young woman performed something of a service, you might say," Mrs. Maring snickered and watched to see if I might blush and give myself away as one of Alexis's teenaged conquests.

"Did she explain her interest? Surely, she has worked her way through our class by now," I inquired while trying to maintain our running theme of Alexis's past to distract her from asking any other questions.

"Apparently Brian has gone missing, and she believed he may have reached out to you," Mrs. Maring informed me. I was barely able to maintain a straight face.

"Did she ask for anyone else's contact information?" I asked.

"No, yours was the only one she requested. The way she talked, I assumed she already knew how to reach everyone on your own list," she informed me. Mrs. Maring accessed the database and wrote down the last-known phone numbers and addresses of my former classmates. She passed me the notecard and leaned back in her chair. I glanced at the card and noticed all three names had addresses in the Kansas City area.

"Out of curiosity, how did you know where I am living these days?" I asked her. Alexis's walking into Strada so casually had rattled me more than I let on.

"All we ever had is your parent's phone number. Your mother was nice enough to fill me in on your life. You seem to have done quite well for yourself."

"I've tried," I said and inwardly cringed. Ms. Maring knew my entire life story before I ever set foot in her office. I was certain to get the academy's newsletters and fund-raising requests now that she knew where I lived and believed I could afford to give back to the school. "I am doing alright in New Orleans, but a little less well now that I am here. Can you recommend a decent bed and breakfast? I passed a pair of motels on my way into town and they both seemed to be fully occupied. I can't say either of them would have been my choice anyway."

Ms. Maring did not say a single disparaging word about either of the local businesses, but she did crack another smile.

"As a matter of fact, one of our administrators and his wife rent the carriage house behind their home. They bought Brian Hollis's parents' place a couple of years ago. Let me give him a call."

"Great," I said with as much enthusiasm as I could fake. I was grateful, but deeply troubled at the prospect of finally winding up in Alexis Hollis's bedroom. Mrs. Maring dialed an office extension and I listened to her explain my situation.

She was smiling at something in the other party's response when she hung up. "Bob says his place is available. He is going to let his wife Carol know you are on your way."

"Thank you for your help," I heard myself stammer. I was lost in thought about this turn of events. Hopefully the rest of my past in Lexington was not going to rise and bite me, as well.

Eleven

I could not miss the place I had been directed to. I had been there often enough that I felt like a passenger pigeon on its way home to roost. The Queen Anne-style home sported massive new planters flanking the short flight of stairs above the curb and unfamiliar statues in the rear garden. The house had also been painted recently, in neutral colors identical to those I remembered.

"You'll need to park in the alley," a slim dark-haired woman in her forties told me when I stopped in front of her house. She pointed towards the circular alley's entrance. I parked alongside the two-car garage behind the house. I could still remember the Hollis family's station wagon and Mister Hollis's Ford Thunderbird squeezing into the narrow bays.

Carol met me at the back gate. The gate was constructed from a pair of heavy wooden doors with iron work in the openings. They reminded me of the European-style patio doors in New Orleans. I turned off the engine and moved to greet my hostess before I unloaded my luggage. She held one of the gate doors open.

"Carol Levy," she introduced herself as she lightly shook my hand. "Do your license plates mean you are a police officer?"

"Yes, a Louisiana State Police Investigator," I replied and produced my badge.

"Are you carrying a firearm?" she asked. I thought this was her real concern.

"I have one, I do not need to carry it if it bothers you," I gamely offered.

"Oh, no, please do. I will rest easier knowing we have armed security so close." This was not the sort of reaction I anticipated.

"Are you having a lot of problems in the neighborhood?" I asked.

"No, but there is a lot more traffic in town than usual for this time of year. Something must be going on," she let me know. She paused and waited for me to comment or voice an opinion on the subject. I was not sure whether she considered me to be part of that worrisome traffic.

"Don't be afraid to call on me, if need be," I offered. I did not take her comfort with my carrying a pistol to mean she was going to find the arsenal in the trunk of my coupe acceptable. I was discouraged to see that the only access to the apartment she was renting me for the next week was a wooden exterior staircase which faced the house. I would need to find a way to sneak the obvious gun cases to my room when she was not looking.

"I understand you attended Wentworth," Carol said to open the topic of the purpose of my visit before she started up the stairs.

"Yes, class of eighty-seven," I confirmed.

"Then you know your way around Lexington?" she asked.

"Not so much," I said. "We were not allowed off campus without a better reason than wanting to stretch our legs. My roommate's parents owned this house, and they invited me for Thanksgiving a couple of years. His sister lived up here."

"That explains a lot," Carol said without elaborating on her comment. "Well, we have cleaned and completely redecorated the place."

Carol led the way up the worn and unpainted wooden stairs. The door had a combination lock rather than a keyed lock. I liked this because it would make picking the lock harder if anyone besides Carol wanted inside in my absence. The large guest space had heart pine flooring and a comfortable mix of antique and traditional furniture. A three-piece bathroom with a slate-tiled shower was next to the compact kitchen. The kitchen was little more than a farm sink flanked by wooden counter tops. There was a coffee machine but no range to cook any meals. The sink overlooked a basketball court and the town's hospital located in the block beyond it. A small refrigerator was set into the eight-foot span of flat-faced wooden kitchen cabinets. Carol opened the refrigerator to show it was stocked with bottled water. She pointed out the plates, cups, and cutlery in the small cabinet beside the drop leaf dining table and its two chairs.

My hostess led me onto the lodging's small deck before

she launched into a detailed list of where she and her husband felt comfortable seeing boarders on their property. The backyard garden, pergola and hammock reduced the size of the lawn I remembered. I was encouraged to make use of the hammock and she offered me the use of the hot tub which I found to be located uncomfortably close to the house. Carol jokingly discouraged my taking up gardening. Paying in cash distracted her long enough to let me hustle her out the door.

I waited an hour to unload my luggage and the gun cases. I wanted to be sure Carol did not decide to double back so she could add anything she forgot to tell me.

I cleaned and checked the Kriss and Steyr rifles and chambered rounds in each before returning them to their hidden compartment behind the panel at the back of the coupe's small trunk. I concealed the loaded Tavor carbine at the head of the queen-size bed before I took a much-needed shower. I put my pants on and secured the compact .45 handgun in a holster in the small of my back before I pulled on the lightweight body armor and chose a casual shirt to wear untucked over it. I decided to carry my badge and ID in my cross-shoulder messenger bag rather than wear them as though I was in Missouri on official business.

I sat down at the small kitchen table and picked up the notecard Mrs. Maring gave me. I began dialing phone numbers and reached Sean Nicholas after striking out with the first two names on the list. Sean sounded surprised to hear from me but invited me to catch up with him at his private club later that afternoon. I noted that he seemed to have no trouble taking time away from his job on a weekday afternoon to visit with a near stranger from his childhood.

Twelve

I drove into Kansas City and went to Arthur Bryant's barbecue place for lunch. It was one of two barbecue places I could remember from the few times my parents came to visit and took me to Kansas City for a weekend.

I imagined scenarios for Alexis and Brian while I gnawed at a pile of burnt ends soaked in Bryant's signature sauce of little more than vinegar and cayenne. I first considered the siblings as individuals and then looked at them as a team in the hijacking scenario I had created using the few things I considered to be facts. I finished my meal while considering what it would mean if the brother and sister were working for opposing sides in an illegal antiquities transaction. All I got from performing these mental exercises was a headache.

Brian was being accused of stealing a vast quantity of cultural artifacts from the specific region of the Middle East where Alexis specialized in antiquities provenance. Their familial link created an undeniable connection, but Brian had not suggested he had spoken with Alexis before calling me and she had gone out her way not to say Brian's name in our conversation, despite Brian being the best topic she could have used to get my interest. Tulip's background dive indicated that Alexis's provenance work for museums and major collectors was not above reproach. Brian owned a private security company that was positioned to know about the shipment, and his men had the firepower to hijack the trailer.

Kansas City is home to several museums. The world-class Nelson Atkins Museum owns and displays a noteworthy collection of Middle and Far Eastern artifacts. It seemed worth inquiring whether Alexis had worked for them in the past, and perhaps someone at the Nelson would be willing to share their opinion of her work if she had blessed any of their exhibits. I washed my hands in the restaurant's restroom and checked myself for flecks of sauce on my shirt before I headed that way. I was relieved to find that the skills I learned from

Café du Monde's powdered sugar carried over to barbecue sauce.

47

Thirteen

The Nelson-Atkins Museum of Art had been built in the golden age of grand museums and its imposing size was meant to dwarf anyone who stepped inside to view the works of grand master painters and the antiquities of civilizations whose downfalls have not taught my own generation of leaders the things to avoid if they do not wish to go down the same paths. The museum had expanded considerably since the last time I toured its exhibits. An entirely new wing had been added to display the Hall family's collection of Isamu Noguchi sculptures, and to add space for other exhibits the museum founders could never have imagined.

The entrance to the original Beaux-Arts building remained through the heavy brass and glass doors of the nearly windowless original building. I paid my admission and headed to the second floor. I asked the uniformed guard at the top of the stairs to put me in touch with anyone who could discuss the acquisition of the museum's collection of Persian antiquities. I fished my badge out of the messenger bag and showed it to the burly Black security guard to imply it was a law enforcement matter. Flashing my badge has a way of shortening conversations and opening doors that an honest explanation does not always accomplish. The guard radioed his supervisor to send someone to speak with me.

"Hello, I am Jack Newsome," a man of about forty and dressed in a suit and tie introduced himself after stepping off the nearby elevator only a moment later. He seemed to be equal parts nervous and wary. "I understand this is some sort of criminal matter?"

"Well, that is the short version of things, anyway," I said and flashed my most disarming smile as I showed him my badge. My casual attire did little to sell my being a cop.

"And the long version, Detective?" he asked and drug out saying my title to suggest I provide my full name and a better explanation of why I had interrupted his day.

"Holland," I introduced myself. "I did not set out to come

here today, but I am hoping you might answer a couple of easy questions for me."

"I will try," he said and motioned for me to follow him away from the security guard. Visits from out-of-state detectives are always a juicy topic on any gossip grapevine.

"I need to know if a woman named Alexis Paradis has done any work for this museum. She is an expert on Persian antiquities, or at least she touts herself as being one," I said. I had nearly referred to Alexis by her maiden name, which he would not have recognized. I handed him Alexis's business card, which I had carried with me from New Orleans. It was the only proof I had that she and I knew one another.

Newsome took the card and read it without showing any emotion. He flipped it over and saw the handwritten phone number. He turned it over again before he handed it back to me.

"And why do you need to know that?" he inquired rather than answer my question or indicate the depth of his willingness to assist me.

"I like to conduct a background check like this in person rather than over the phone. I find people have more to share when we speak face to face. Alexis's brother might be involved in the theft of artifacts which belong to the Iraqi National Museum. I have no evidence Alexis has any role in her brother's potential crime, but I would like to know whether she has the sort of integrity not to be," I answered. Newsome's brow furrowed at the thought the museum might be pulled into an international criminal investigation involving art theft. It would mean negative headlines, which would alarm their donors.

"And that brings you to us," he sighed. "The answer is, yes. Yes, to the first question that is. The museum has used Alexis Paradis's services to authenticate new acquisitions for our collection. She was referred to us by one of our donors, and her living in Kansas City made her well suited to our needs. Provenance is a difficult thing to establish for anything six or seven millennia old, and the rules for acquiring new antiquities change so often it can be hard to build a collection which balances our obligation to educate our guests with the sovereign interests where the antiquities originated. I believe we are approaching a tipping point where more antiquities are headed back to their countries of origin each year than are made available on the legal market. There are billions of dollars' worth of looted antiquities sold to private collectors and less scrupulous museums on the black market. We do our very best not to let any of those artifacts into our collection, nor to accept any from collectors who failed to do their own due diligence. It is why people like Miss Paradis are so important in our world."

"I understand the tight rope act this must require," I assured him. "It is why I am interested to know your museum's opinion of Alexis Paradis. I could not help but notice you referred to her in the past tense. Has the museum stopped using her services?"

"Her professional opinion is both valued and trusted, but we have chosen to hire experts of our own." The tone and semantics of his response invited additional questions.

"How about Alexis as a person?" I inquired more directly.

This time he paused before answering. "She has a certain zest for life. Can we leave it at that?"

"I knew Alexis as a teenager. Her zest for life apparently seems to have remained a defining part of her character." I said and chuckled to ease the tension in his face.

"I wish we had known about her proclivities in advance," Newsome said and frowned. "She managed to compromise a couple of promising careers here before we were instructed to hire a different expert to use in the future. She tends to blur the lines between professional and personal relationships."

"My apologies," I said. "Not that I had anything to do with that. It is just sad to hear that she has accomplished so much as an adult without overcoming her childhood impulse control issues."

"That pretty much sums her up," Newsome said and took a step back. He clearly felt he had answered my questions and may have regretted sharing what he had about the damage Alexis had caused to the museum's antiquities office.

"Have you dealt with her yourself?" I asked. I sensed I could ask no more than two additional questions before he bolted on me.

"No, detective. I arrived after the previous director resigned and the museum began to rebuild the department," he replied. He did not state that Alexis played any role in the reshuffling, but his previous statements indicated as much.

"Would you happen to know how many artifacts Alexis recommended the museum acquire during that transition period?" I asked solely to play a hunch.

"Not offhand. I do know that we continued acquiring new antiquities during that time. Alexis handled the provenance on a handful of those." An ugly thought came to the administrator as soon as he said this. It was the same possibility that troubled me. Had Alexis intentionally sabotaged the museum's antiquities department to create an opportunity which helped her clients sell the museum items which had less than stellar provenance?

Newsome hastily excused himself. I decided to stay and study the museum's collection. Viewing the craftsmanship in everyday objects like pottery and the fine art of Pharaoh-era Egypt, Babylonia, Samaria, and Imperial Rome and Greece, as well as statuary from Nimrud in modern-day Iraq left me in a mild state of awe. I only knew the nations where these antiquities originated in their modern, war-torn incarnations.

The three bronze artifacts from the Lakhmid Kingdom, dating to about 400 A.D., which had been loaned to the museum by the Peter Yoder Trust stood out as much because of their beauty as the familiar name attached to them.

Fourteen

It took me nearly an hour to find the address Sean had texted me. I found the city's street grid to be complicated by its multitude of parks, its impressive collection of fountains, and its network of expressways. Sean's club was on the west side of a busy four-lane street linking the Gatsbyesque mansions lining Ward Parkway and the Country Club Plaza shopping district to the city's downtown office towers. The expressway is bisected at only a handful of locations, and finding an opening into the neighborhood where Sean's club was located proved to be harder than I anticipated.

I was mildly surprised that the private club was operating in a former residence. The homes closest to it mostly dated to late in the nineteenth century when mansions were still built using the same local limestone used to build the museum I had just visited. The remainder of the neighborhood's homes consisted of large 1930s bungalows and a couple of substantial newer, custom-built homes.

The streets were well maintained, the acres of immaculate lawns were likely professionally tended, and the cars in every driveway were expensive imports. And, like all communities of highly successful people, the place showed no more signs of life on a weekday afternoon than a cemetery. This was not a place where people hung out on their front stoop to gossip about the comings and goings behind the gates of the private club in their midst.

The address proved to be one of the stone mansions. The three-story residence was so immense that it dwarfed the neighboring homes built in the same era. Housing a private club with even a moderately sized membership should have posed no problem. Despite its use of local materials in its construction, the mansion's design and architecture had distinctly European touches, as a surprising percentage of homes in Kansas City do. Its roof of rounded red tiles and the leaded glass attic window were found on nearby homes.

The home was set back from the street and secluded from

view by the trees surrounding it and the small ravine it backed onto. A stone wall ran the length of the property's frontage. The thick wall began at waist height and increased in height as the yard sloped downwards towards the shallow ravine. Its paved driveway was large enough to accommodate a half dozen cars at once, and there was additional parking to the right side of the home. The carriage house was the size of smaller homes in the neighborhood.

While the home blended into its surroundings, the rolling metal gates and gatekeeper in a suit and tie standing beside the entryway's electronic keypad stood out like a neon sign.

"May I be of assistance?" the gatekeeper asked as politely as my potential intrusion allowed. The man's clothes did not hide his muscular build, nor the large revolver nestled in the shoulder holster beneath his pin striped jacket.

The Louisiana plates on my Cadillac coupe and my slacks and open shirt wardrobe were dead giveaways that I was not a club member.

"I am supposed to meet an old classmate of mine here," I responded without any annoyance at being challenged. It was a private club, and tight security was how they maintained their privacy.

"Your name?" he asked and raised his clipboard to confirm I was on the day's guest list.

"Cooter Holland," I offered no more information than he requested. He matched my face to the photo on my state police ID and announced my arrival on his two-way radio.

"The valet will park your car for you, sir," he directed, and pointed me towards the unusually tall and muscular valet already waiting to take my keys.

I shook my head at the beefy valet as I pulled abreast of him. It seemed like whoever oversaw hiring the staff did their recruiting at Gold's Gym.

"If you don't mind, I will park it myself," I said with a bit of firmness. I did not care if he mistook my insistence for rudeness. Wanting to park my own car was not an act of pettiness. I always prefer that strangers not touch my car. The valet clearly wanted to say and perhaps to do something to compel my cooperation, but he paused to assess the situation. I was the guest of a club member and I had not been so intimidated by the armed gatekeeper that I had passively followed his parking instructions. To complicate the valet's decision, I was driving a vehicle with license plates indicating a level of involvement in law enforcement.

"If you would, then, please park in any of the open spaces around this side," he decided and made a sweeping gesture to show the path of the driveway.

"I don't plan to stay long. I am going to park right over there," I countered and pointed to an empty space near the front walkway.

I did not wait for his response before I pulled forward and parked. I paused after I got out of the coupe to place my badge on my belt. I had no legal authority and was not there on an investigation. I just wanted to wield it as I had with the man at the museum. I closed the convertible's hard top and set the car alarm to secure the vehicle's interior and trunk from any prying eyes or hands.

My next encounter was with the private club's swarthy doorman and the additional members of the club's security detail flanking him on the covered front porch. The doorman was a blonde-haired American but the pair behind him had the size and tattoos of Samoan fullbacks. They had witnessed my interaction with the gatekeeper and valet and undoubtedly overheard their radio conversations. The trio were prepared to defend the door to the death.

"Please extend your arms straight out from your side, sir," the doorman instructed me with exaggerated politeness while one of his companions turned on a magnetic wand and stepped towards me.

"I think not," I politely refused and sidestepped the wand. I pivoted slightly to display my badge and showed the trio my state police ID. I did not allow the doorman to handle the ID, but he did not challenge that I was who I claimed to be. The distant Cadillac's vanity license plates helped sell my story.

"We do not allow weapons on the premises, detective,"

he informed me.

"Except your own," I pointed out without caring if this antagonized the trio. They had enough muscle in place to impose the club's will. "I assure you I am not here to harm anyone, but I am a police detective and I suggest you reconsider your club policy."

"Why is that?" the doorman huffed.

"You assume that I am armed, but you have no idea how I might resist any attempt to disarm me. Physically enforcing club policies against a member's guest is surely a worse idea than assaulting an out of state police detective," I reminded him while silently reminding myself that I was the guest and causing a scene was unlikely to reflect well on my host.

"It is still club policy," the doorman refused to budge.

"Then you can explain to my host why I left," I instructed him and took two steps backwards, but with my hands loose at my side to appear as unthreatening as possible. I was busy formulating a plan in my head for how to reconnect with Sean if the trio did not relent. The door opened before I stepped off the porch. Sean placed his left hand on the doorman's shoulder and flashed me a broad, but not especially welcoming, grin.

"I invited the man here, Charlie," Sean declared. "I will vouch for my friend, but you are free to shoot him if he makes a scene inside."

I was not at all certain my former classmate was joking. Sean shook my hand and steered me past the still fuming doorman. I felt Sean's hand move to my shoulder before his fingers trailed down my back to tap the pistol holstered in the small of my back. He stepped away and gave me a conspiratorial wink as he pointed to his left.

The home's high-ceilinged entryway included a marble double staircase with a brass and mahogany railing. It took a moment to realize the home was devoid of rugs or furniture. Heavy drapes hung at each window to give the illusion of occupancy to anyone driving past. Sean led me through a sizeable parlor and slowed as we entered the home's large library. Our leather shoe soles echoed off the oak parquet floor and bookshelf-lined walls. The expanse of empty shelves looked odd and more than a bit depressing for a reader like me. I noticed that the Italian marble fireplace was clean of any trace of wood ash.

"You will have to give me the name of your decorator," I laughed and smiled uncomfortably. My hyper-vigilant PTSD began to kick in and I braced myself to step into a room with a large plastic sheet laid out for me to stand on.

"We just leased this place. The furniture will be here later this week. I thought it best that you and I meet somewhere private," Sean attempted to explain the emptiness.

"Somewhere with private security, anyway," I mumbled to myself and then rephrased it as an observation. "You have impressive security for an empty clubhouse."

"They are rentals, as well," Sean shrugged and closed the subject.

Sean opened a door onto the home's porte cochere and led me outside. I followed him across the driveway to a pagoda which overlooked a swimming pool. The pagoda was built of rougher stone than the house and was probably a recent addition to the estate. The concrete floor had been stamped and stained to resemble mahogany planks. An indoor/outdoor rug designed to look like a Persian rug matched well with the faux wood finish. The sparse furnishings were genuine rattan with plush floral cushions. A round teakwood coffee table separated our chairs. Sean made a point of sitting where he could face the house, forcing me to sit with my back to the security team watching us from there. I was sitting at a right angle to the carriage house and noticed additional guards standing at the ready.

A tuxedoed member of the staff appeared and took our drink orders. This one looked like the sort of college-kid waiter I would expect to find working at a catered event. Perhaps the service staff had been hired for the day as well as the security detail. I surmised that Sean was more concerned with his perimeter security than potential attacks from the household staff. The server returned moments later to set down crystal tumblers holding a gin and tonic for Sean and an Old Fashioned for me before excusing himself to walk back inside. It was early in the day for me to start drinking, but I was impressed that the unseen bar in an empty mansion was equipped with ingredients beyond a highball. We both waited to speak until the server was inside the house, as though what either of us might say involved some sort of national secret.

"Quite the security detail you have here," I repeated myself when Sean did not immediately open the conversation. I was hoping he might explain their presence in greater detail, such as where had he 'rented' such men.

"I told them to be extra careful with you," Sean admitted.

"Why is that?"

"You are the only friend of mine to ever reach out to me from the grave," Sean finally explained the tension that hung over the property from the moment I arrived.

"What made you think I was dead?" I asked because this was the most curious of reasons to surround himself with so many guard dogs. He obviously had not made this wild assumption based solely on our having lost contact.

"We live in an information age," Sean cryptically replied. This was certainly not an answer to my question. "You look like you came back to life as someone else."

"I needed reconstructive surgery, and my sister used the opportunity to give my looks an upgrade," I told him without elaborating on why the surgery was necessary. Sean just nodded at my thin explanation. His angular face and receding hairline of faintly curly brown hair made him look much more like his father than he had at eighteen. Sean stood roughly six feet tall and obviously worked out as he was not just slim but also quite muscular. His handshake had been meant to make a point.

"So, you understand why I was surprised to hear from you."

"And it probably explains why I have been unable to contact Peter Yoder or Hank Grainger," I mentioned.

"Yeah, our concern was that someone was running some sort of scam, and they asked me to check you out. That's why we are meeting here and not some place more public," Sean let me know. "I suppose we could have met in Lexington, but I wanted the home court advantage."

"Well, this place is certainly impressive, I must say," I told him honestly. I did not believe the high quality of the protection he surrounded himself with for our meeting had anything to do with his suspicions about who I was. I bit my tongue rather than press him on why he believed I was dead, or to question how he knew I was staying in Lexington. I did not remember having told him so, but I may have let it slip. I decided to demonstrate my own capacity for staying informed. "You seem to be doing alright despite your family's bank folding."

"I was handling the loan department when the bottom fell out of the housing market. We managed to stabilize the situation, but my father was willing to sell when a generous offer was made. He sold out to one of those banks who make their money issuing credit cards to anyone too stupid to check the interest rate. I took my share of the buyout and opened a real estate company specializing in selling high-end properties. It has proven to be the one level of housing which remained stable throughout the crisis. The only problem with properties like this beast is that a house might sit on the market for a year or more waiting for the right buyer, or some lottery winner with enough money to take it off my client's hands. I recently began leasing my clients' properties to house a discreet club that I operate on the side. It pays their mortgage while they wait for the house to sell and lets me move the club about, so that it attracts less attention. It makes for a win-win. I have an A-list of male members willing to pay a pretty penny for a discreet place to misbehave. I keep my ear open when I am around them for other business opportunities." Sean may have wanted me to know how well connected he was in addition to his wealth, but the way he flipped his wrist to draw attention to his Rolex Yacht-Master watch and the black Mercedes Maybach parked under the porte cochere struck me as talismans against his newfound fear of poverty. It sounded to me like he had unwittingly replaced one risky form of finance for another. I did not bother showing him the ridiculously expensive Breitling watch on my own wrist or mention my partnership in Strada Ammazarre, or the trust fund left me by filthy rich maternal grandfather that I have never touched. I was not here for gamesmanship and was not willing to waste time indulging Sean's ego. All his posturing did was give me a way to get under his skin if need be.

"I got a strange visit from Alexis Hollis and was wondering whether anyone else did as well," I said to refocus the topic of conversation. I did not include the date we crossed paths, but my sudden presence suggested it was a recent event.

"Interesting. Did she say why she looked you up?" Sean asked and reached for the crystal tumbler sweating on the coffee table between us. He took his time sipping the gin and tonic, obviously using it to hide his reaction to my response.

"I did not say she sought me out," I noted his assumption. "She may have happened upon the place where I was drinking on her own."

"Do you really believe that was the case?" Sean scoffed.

"Not at all," I concurred with his unstated opinion. "I would not be here now if I did."

"What did she do that brings you to town?"

"Like I said, my curiosity got the better of me when both Alexis and Brian contacted me on the same day. Neither of them mentioned the other to me. I found that to be especially strange considering how close they were as kids. I have since heard a suggestion that Brian was involved in the theft of part of the Iraqi National Museum's collection. Alexis told me that she had been hired to handle the provenance on a large collection of Persian antiquities that are about to go on the market. In police work we call that an unlikely coincidence," I padded what I knew about Brian and the missing antiquities and paused to see how surprised he was. He did not seem at all shocked or disappointed at the news. "What did she tell you about that?"

"What makes you think she and I have spoken?" Sean was quick to challenge me.

"Alexis made a special trip to see Mrs. Maring at Wentworth to ask whether Brian had contacted her for my address and phone number. She told me that Brian had, but that Alexis only asked for my contact information, so she must already know how to reach you," I explained. Sean began nodding part way through what I told him without realizing he was doing so.

"Okay, we spoke last week," Sean confirmed. "Alexis told me that Brian was in trouble and to avoid him like the plague if he reached out. The way she talked led me to think someone besides Interpol is on his tail. He may have double crossed someone he should not have."

"Do you suppose Brian might have smuggled those artifacts to the United States?" I asked. His ability to answer any of my broad questions was going to betray his own level of involvement.

"I hope he isn't that crazy," Sean said in a near mutter. I could not tell if he was answering me or opening a fresh topic, but I sensed something in his tone.

"You say that like you know someone who is crazy enough to try and do so," I suggested and leaned towards him as I do when interrogating a tough suspect.

"His sister certainly is," Sean assured me.

"How could she, though?" I pressed him.

"She has all the contacts she needs to pull it off. She claims to be an expert on old stuff and always seems to be making deals of some sort all over the globe. I bet she knows people who could move stuff for her if she wants." I was curious how Sean knew so much about Alexis's business life.

"Smuggling antiquities into the United States would involve crossing multiple borders and bribing customs officers in two or three countries as a starting point. She would also need a ship willing to carry them to a friendly port in the States," I explained the intricacies that I imagined were involved in antiquities smuggling. Alexis struck me as a lot of things, but being an international antiquities smuggler was not one of them. Tulip claimed Alexis had flexible ethics, but it would take more than that to take so large of a large leap into the black market.

"She knows people who could do all of that," Sean strove to reinforce his opinion. "But this is just a wild idea, anyway."

"Wild, yes, but you sounded pretty convinced your theory was good just now. What sort of shenanigans have you been up to with Alexis since we graduated?" My tone and expression were not those that he might confuse for casual conversation.

"She showed up at one of these party houses three years ago with some client of hers from New Jersey. Alexis made it clear to me that they were not an item. She left her number, and I called her a week later. Now we hook up whenever she is in town. She likes to brag to me about all the other men she has entertained at her condo in the River Market. She is still collecting scalps as well as artwork, let's just leave it at that," Sean elaborated. He did an admirable job of being discreet by not identifying the club member Alexis accompanied, but he was less successful at hiding his displeasure with having to share Alexis's bed.

"She went for mine in New Orleans," I let him know. "So, you already know she is an antiquities expert."

"Expert may be a stretch," Sean scoffed. "She has an impressive business card, but she only does freelance work. If she was any good at her job, some museum or auction house would have put her on their payroll."

"Maybe she is like her brother and prefers to work for herself. She seems to be making a very good living at it," I reluctantly defended Alexis.

"I know she does. She has sold stuff to me, and to Peter and Hank. I am sure she has quite a client list of private collectors. She is one helluva a saleswoman. She shows you something old and gold, as she likes to say, and convinces you that buying antiquities is just like investing in real estate, but you never have to mow the lawn or pay property taxes. Stuff she sold me from Mexico and Peru tripled in value in just a couple of years. I gave a few of the club members her number and told them what she had done for my portfolio, so I am sure she sold antiquities to a lot of them, as well. She managed to hook Peter and Hank on buying Persian artifacts because both of their companies do so much work over there. She started out by selling them rugs and then moved them into buying old pottery and statues. I don't know what Hank does with his but Peter likes to show his off.

"I take it that all three of you are still sleeping with her," I stated as though the answer was clearer than it was.

"Oh yeah. She is an absolute tiger in bed," Sean laughed and slapped his leg.

"I had a conversation with a guy at the Nelson Atkins earlier today. He thinks Alexis may have used her feminine wiles on one or more of their curators to slip a few pieces of hot art into their collection. She has the credentials of a professional, but the mind of a huckster," I shared. His brow furrowed again.

"What are you trying to tell me?" Sean asked and set his drink down. His inability to disconnect the Alexis he still viewed in the dismissive way we all did in high school from the well-educated adult woman who traveled the world was probably his undoing.

"Consider for just a moment, if you can, that Alexis showed you shiny gold artifacts from the Mayan and Incan civilizations and cooed in your ear that you could own as many as you wanted to buy. All that precious metal and sweet talking might make you overlook the obvious flaws in her sales pitch," I began to unspool Alexis's possible deception at a pace he could follow. "I am nowhere near the expert on the subject that Alexis is, but I do read newspapers and keep up with things. Mexico and Peru are clawing back every artifact they can get from every museum and collector they find holding pieces of their heritage. They have shut down the export of any new artifacts and the penalties for trying to smuggle antiquities out of either country is heavier than you would face for doing the same thing with drugs. Yet, Alexis just happened to know about a large collection of artifacts that the Mexican and Peruvian governments are unaware of that you could legally buy. What were the odds of that? I will even bet you that she is the one telling you how much your collection has appreciated in value. Does that sound about right?"

Sean became wracked with a combination of guilt and anger. He started to answer me twice before taking a long swig from his gin and tonic and falling back in his chair. He held the glass aloft and another round of drinks arrived before he had formulated his answer.

"She gave me paperwork claiming that these were all

legal transactions," Sean sighed and then huffed. "That dirty bitch."

"Alexis was just making a living. You should have done your due diligence and found a second opinion on whatever she sold you," I said without laughing in his face. "You let your wrong head make the decision to buy from her."

"What happens now?" Sean demanded. "You're a cop. Am I under arrest?"

"I am not a cop in Missouri or Kansas. I am a cop in Louisiana, but even there I do not think this would fall under my authority. You are in federal trouble if you are in trouble at all. Maybe Alexis is right and all the stuff you bought from her has some sort of grandfathered provenance, so you are fine. I think the Mexicans would probably still want their stuff back if they knew you had it, though," I did my best to soften the blow. I could tell his mind was filling with imaginary headlines, and that he realized he was about to be confronted with the sort of professional and financial ruin he was convinced never happened to bright guys like himself twice. It is better to be thought of as a bank robber than a grave robber any day.

"Oh, hell," he blubbered and gave me the opening I was looking for all along.

"I should probably get in touch with Peter and Hank about this, don't you think?" I suggested as tactfully as my ulterior motive allowed.

"Oh, yeah," Sean agreed. "Here, let me give you those numbers."

The phone numbers he wrote on the back of his own business card were not the same as the ones Mrs. Maring had handed me. She had provided their home and business numbers. Using those numbers would have taken me longer to connect with the pair, if at all. These were their personal cell phone numbers.

"Can you give me Alexis's address?" I prodded him while he still had the pen in his hand. He wrote the address down without any discussion. I calmly finished my drink as he frantically scrawled her address beneath the two phone numbers. I silently picked up the card from the middle of the coffee table.

"Do you think whatever Brian is up to is connected to his

sister?" I asked to break the silence which now filled the pagoda. I was trying to increase Sean's anguish by timing my departure to look like I had nothing else to do with my own day. It was difficult because I was becoming increasingly aware that a clock was ticking, and I still had no idea what Brian intended to do on Saturday.

"I cannot say for sure, but it makes sense, doesn't it?" Sean surmised. "Do you think Brian is mad that we have been sleeping with his sister?"

"He didn't when she was a minor, so I doubt he cares now that she is an adult. Still, it was a dumb thing to do," I chastised him.

"Most expensive piece of tail I ever had," Sean grumbled but managed to force a wry grin. He was grasping for any way to save face at this point.

"Hopefully she is not your last," I burst his bubble. Sean would not do well in even the most country-club of minimum-security facilities. I was a little jealous that his arrogance and bad judgement would come as a balloon payment. I have spent my entire life being punished for every wrong move I make on a pay-as-you-go basis.

Fifteen

Alexis's having an apartment in Kansas City was a revelation. The addresses on her business card listed New York City as her home in the United States. Her place in Kansas City was not going anywhere, and I did not even know whether she had returned to Kansas City after leaving New Orleans, so I dialed the first number on the back of Sean's business card before I performed a U-turn in the driveway.

Peter Yoder let the call go to voicemail.

"Peter, this is Cooter Holland. Sean gave me this number to reach you and we need to meet at your earliest convenience. I think you know why. Call me today," I said in a calm and even tone. I hung up and considered calling Hank Grainger so I could meet with whichever of them answered first. I chose not to. Peter Yoder was my primary person of interest because of the antiquities that Alexis had convinced him were legal to donate to the museum and for the museum to accept.

Sean seemed certain that Alexis knew people who could move a trailer of stolen goods. He also mentioned that both Peter and Hank had business interests in Iraq, or at least the Middle East. There are not many types of private business that can operate amid social collapse or civil war. I was curious what theirs might be. I felt optimistic that I could get Peter or Hank to implicate themselves in what was going on, but all that I knew for certain that this pair had done wrong was to have bought what Alexis sold and enjoyed what she gave away for free.

My phone rang as I pulled out of the driveway and turned towards the nearby expressway. I asked Peter to hold on for just a moment and veered to my left to follow the road running parallel to the mansion's rock wall as it descended into the ravine behind the estate. Trees blocked my view of the pagoda where I imagined Sean was continuing to melt down.

"I hope I didn't take you by complete surprise," I half-apologized to start what I had reason to believe might become a testy conversation.

"You certainly did," Peter admitted. "I guess Sean considers you to be legitimate. I will call him later and get him to fill me in on the conversation you two had. What are you doing in town?"

"Brian Hollis asked me to meet him here this weekend," I informed him. I added no details about Brian's legal issues and made sure not to mention how long Brian and I had been out of touch or where 'here' was. "Have you heard from him lately?"

"I haven't heard from you since we graduated from Wentworth and now you show up in Lexington and call me to ask about Brian. All I can say is that he is in deep trouble with the Iraqis. Why are you here?" Peter was the second person to tell me I was staying in Lexington, and I knew for certain that I had not offered him that information. Peter had just said he planned to call Sean when we hung up, so Sean was clearly not his source. This was troubling, but demanding answers might make this a short conversation that yielded nothing useful to my search for Brian.

"I had not spoken to Brian in years until he called me on Monday to say he is in trouble. Alexis looked me up in New Orleans the same day and that made me curious enough about Brian's situation to come here," I said to offer Peter multiple topics to pursue. I fully expected him to choose the one he thought would trick me into admitting I was involved in Brian's caper. He would do that or do his best to distance himself from Brian.

"Is that why you are in Lexington? Do you think Brian is hiding out there?" Peter asked. I had not chosen to stay in Lexington because Brian asked me to meet him there on Saturday but because I am more familiar with Lexington than I am with Kansas City. I could not believe a wanted man would decide to hide in the one place where he is most likely to be recognized. The sheriff's personal welcome to town and the FBI surveillance on the two motels suddenly made a lot more sense.

"I am not aware that he is," I answered honestly. "What makes you so certain Brian is there?"

"Oh, I am just hypothesizing. I mean, where else is he

likely to try to hide?" Peter did his best to retract his comment.

"All I know right now is that antiquities belonging to the Iraqi National Museum went missing and Brian's name is attached to their loss. His sister told me she is expecting to have the opportunity to do provenance on a new collection of Persian antiquities coming into the country, and I cannot imagine those are unrelated matters," I said to add to the topics Peter might be willing to discuss.

"Brian absolutely stole the stuff you are talking about. I know that for sure, and I can even tell you the exact contents of the shipping container he stole," Peter emphasized his confidence in the little he was sharing with me.

"How can you do that?" I challenged him.

"Well, he stole one of my containers," Peter dropped a bombshell.

"Your container?" I blurted out more than asked.

"The container he swiped belongs to P-Y International Shipping, so yeah it is my container," Peter repeated, adding a little more detail. "A division of my company operates overseas. We have a very lucrative contract with the Pentagon to securely move their materials in-country and to ship things in and out of Iraq and Afghanistan as need be. We also have contracts with the new Iraqi government to haul anything they need transported under a security blanket. You know, things like a twenty-foot-long container of their priceless cultural artifacts."

"How did you get into trucking?" I was curious enough to sideline the more important topic. Trucking was a great career choice for anyone with a talent for hustling, but it seemed too blue collar for the Peter Yoder that I remembered.

"I got a degree in logistics and saw the future was in government contracts. I created a company on paper and secured a place on FEMA's post-disaster call list. I used that potentially lucrative position to convince a friendly bank to loan me the money to buy Brian's father's trucking company. I paid off the bank note in just two hurricanes and handled things well enough that I started getting work with the Pentagon. It is like having a personal Treasury printing press," Peter proudly bragged. I suspected the friendly bank had belonged to Seans's family. That possible connection was not the gem in this disclosure. Peter buying out Brian's father was. There might be some unresolved animosity there that had led to the theft of the container.

The loss of these irreplaceable artifacts of Iraq's ancient history would surely be viewed as a breach of faith between Peter's company and the Iraqi government. It also reflected poorly on Peter's security arrangements. The Iraqis trusted Peter to securely transport their national heritage, and their container could no longer be accounted for thanks to Peter's former classmate. There was a slim possibility that the Iraqis were not aware of Peter's childhood connection to Brian Hollis. It would not be long before the Pentagon began to question whether Peter could securely deliver their weapons systems or move sensitive materials between two points without this happening to their own shipments.

"How did Brian get hold of your container?" I asked to refocus on the topic at hand.

"He used to handle security for me. He knew the truck dispatchers well enough to convince them it was alright for him to drive off with the container. I hired Brian's company to provide overwatch for our convoys when we moved our operations into Iraq in 2003. His men rode shotgun on all those convoys you saw on the news after Bush invaded the country. Hank Grainger and I were having dinner in the Green Zone one night and I mentioned that we were spending a fortune on security. Hank bought Brian's company because owning a private security company dovetailed with Hank's operations in Iraq, and he also bought the respect the Iraqis had for Brian's company," Peter overshared.

I found it especially odd that Brian never mentioned he was working with Peter when I tried to work for him in 2003. It seemed credible that Sean had called up Hank to surround him with the hired guns at our meeting. I also noted the calculating way Peter and Hank thought things through when it came to business. It seemed inexplicable that they had failed to do their homework when dealing with Alexis.

"Hank encouraged Brian's shooters to leave with him

when Brian started his new company. The guys working for Hank now are mostly veterans of the special forces from foreign armies. Brian's new company has a personal protection contract with the State Department and Pentagon. I was as surprised as anyone when people pointed fingers at Brian after the container went missing. I must have misread him."

"Do you really see Brian as a truck hijacker?" I asked in disbelief despite the clear evidence to the contrary.

"Brian was filmed at our shipping terminal in Kut with a driver and an armed escort. He handed the dispatcher what looked like proper paperwork and drove off with the container. Brian knew how to make the container vanish by disconnecting its satellite GPS link. The satellite's last reading showed them headed east, but there is nothing east of Kut but the Iranian border. I cannot imagine he struck a deal with the Iranians for the shipment. That would be enough to start another war between Iraq and Iran. The Iraqis claim the cargo is worth a quarter of a billion dollars and are insisting that Hank and I pay for the loss before they let us get back to work. They have shut us down until we either pay up or find the container. What they want is considerably more than my insurance company wants to pay or I can afford," Peter lamented.

"Has Brian offered to ransom it back to you?" I wondered. I could imagine no use for the container or its contents beyond leveraging them for cash or gaining some sort of situational advantage. None of this made much sense and I was having trouble disconnecting the people I last knew as adolescents from the middle-aged adults embroiled in international politics. This was no childish prank.

"I have not heard word one from whomever has the container, but I assume it is still in Brian's hands. I thought Interpol had a bead on the container when its number appeared on the manifest of a container ship sailing out of Kuwait. The ship docked in Baltimore a week ago, but the container was not on board when Customs and the FBI searched the inventory. We wondered if it had fallen overboard, but the FBI suspects that Brian may have painted a different number on the container while it was in transit. I have no idea, but I do know every container that arrived on that vessel has left our Baltimore yard. My guess is that Brian and the container are somewhere in this country."

I was not sure why Peter was being this forthcoming. The theft was likely an active FBI investigation, and the agency would have undoubtedly instructed him not to discuss any details with the likes of me. Our relationship was neither close nor professional enough to explain Peter's telling me any of this. Maybe he needed to share the tale with someone he knew in hopes that saying it out loud might make it seem like more of a bad dream than the legal nightmare it must be for him. I know from personal experience how unforgiving and tenacious the Iraqis can be when they feel wronged. Perhaps he hoped mentioning the FBI would rattle me enough to scare me off. If that was Peter Yoder's hope, then he failed. I came away no less confused by what was going on than he and the FBI seemed to be, and our conversation made me more determined than ever to be the one to sort things out in time to save Brian from prison in either country.

"Does the FBI think he is headed to Lexington?" I asked in serious doubt. If he said yes, then it explained the surveillance I had spotted when I arrived in town.

"I don't think they have any better idea about Brian's intentions than I do. My personal guess is that he lined up a buyer and has already delivered the container. Our last hope is to catch somebody when the contents start showing up on the black market," Peter sighed. He did not need to tell me how ruinous things would be for his company and diplomatic relations between Iraq and the United States if the container was not recovered and delivered with an intact seal on its doors.

I decided not to add to Peter's woes by telling him that Alexis's provenance on the antiquities he loaned to the Nelson-Atkins Museum was being questioned.

Sixteen

I hung up and made my call to Hank Grainger. I left the same voicemail as I had on Peter Yoder's service and waited ten minutes to see if he would call back before I drove downtown to search Alexis's apartment.

Alexis's choice of neighborhoods had been referred to as The River Quay in the late 1970s, which was eons ago in real estate marketing. There had been a renewed effort to create an upscale entertainment district among the former storefronts and warehouses sometime in the last decade. Only a handful of produce vendors and long-standing warehousing operations had survived the gentrification of the previously all-commercial area north of Interstate 70. The interstate's running east to west formed a moat between what was now being called The River Market and the office buildings of downtown Kansas City.

The urban pioneers of the 1970s had failed to consider the interest Nick Civella's crime family had in controlling this part of town when they sought to create the entertainment and urban living combination that was finally taking shape thirty years later. The mobsters had made their position on redevelopment known by using enough dynamite to level nearly an entire city block to graphically eliminate a single bar which had refused their protection. That level of organized crime was gone now, which allowed the area to finally become a bustling mini-Soho with trendy shops, specialty grocers, overpriced bistros, and condominiums. I was not surprised to find Alexis had chosen to live in one of the oldest buildings in the district.

I followed the parking pattern on Alexis's block of Delaware and carefully backed into a vacant space diagonally, much to the annoyance of the line of cars behind me. It took a moment to realize the odd arrangement allowed for more available spaces than parallel parking would in the overcrowded neighborhood.

Alexis's loft was in a four-story brick building facing east across Delaware Street. The lower stories of her building faced a building directly across the street and the few windows on the north side overlooked a parking lot. Only the units on the top floor looked like they might have a view of the Missouri River or the skyline of Kansas City. There was a pleasant-smelling bistro on her building's ground floor and a large farmer's market barely three blocks away. Everything was crisp and clean, which made it feel soulless compared to the French Quarter. I prefer the patina of age and a touch of decay in my neighborhood. History makes the place feel like it is lived in.

I rang the buzzer with Alexis's maiden name beside it. There was no answer. I rang the buzzer a second, and then a third time with the same results. A resident in his late twenties approached the door with a bicycle over his shoulder and a cloth bag full of groceries and craft beer in his hand just as I was prepared to leave.

"Need some help?" I asked as he struggled to reach into a pocket for his keys.

"No, I think I have it," he said and waved me off.

"Well, let me get the elevator for you," I offered and smiled. I held the security door open for both of us once he unlocked it. I stayed a step ahead of him and punched the button for the elevator. We waited in silence for it to arrive.

"Are you new here?" he finally asked once we were on the elevator. "I don't remember seeing you before."

"No, I am visiting an old friend," I answered. I noticed he glanced at the elevator buttons and saw which floor I was headed towards. The look that crossed his face for just an instant suggested he knew who my friend was. I must have looked old enough to be one of the clients Alexis entertained if what Sean had told me about her was true. The guy had nothing else to say before he juggled the bike and groceries out of the elevator. The doors closed and I had a moment to reconsider my next move.

I had pulled a lock-pick set from the messenger bag set behind the passenger seat of my car. The canvas pack over my shoulder was certain to be something anyone I encountered would remember if the police interviewed them about a burglary on the third floor.

The carpeted hallway muted my footsteps as I made my way to the front of the building. Alexis had one of the premier lofts on the third floor, and only the one across the hall would have shared the building's original tall, curved window casings.

I knocked on Alexis's door even as I was opening the lock-pick case I removed from my pants pocket. Nobody poked their head out to see who was in the hallway and I did not knock a second time. It took me only seconds to pick the single lock and open the metal door into Alexis's apartment.

I was committed to the break-in, but I paused just inside the door to look for an alarm panel and to scan the doorframe and floor for any tricks Alexis may have used to tell whether someone had entered her apartment in her absence, such as a coin wedged in the doorframe or a piece of strategically placed tape in a corner to show the door had been opened. These were just a few of the ways I alert myself to any unwarranted intrusions in any hotel rooms I use.

The absence of an alarm system and the lack of any apparent precautions suggested that this was not Alexis's primary residence. This might have only been a place for a layover between continents and a place to hustle some business from her brother's acquaintances and their friends. It was tastefully furnished, though a little modern for my own taste, and I envied the massive windows that dominated her living room, even though her view was limited. This was a one-bedroom unit, but newly installed windows in the living room and her bedroom offered a nice view of downtown.

The exterior walls were stripped to the original brick. The original thick, wide-plank wood floor showed its years of use, but a thick coat of glossy varnish smoothed its surface. Alexis's collection of Afghan rugs covered the higher traffic areas to prevent slipping on the floor's slick surface. The ceiling had been painted in a flat black tone to conceal the exposed plumbing and duct work. I perused Alexis's bookcase and found it was full of coffee table-style picture books and a few authoritative tomes covering her narrow area of expertise. I picked up a couple of the antiquities she had on display and was amused, but not at all surprised, to discover they were fakes. The few plants in the room proved to be silk, so Alexis was not paying anyone to water her plants in her absence or leaving anything of value to be taken.

I stopped to look inside the galley kitchen's small refrigerator. There were no perishable vegetables, milk, or fruits and surprisingly few condiments. The freezer was stocked with frozen dinners sold by popular chain restaurants, but the total inventory was barely enough to allow her to survive more than a day or two without shopping. I checked out her wine cooler and noted that her own budget did not allow for a supply of the sort of expensive champagne she had ordered at Strada. Her liquor cabinet was stocked with upscale but affordable brands of alcohol. A partial bottle of eighteen-year-old Macallan Scotch stood out. It suggested Alexis had at least one regular visitor with exquisite taste in Scotch despite their poor taste in drinking partners.

I did not have a specific plan or piece of evidence in mind that I hoped to find when I picked the lock. I certainly did not believe Brian was holed up there. I was simply curious what Alexis's apartment could tell me about Alexis. There was a lot to learn, and I belatedly realized Tulip had been reading my own apartment to me as I was leaving town.

Alexis, though, had photographs on her walls, in addition to works of original art and a few framed posters which must have meant something to her. Most of the photos seemed work related, as she was invariably standing next to someone holding an antiquity. The artwork outnumbered the posters, but the posters chronicled museum showcases of artifacts she may have done the provenance work on or were where she had attended an exhibition. There was an unexpected New Orleans Jazz Fest poster of Harry Connick, Jr. hanging outside of her bedroom. It was numbered and signed. I wondered if she had attended Jazz Fest that year or simply bought the poster because of her appreciation for the musician. None of the museum posters were likely to become collectibles, but this poster was probably as valuable as any of the artwork. It commemorated what proved to be the last time the New Orleans music festival was held before Hurricane Katrina.

I could not locate a wall or floor safe, but I did find a phone book in the drawer of her nightstand along with a few very intimate items I avoided touching. I used the lock-pick to flip the pages in the phone book and spotted my name and Strada's address under the letter H. She had my cellphone number as well, which confirmed her decision to blindside me at the bar was a deliberate act.

Maybe she had only dropped by to confirm I was not dead. I vowed to get to the bottom of why everyone believed I was dead before this field trip ended. I had not failed to notice that no one I had spoken with since I arrived in Kansas City seemed happy to learn I was still alive.

Seventeen

I backed out of Alexis's empty condo as I told the empty space goodbye to make it look as though I were in conversation with an unseen occupant. I pulled the door closed and listened for the lock to engage. Anyone who knew Alexis was out of town would have debated calling the police if they spotted a burglar leaving or the had reason to believe someone else was using the unit. It was barely four o'clock, so her neighbors were still at work for the most part, but it was still a wise precaution.

I stepped outside and took a deep breath of the exhaust odor from the bistro's kitchen. It made me homesick for Strada Ammazarre's aromatic blend of garlic, grilled meat, and simmering pots of gumbo and red sauce that constantly find their way into my apartment two stories above the kitchen. I also took a moment to look around. None of the pedestrians gave me reason to believe they even noticed me. There were no cars parked with their engines running and drivers ready to follow me to my next stop. Nobody appeared to be looking down upon me from the windows across the street. Yet I felt watched. I have learned to trust this instinct rather than write it off as a manifestation of my PTSD. As the saying goes, you aren't being paranoid if someone is out to get you.

I unlocked my Cadillac coupe and replaced the lock-pick in the messenger bag before I locked the car again and began walking against traffic. I checked the side mirrors on the cars I passed for reflections of anyone tailing me. I kept one eye on the other side of the street and checked the cars I strolled past for extra antennas. Cellphones have rendered this former way to spot police cars obsolete. I walked two blocks towards the river and then circled the next block before abruptly reversing direction and retracing my steps. I did not spot anyone making the same about-face. There were far too many people using their phones to isolate anyone who may have been relaying details of my path.

I had just opened my car door when I heard a couple shouting after an albino pit-bull headed my way. I stopped in my tracks as the dog approached me. The good-sized dog must have sensed I was a dog person because it slowed its pace when it spotted me and sat down at my feet. I did the first thing that came to mind and grabbed its leather lead with my left hand before I began stroking its head with my right hand.

The man was already thanking me before he reached me and immediately took hold of the dog's leash. He wrapped the lead around his own hand but allowed the dog enough slack to sit where it was while we waited for his companion.

"What's his name?" I asked the couple after glancing between the dog's hind legs.

"Bruno," the woman said. "After Bruno Mars."

"Of course, it is," I laughed without meaning to openly mock them. Bruno was still sitting at my feet with his mouth open. This created the illusion of a smile as his spotted tongue rolled out of his mouth and he wagged his stump of a tail. His eyes were bright red and friendly. I suppose he looked like a Bruno, but I don't know many albinos named Brunos.

"Do you own a dog?" the woman asked as she maneuvered herself until she stood at a right angle to me. I was effectively boxed in, with my own car behind me, the pair flanking me, and Bruno directly in front of me. I suspected the pair were experienced pick pockets. I anticipated that the dog would 'unexpectedly' jump on me at some point and one or the other of them would help me adjust my clothes while doing their best to empty my pockets.

"A pit-bull named Roux. He's a New Orleans dog so there wasn't much choice when I named him." I made conversation to kill time until they made their move.

"Oh, you're from New Orleans?" the man asked. "We love it down there."

"It's probably the only place you will ever go that you understand whether you belong there within five minutes. It has a definite vibe," I asserted.

"Not so much here," the man laughed and waved his free hand to indicate the neighborhood while he silently gave the dog's leash some slack with the other. I did not expect the dog would prove to be aggressive. I braced myself for the dog's lunge, and when it did not happen as I expected, I stopped petting Bruno and abruptly stood up. Neither of the pair anticipated this move.

I straightened my jacket and stretched slightly to feel whether my handgun was still in place. I did not sense a physical threat from the pair that warranted drawing the handgun, but I wanted to be sure I could get to it if the situation changed.

"Well, it was nice meeting you, Bruno," I spoke to the dog and smiled at the man holding him. He seemed disconcerted that I was not following their script.

He reached his hand forward as though he wanted to shake my hand just as the dog finally made its jump and knocked me sideways into the woman. She grabbed me with one hand across my shoulders from behind until I could regain my footing and twist away from her. The incident lasted three seconds and the pair were very convincing in their apologies. I patted Bruno on the head one last time and stood my ground until the pair were standing with one another.

"Do you mind if we get a picture with you and Bruno? You were his savior today. I think anyone else would have thought they were being attacked and called the police," the woman asked and held her phone up to take the picture.

"Sure," I consented against my better judgement. I had my doubts that this was a funny story they would tell their friends over dinner. The woman took at least two photographs and then the pair thanked me one last time before they continued walking towards the interstate overpass. Perhaps they lived in a loft apartment across the bridge, but they carried no groceries, and the woman did not carry a purse or shoulder bag. I paid attention to the hairs tingling on the back of my neck.

I patted myself down. My badge was still on my belt and my state police ID was still in my left pants pocket. The handgun remained holstered in the small of my back. My cellphone was still in my other front pocket, and my wallet was in my right hip pocket. I had everything I started with, but still felt as though these two took whatever they wanted from me. Then it occurred to me that perhaps they were not trying to steal from me at all. Perhaps they meant to plant something on me.

I waited until I was locked in my car to feel myself for any metallic objects. Modern bugs and trackers are deceptively small and easy to tuck under a lapel or jab into a lining. I found nothing.

I drove to the nearby downtown airport and found a place to park outside of the TWA museum. I opened the Cadillac's trunk and visually inspected the hidden compartment containing the two rifles. The panel showed no signs of having been pried open or otherwise disturbed. I checked the trunk and engine compartment for tracking devices before doing the same thing at each wheel well. I ran my hand under the front seats and pulled them forward to look for anything I had not placed there and still came up empty. Lastly, I removed both license plates and checked behind them, and only then did I feel satisfied that my vehicle had not been disturbed.

I was not satisfied that I was not physically compromised. I knew about highly sophisticated tracking devices from my work in Iraq but I found nothing suspicious on my clothes. I wish I had found something because it would have saved me quite a chunk of money.

The only other means of tracking me that I knew of was through my phone, so it had to be destroyed. I could have tossed it in a dumpster or under the seat of a taxicab to confuse anyone tracking me, but I chose not to do so.

I made sure my phone contacts were backed up on the carrier's server before I placed its SIM card behind the driver's side rear tire. I started the car and slowly backed over the iPhone with both tires on that side of my car. It was not designed to survive such abuse, and it did not. I left it where it was and drove to the nearest retailer to replace it. I realized I might have to repeat most of these steps every time I met with Sean, Peter, or Hank. I needed to avoid allowing any of them, or their operatives, to get close enough to touch me or be close enough to my phone to clone it or learn its ISP to track it. Constantly replacing my phone was going to run into a considerable amount of money and inconvenience. I had not packed any of my burner phones because it never occurred to me that Brian's situation might involve the need for one. Besides that, none of the people I knew were involved in this were likely to answer a call from an unrecognized number. I also did not care to explain why I saw fit to carry multiple phones if anyone searched my car.

I left the phone store and headed to the Country Club Plaza to do some window shopping among the pseudo-European buildings. I thought I spotted at least two teams following me, but I did not care. Surely none of them believed I would meet Brian Hollis when I suspected I was being watched. If I was not being tailed, then someone saved a lot of money and manpower by making me imagine things so I might destroy my mental well-being all on my own.

Eighteen

I drove back to Lexington on Interstate 70 at fifteen miles an hour over the speed limit, not because I was worried about being followed but because I needed to do so to stay with the flow of traffic. I checked my rear-view mirror from time to time, but I no longer believed anyone was following me. Sean and Peter had already disclosed that they were aware I was in Lexington, so they had no need to track to know where I was staying.

Carol was washing her Volkswagen sedan when I pulled into the driveway. I parked in the space we agreed upon and locked my car again. She said nothing to me before I headed upstairs but I noticed the anxious look on her face.

I opened the door just enough to poke my head inside and confirm that the half-full glass of water behind the door was still upright. Another well-trained operative would have anticipated something being wedged in the doorframe, as I had at Alexis's, but probably would not have anticipated my placing a glass of water so close behind the door. I opened the door far enough to pick up the tumbler before I entered the apartment. Knocking the glass over would have left a damp spot on the rug even if someone set the glass back in place. I confirmed the windows were still locked before I opened the one above the sink to let in some fresh air.

I undressed and took a shower after hanging my pants and shirt on the wooden valet beside the bed to air dry. I had sweated more than I realized, and knew it had nothing to do with the heat. There was something going on beyond what I had gone into the city to learn.

I turned on the shower and did my best to sort out what that might be while I let the hot water relax my neck and shoulder muscles. I was bone tired from the drive, but I was also beginning to grow tense about the situation everyone seemed determined to make me believe Brian had brought upon himself. I doubted the versions of events that Alexis and Peter had shared. For one thing, Brian had never shown much initiative or interest in risking his life in the three years we served together in the

Rangers. We both left boot camp to take positions in a Ranger battalion that kept us tied to headquarters operations, which was why I eventually decided to lead a platoon in combat, attend sniper school, and join the Green Berets during my second enlistment. I was eventually selected for the only detachment the Army refuses to acknowledge exists, but which serves as their own Seal Team Six.

Brian, however, never felt the need to test his mettle in battle. He enjoyed the status of his position at headquarters, but he enjoyed the perks of life in the rear even more. Peter Yoder was clearly more interested in making money than in old friendships, and Alexis seemed unwilling to honestly explain her role in her own brother's situation. In the end, I realized I was no closer to finding an answer to Brian's actions or whereabouts than I was before coming all the way to Lexington.

The current list of facts was sparse and barely justified making the drive from New Orleans. Sean, Peter, and Hank were all sleeping with Alexis on a casual basis. That was none of my business, and frankly did not surprise me in the least. Alexis had persuaded all three men to purchase antiquities, and they had blindly trusted her word that the sales were above board and that the artifacts were genuine. The museum was not as enamored of her as my former classmates, and I imagined the man I spoke with about her history was already arranging for a second opinion on everything Alexis had vouched for under the previous director.

Sean had struck out on his own following his family's financial downturn. By all appearances he was able to finance himself on his stake from the sale of his family's bank. Sean may have leaned on the bank's loan officers under him to furnish Peter Yoder's purchase of Sean's father's trucking company before the bank collapsed, but Peter had paid the loan off well before its contracted maturity. Sean's club meant he was still looking for ways to make connections that he could profit from, just as he had at Wentworth.

I had no idea what Brian's opinion of his father selling out to Peter was, nor did I know Alexis's reaction to the sale. I could not imagine that Brian harbored any objections, considering he was never going to leave the military to run his family's small-time trucking company. It was ironic that he wound up working for his father's company all the same, having been paid to protect convoys of Peter's trucks six thousand miles from Missouri. There was a potential conflict with Hank because he had bought Brian's security outfit to benefit himself and Peter. That was unlikely because Brian's new contract suggested that his deal with Hank must not have included a non-compete clause.

Brian and I had drunk and talked for hours about what we had done as Rangers when I sought him out in Baghdad after taking a medical discharge, and I had shared the barest of details of my exploits in the Special Forces. We had eventually discussed our days together at Wentworth, but I do not recall Brian's even once bringing up that Peter Yoder had bought his father's business, or that Hank Grainger had recently bought his own private security company. Why had Brian decided to withhold information that should have been nothing more than a casual topic of conversation when we spoke? Did Brian's real reason for recommending that I work for someone else when I approached him in Iraq have something to do with an arrangement that he had with our former classmates that he did not want me to know about?

Chef Tony and I had put our lives on the line tracking down the insurgents who were targeting the same convoys Peter paid Brian and Hank to protect. It would have been nice to know I was doing my friends a favor in the process.

Peter Yoder most notably failed to mention what Hank Grainger's 'operations' were in Iraq when we had spoken. His description of the timeline for everyone's presence in Iraq suggested that Hank was already doing something in-country before he added Brian's company to his portfolio. Businessmen generally like to buy companies which enhance the ones they already own, and Peter had stated that Brian's private security firm 'dovetailed' with whatever Hank was doing at the time.

I stepped out of the shower focused on what Hank Grainger's

activities in Iraq might be, and why nobody wanted to discuss them. If anything, my classmates had gone out of their way to avoid mentioning Hank or the name of his company. Hank was an electronics geek in high school, at a time when knowing how to fix VHS players was considered a valuable skill. What had he become as an adult in a world which had become totally reliant on electronics to survive?

And why was he the only one still avoiding my calls?

Nineteen

I was hungry and decided to make up for my lack of exercise in the past two days by walking the half dozen blocks to Maid-Rite for a sandwich and an order of onion rings. Lexington's city blocks running north and south are twice as long as the blocks running east to west. I did not remember ever noticing this anomaly while attending Wentworth, because 'city block' was never a unit of measure on campus and I had few chances to explore the town.

The homes along Seventeenth Street, where I was staying, were all modest but largely well-kept. The homes lining Main Street were older and statelier, but not all of them were in good repair. The brick house on the corner when I reached the town's main drag had rotting boards and a crumbling driveway. Main Street sloped downwards from there before rising again just past the Maid-Rite and I knew I was going to feel a lot less like walking when it meant trudging uphill with a belly full of greasy food. I also felt awkward to be walking without Roux by my side.

Lexington's cramped Maid-Rite diner had opened its doors right after the Second World War. The floors, walls and the half dozen stools lined up along the worn Formica counter all looked original. The cooking equipment was probably only second or third generation and showed signs of heavy use. There was a McDonald's just a block away, but the diner's carhop was kept busy getting orders to the rows of cars parked behind the building.

I ordered two sandwiches and a single portion of onion rings with a large soda and watched the cook's practiced motions as he prepared my meal. He and Tony shared the learned capacity to be in constant motion without making a single wasted gesture. It was like watching a gifted artist at work, but this cook's creations smelled better than oil paint.

The arrival of two men in dark suits and white shirts was unexpected enough that every employee stopped to look at the pair. I glanced at them and immediately knew who they were but did not move or say a word. I doubted that they were there for anything to eat. Hopefully I had time to get my order as take-out.

"Detective Holland?" the older of the pair asked and stepped forward. He looked to be pushing sixty. His crew-cut hair was silver, and his muscle tone was getting soft. There was a time when he would have filled his suit as impressively as the thirty-something year old agent accompanying him fit into his pin-striped Brooks Brothers suit. The younger agent blocked the door and the older one maneuvered into position beside and slightly behind me, boxing me in just as the dog walkers had done earlier. There was no exit to my left and jumping the counter would have been senselessly dramatic. A third agent may have been posted at the back door on the off chance I did not accept the reality of my situation.

"Agent...?" I asked but did not fully turn to face the senior FBI agent.

"Bennett," he stated but did not offer any proof of his name or of actually being an FBI agent. The cook and two servers remained transfixed, and my food was going to burn on the griddle if things didn't get back to normal soon.

"What can I do for you, Agent Bennett?" I asked and pivoted enough to size up the junior agent. He was no rookie, either, but I could have taken either of them down if this proved to be anything but a rousting.

"Are you free right now?" Agent Bennett inquired with unusual etiquette.

"It looks like my order is just about ready," I said and turned to the cook. He was transfixed by the confrontation occurring before his eyes. "Can I get that to go?"

"Yes, sir," the cook stammered and motioned to the nearest waitress, a weary looking woman in her mid-forties that looked like she may have worked there half her life and seen her share of weird moments. She calmly wrapped and bagged my order before she refilled my soda and dropped a lid and straw on the counter along with my tab.

"You boys paying?" I inquired as I stood up. Their blank stares answered the question, so I tossed a twenty-dollar bill on the counter and told the server to keep the change before

I allowed myself to be escorted out between the FBI agents and walked to the black Ford sedan I recognized from the motel at the edge of town.

"Don't make a mess," Agent Bennett said and opened the back door. I slid across the vinyl to sit in the middle of the rear seat with the already greasy sack set on the floor between my knees. Neither agent had bothered to pat me down nor bothered to disarm me. This was becoming a very interesting interview.

The two agents took their seats in the front and Agent Bennett started the car. He exited the parking lot and turned to the right on Main Street, only to pull into the car wash a block away and stop the car in one of the brick-lined stalls. It occurred to me that they could hose my blood out of the Ford sedan's vinyl interior without anyone noticing.

"You know who we are," Agent Bennett said and turned to look at me over the seat. I opened the bag and removed the onion rings. They were best eaten while still warm. The Maid-Rites could wait.

"I know who I hope you are. How about a show of badges all around?" I asked him and pulled mine from the pocket of my sweatpants. They were visibly unimpressed with the shiny badge shaped like a golden model of the state of Louisiana, but it confirmed they had found the guy they were looking for when they entered the Maid-Rite.

They produced their own credentials in turn, and I nodded that I was satisfied I was talking with genuine federal agents. Normal citizens always demand to see badges and credentials but usually have no idea whether what they see is genuine or fake because they don't know what to look for when presented with a federal agent's credentials. Agents from the FBI office in New Orleans had shown me theirs enough times that I knew what to check.

"What is this all about then?" I asked and leaned back to enjoy my dinner. I offered to share the onion rings but they both shook their heads.

"What are you poking your nose into?" Agent Bennett asked. His tone was level, almost curious, but he was not in a mood to be toyed with.

"Honestly, I was hoping you might tell me." This was not the response either of them had expected and it was certainly not one that they were prepared to accept.

"You have no idea why you drove non-stop from New Orleans to Lexington and began asking your former classmates about Brian Hollis?" the younger agent snarled. I doubt he grasped how much information about the FBI's level of interest in Brian and my movements his question revealed. Agent Bennett did and flashed his partner an angry look that prompted the younger agent to turn around and look out his side window while the two adults discussed business.

"I came here hoping to convince Brian to turn himself in if I was sure he had committed a crime," I told them. "But now I do not think Brian is anywhere near here and, now that I know what he allegedly did, I am far less convinced he has done anything wrong. I think he may be the fall guy for some larger conspiracy."

"What makes you think that?" Agent Bennett asked. I assumed he knew things he was not going to share with me because he did not sound like he doubted my theory.

"His kid sister is working for a client who needs provenance for a shipment of Middle Eastern antiquities. Those may be the artifacts in the container her brother allegedly stole. That container is owned by a former classmate of Brian's and mine who has been sleeping with Brian's sister and buying antiquities from her," I told them. Neither of the agents blinked so this was likely something the two of them already knew. "I think Alexis and Peter Yoder are colluding on the sale and he needed someone to take the container from him so he would not have to find a way to steal it himself. I think they made Brian their fall guy. Brian figured it out and has gone into hiding, but he took the container with him and is looking for a way to stay out of an Iraqi prison."

"Do you really think they would double cross him? I mean, do you think Alexis Paradis would set her brother up like that?" Agent Bennett tried to poke a hole in my wild theory. I didn't believe my theory either, but it fit the facts at my disposal.

"Have you met Alexis Paradis?" I challenged his argument and noted that the agent had used her professional name even though he knew she was Brian's sister. "She would do worse than that if she stood to make enough money. Peter Yoder may have decided that it was better to make Brian the bad guy when he gave the Iraqi authorities his own version of things. Does that make sense?"

"We're not here to answer your questions," Bennett's partner snapped. The two federal agents used facial expressions to concur I was of little to no use in their quest for Brian Hollis.

"You should pack up and go home. You are only going to be a fly in the ointment, and the next time we talk it will be in our office and the topic will be your obstruction of justice," Agent Bennett warned me. The junior agent got out and opened my door.

"I'll take my chances on you making that stick." I told Bennett and then crossed my arms. "You interrupted my supper. You owe me a ride home."

Agent Bennett glared at me in the rear-view mirror and started to say something, but then he sighed again and started the car.

The fact I did not have to give him an address was my second freebie. Now I knew I had been tracked since the sheriff stopped me that morning. My hostess had just returned from shopping and was standing in the garage next to her car when the Crown Victoria pulled into the driveway. Carol took a hard look at the agents and then at me. Nothing was said between us before she collected her grocery bags and headed inside. I knew my presence was proving to be more than the couple had counted on when they rented me the space, and I hoped my hostess had not seen enough just then to boot me out.

I leaned back inside the car before I closed the passenger door.

"One more thing," I said. "A real interview would have taken place in your office or my room upstairs. This was an ambush. Whoever you guys are working for on the side needs to know I have no idea what is going on. You can tell them that I intend to stay here just because of your rousting. I intend find Brian Hollis and I will be here until I do."

"I'll pass that along," Agent Bennett assured me. "You best hope that we never drag you in officially. That sort of interview isn't a place for giving the sort of non-answers or making the wild accusations you just made. You don't want to dig a hole you cannot climb out of, Detective Holland."

"I don't plan to wind up in the hole anyone is digging for me, Agent Bennett," I said and slammed the door behind me.

Twenty

It was after normal office hours, but I called the local FBI office anyway as soon as I settled into the marvelously wide wing-backed chair in the carriage house's small living room. My hosts had stocked the bookshelves with a selection of books on the town's history and the biographies of a half dozen of the politicians and high-ranking members of the military who had either grown up in Lexington or had graduated from Wentworth Military Academy. It was an impressive array of literature and a cast of characters that few towns as small were likely to match.

"How may I direct your call?" the switchboard operator asked in a pleasant yet businesslike manner.

"I would like to speak with Agent Nathan Bennett," I told her. She placed me on hold. I began counting seconds. If she came back in under ten seconds, she would tell me there were no agents by that name in her field office. If she needed more than thirty seconds, there was a decision being made on how to approach my call by a supervisory agent.

She came back on the line in eighteen seconds.

"Agent Bennett is on vacation," she informed me. "Would you care to leave a message?"

"No," I said and paused as though I was considering my options. "I don't suppose you know where Nathan is vacationing?"

I did not believe using an agent's first name would be enough to convince an FBI telephone operator to share any personal details about that agent with me.

"I'm sorry, no," she said with perfectly feigned empathy.

"Could I perhaps speak with his supervisor?" I asked and did my best not to sound like I intended to escalate the situation.

"I'm sorry, they have left for the day," she immediately replied. That sounded like the truth, but I envisioned the night supervisor standing beside her and waving their arms to show they did not wish to speak with me. "Sir, would you care to leave a message for Agent Bennett?"

"Sure, why not," I decided. "Tell him I enjoyed having dinner with him this evening and look forward to following up on the case with him."

"Okay," she said in obvious confusion. "Why did you think he was here and then asked where he went on vacation when you just had dinner with him?"

"I wanted to be sure we were talking about the same Agent Bennett," I told her. "Do you have more than one member of his family working there?"

"In fact, we do," she unintentionally opened a door into the local office.

"Father and son? Father and daughter?" I wondered. I did not anticipate hitting pay dirt with my off-hand question. Perhaps she was alone at the switchboard.

"Uncle and nephew," she unexpectedly replied. She did not offer the younger agent's name. I had a good idea of what it was, though the last name didn't match. The facial triangle on the younger agent was very similar to his uncle's face.

"None of my business, really, but are they perhaps on vacation together?" I asked.

"I cannot answer that," she immediately slammed the door closed on the topic.

"Well, how much trouble would it be to get Agent Arthur Kinsey on the phone this evening?" I asked. She gave an audible gasp when I spoke the name of the agent accompanying Agent Bennett. Her reaction was enough to confirm both men were legitimate federal agents, but it did not absolutely confirm Arthur was Nathan's nephew. I still filed away that there was a family connection as being a fact.

"Fairly difficult," she allowed. She knew she had just disclosed something, but she and the supervisor she played this recording for were going to be bedeviled trying to figure out what I wanted to learn or accomplish in making the phone call. "And did I hear you correctly, that you discussed an investigation with Agent Bennett?"

"Yes, ma'am. I am an investigator with the Louisiana State Police and apparently your agents and I are in pursuit of the same individual. Agent Bennett wished to dissuade me from interfering in your own investigation," I gamely offered. With any luck, this would be gasoline on a fire.

"What is the name of that individual?" the operator inquired. Her tone was one of concern and curiosity.

"Major Brian Hollis, United States Army, Retired," I said. I tossed in his rank to help them confirm we were discussing the same individual. "Well, you have a pleasant evening and thank you for your assistance."

I was on the line long enough for the call to be traced, and I had used my own cellphone to make the call, so the FBI knew who had contacted their office about Agent Bennett. The phone operator failing to ask for my name when I left my message was my confirmation that I was already on their radar. All those times she put me on hold or paused a little too long were likely spent alerting someone that I was on the line, or the supervisor coaching her needed time to decide how to answer my questions.

One of two things would happen the next morning.

The first was that Agent Bennett and his nephew were going to be called to the local supervising agent's office to explain why they chose to spend their vacation in Lexington, Missouri during a manhunt in the area. The amount of trouble they were in would depend on whether the FBI was even aware that Brian Hollis might be in the area. No review board was going to forgive an agent's bounty hunting during their vacation.

The more likely scenario was that the supervising agent was going to have to deal with the presence of his agents in Lexington exposing the agency's interest in Brian Hollis. The unanticipated revelation of the FBI's investigation and its search for millions of dollars in stolen Iraqi antiquities would require a press conference to address the questions the media were sure to have. Perhaps I could get some work done while the FBI busied itself with shuffling its agents and wording a public statement about the case that could distract the newspaper reading public without fully informing them of what was happening.

95

Thursday

June 24, 2010

Four things I am wiser to know:

Idleness, sorrow, a friend, and a foe.

-Dorothy Parker

Twenty-One

There was a not entirely unexpected knock at my door the next morning. It was just past seven o'clock and I was preparing to take a shower after my morning exercises. I was still waiting to learn what my hosts' reaction to the agents who dropped me off the evening before would be. There was also the possibility that Hank Grainger had decided to speak with me in person. Brian must have known I was in town if he was in the area because everyone looking for him was beating a path to my door.

I opened the door to greet a well-dressed male with an intense expression. He looked to be in his late thirties, with a Middle Eastern complexion. He was a foot shorter than I, and his impatient attitude made it clear that he expected me to step aside and allow him to enter the apartment.

"May I help you?" I asked and glanced past him. There was a stocky bodyguard, who also looked Middle Eastern, at the top of the stairwell. He barely glanced at me. He was focused on not allowing anyone to interrupt our meeting.

"Detective Holland?" my unannounced visitor asked. I nodded to confirm my identity. I did not look particularly detective-like standing barefoot and dressed in baggy sweatpants and a sweat-soaked Funky Meters t-shirt. "Do you have a few minutes to discuss Brian Hollis?"

"I have all day to discuss Brian Hollis," I assured the man but held my ground. "What is your interest in him?"

"Do you mind if we speak in private?" he asked.

"I thought we were speaking in private," I told him, but then relented and stepped aside. The man gave the studio apartment a quick once-over. My shirt and pants from the day before were still air drying on the wooden valet beside the queen-sized bed. The bed was freshly made, and my dirty laundry was folded beside my carry-all full of clean clothes. These were habits developed over years of military conditioning and not because I expected company.

"Coffee?" I asked and waved the pot in the stranger's direction before topping off my own cup. I travel with a sack of ground Community Coffee because my taste buds reject the swill hotel chains provide.

"No, thank you," he said and made himself comfortable on the sofa, facing the wing chair he motioned for me to occupy. I remained standing because I saw no reason to trust him. I rested my forearms on the high back of the chair instead.

"You have thirty seconds to explain why you are here," I told him and glanced at my watch as though I were marking the time.

"My name is Sami Habib. I represent the interests of the Iraqi government," he declared, which bought him enough time to finish what he was there to say. "I came to tell you to go home while you still can."

"I just got here. Why would I do that?" I asked and managed not to flinch at the man's last name.

"Your presence might be considered to part of a conspiracy to aid Brian Hollis in his efforts to sell artifacts stolen from my country's museum. We have no time to decide what your real purpose is in being here, so it is easiest for us to assume the worst possible reason. Leaving will prove that you are innocent," Sami suggested.

"Who is this 'we' that doesn't have the time?" I asked Sami and then lied to his face. "I do not believe most people care why I am here or what I do next."

"You are clearly a problem for the authorities seeking Brian Hollis and the whereabouts of the container he stole," Sami elaborated without answering my question. It wasn't hard to guess that I was lying about the FBI being ambivalent.

"And how, precisely, do you represent the Iraqi government?" I asked. Sami had so far failed to produce any ID or proof of any legal authority. I also knew the proper name for the government Sami claimed to represent was the Iraqi Ruling Council, and that they prefer to refer to themselves as such rather than use the more general term he kept repeating.

"I am responsible for transferring the artifacts recovered from the thieves who robbed the museum after your country senselessly invaded ours," Sami offered as an explanation. None of this sounded as though he was in any position to tell me what to do. I did not share that we held identical positions on the invasion of Iraq.

"Good for you," I shrugged and took a drink of coffee. "That does not explain why you are knocking on my door at this hour of the morning."

"I am here because it would be unacceptable for you to interfere in the recovery of the antiquities your friend stole, or to help him escape from justice for what he has done," Sami finally explained his persistence on the matter.

"I have no intention of doing either of those things," I said. "I hope to convince Brian to turn himself in and to surrender the container you have accused him of stealing without bloodshed or incident. To be honest, I am still in the dark about Brian's motive for taking the container. It strikes me as being against his nature."

"I have proof that Brian Hollis stole the cargo container. It contains three hundred and forty-three pieces of our national heritage that were entrusted to a company owned by another friend of both of yours, and a third friend of yours was responsible for securing the trailer from theft," Sami Habib assured me. It was not good that the Iraqis already knew about our connections. "The Iraqi government has suspended the activities of the companies these men own until the container is recovered and the thief is delivered to the Interior Ministry for prosecution."

"I spoke with Peter Yoder yesterday. He told me about the theft, but he failed to mention his operations in Iraq were suspended." I mentioned this merely to inform Sami that I was in touch with the man who owned the company that he spoke of so obliquely, and to challenge his statement about Peter's business being sidelined. Peter *had* told me the same thing, but I did not want Sami to believe I trusted his version of things. "How is your government treating you for losing the container?"

"There is no reason to suspect I was involved in this theft. This occurred before I was in control of the container," Sami said. "The Interior Ministry is convinced that I am not involved.

I promise you that I am innocent."

"Innocent men go to prison every day, especially in places like Iraq," I weighed in. I was tired of this man's presence and his presumption that he could tell me what to do. I was not concerned whether Sami slammed the door, so long as it closed behind him.

"And guilty men walk free in your country because of policemen like you," Sami snarled.

"The ones I shoot don't," I fueled the fire just a bit more. "I have things to do this morning. Swapping this sort of crap back and forth with you is not one of them. You said your last name is Habib. Are you related to Colonel Ahmed Habib?"

"I am his nephew," Sami informed me, "And I am aware of your involvement in my uncle's disappearance."

"I don't know what you think you know, but I assure you that your uncle was not missing until there was a violent attempt to free him from our custody," I informed the colonel's angry nephew. Informing Sami that my partner Tony had traded his gravely injured uncle to members of Iran's Pasdaran in exchange for our safe passage to Italy via Syrian airspace would undermine the strength of my denials about knowing his fate or whereabouts.

"You had no reason to kidnap him," Sami sought to argue.

"Nobody kidnapped your uncle. He was being detained for questioning about the millions of dollars that he stole from your own country's treasury to finance attacks on Coalition troops and his attempts to disrupt the transition of power back to your own country," I said without a single hope of convincing him.

"What proof did you have that he did that?" Sami demanded.

"The pallet of hundred-dollar bills in the shed out back of his house matched the serial numbers of money transferred to your treasury by our government," I informed him. "I am sure your parents and aunt have spun this entirely differently. We were instructed not to speak with your uncle because his brother, who I am going to assume is your father, was about to be sworn in as part of the transitional government which preceded the election of the Ruling Council and we risked creating a political incident."

"My father is the Deputy Minister of the Interior," Sami informed me with a bit too much pride. The young man seemed entirely comfortable knowing his family held a position on the Ruling Council because of its comfort with corruption.

"And what are your intentions towards Brian? I doubt that you have any legal authority here, so I doubt you can extradite him to Iraq," I pressed Sami.

"He will be returned to Iraq with the pieces of our national heritage he stole to answer to my father," Sami declared firmly. I understood exactly what he meant to convey. He was not concerned about the due process in our court system. Sami had a fully fueled jet ready for departure somewhere close by.

"And if our government does not wish to see him extradited?" I wondered. I had to doubt that the Department of Justice or the State Department would rush to protect any American citizen who stole millions of dollars in antiquities from Iraq.

"I am taking Brian Hollis to Iraq with me, and they can ask for his return," Sami doubled down on the purpose of his mission.

"And will he disappear when he gets there?" I prodded him.

"He will receive a very public trial," Sami promised. "And a public execution."

"And you come here wondering why I might want to help my friend," I said and gave a hollow laugh. "I think my reasons are pretty obvious now, don't you?"

"You and the criminals you worked with in my country are still wanted men as well. You should be careful not give me a reason to take you back with me," Sami threatened me personally. My confidence in the State Department denying Iraq's requests for the extradition of Tony and myself if things went wrong here was not strong enough to allow me to laugh. Ralph had warned me not to come here.

"I will not go quietly," I growled and glanced at the holstered handgun hanging off the corner of the chair I was standing behind. Sami followed my eyes and then turned back to face me.

"I hope not," he said and smiled a tiny bit.

I did not allow the thick silence that followed this exchange to hang in the air.

"Then we are clear. Thank you for stopping by," I said and walked over to open the door.

Sami rose slowly, straightened his tie, and left without another word.

Twenty-Two

I telephoned Tulip at home.

I did not need legal advice. I just wanted to hear the voice of someone who would take my call and had not traveled half-way around the world to threaten me or was not hiding behind their badge to boss me around and was unlikely to express any suspicions that Brian and I were in cahoots.

"It is eight o'clock in the morning, big brother," Tulip complained. I knew she had been up since six o'clock and had already spent an hour on her rowing machine and eaten a light breakfast. "Are you in jail? Do you need bail?"

"No, I just wanted to check in," I reassured her. "But hold that thought."

"Oh, dear," she sighed. I imagined her sitting down at the breakfast counter and bracing herself for bad news.

"Brian is clearly guilty of taking the antiquities. They were in a shipping container that he stole from a company owned by one of our old classmates," I informed her.

"Then leave well enough alone. Let him get caught and come on home," Tulip pleaded and added her name to the list of people who wanted me off the case that was still not even a case as far as I was concerned.

"Yeah, I would, but things are weird," I lied. I was certain that I was not going to leave. "Like I said, the container Brian swiped belongs to a guy named Peter Yoder. Yoder bought his trucking company from Brian's father years ago and made it into something a lot bigger than it ever was."

"Peachy," Tulip sighed again. "I assume there are conspiracy theories?"

"I don't know that there are any on this side of the Atlantic. The Iraqis have suspended their contracts with Peter Yoder until they get their antiquities back because they don't like the link between him and Brian. That must cost Peter quite a bit of money every day this goes on. The Iraqis clearly think there is some sort of connection, and one of them visited me this morning to say my being here made me part of their conspiracy theory about the theft," I elaborated.

"I repeat, you need to come home," Tulip recommended. "Take yourself out of the equation. I am still not clear what you hope to accomplish by being there."

"I don't know either, unless I find Brian," I admitted. "It gets worse. The company that was responsible for securing the container is owned by another guy we went to school with, a guy named Hank Grainger."

"I am starting to like the Iraqis' theory," Tulip let me know. "And I know for a fact that you had nothing to do with any of this."

"It might be possible that Peter, Hank, and Brian are in this together, maybe with Alexis, but I do not believe any one of them has any idea what to do with a container full of antiquities the Iraqi National Museum can identify. I just do not see any of these guys being black market types," I lamely argued. I had not been in touch with any of these former classmates in decades and had no idea what their current ethics were. Buying antiquities from Alexis told me there was as much moral flexibility on the part of Peter Yoder and Hank Grainger to buy them as there was for Alexis to sell them. The possibility of a combination of any of these classmates plotting with Brian to take the container did seem to be more credible than the counterargument that the association these former classmates had with the missing container was nothing but a coincidence.

"We are talking about a lot of money. People do mighty stupid things when this much money is involved," Tulip shared her opinion, based no doubt on her experience as a civil attorney.

"Alexis is my only lead to Brian," I confided. "But that means accepting the possibility that he stole the container and that she is selling it, and that they are in touch with one another. She tried to convince me they haven't spoken in years when we saw each other New Orleans."

"Maybe I should speak with her," Tulip suggested.

"That couldn't possibly scare her," I said to discourage the idea.

"Is there anything else I should know or that you need for me to share with Tony?" Tulip wondered now that she accepted that I was not returning to New Orleans.

"Let Tony know that Colonel Habib's nephew is in the country. Sami Habib was the guy who was supposed to deliver the missing container to the museum. He just threatened to gather me up when he finds Brian and to spirit both of us to Iraq. Sami is here on his own, but I think he brought some of his father's agents with him." Tony had filled her in on our activities in Iraq enough that the name Habib sent the same chill down her spine that shot down mine when I heard it that morning.

"He will want to join you in Missouri if I tell him that," Tulip pointed out. "Maybe you should wait to tell us about him when you get home."

"Tony needs to know to keep his eyes open," I insisted.

"The man literally sleeps with his eyes open, Cooter," Tulip audibly shuddered over the phone. "He weirds me out sometimes, I gotta tell you."

"Yeah, I should have tipped you off about that, sis." I laughed at the only thing I had found amusing so far that morning. "I spoke to him for half an hour one time before I realized he was asleep."

"My lips are sealed for now," Tulip told me. "But let me know if you need legal help or if you need me to send the dogs of war. Roux misses you, by the way."

"I will be home soon. Tell them both hello, okay?" I requested.

"Sure thing," Tulip agreed. "Now, go be careful."

She hung up before I could find anything pithy to say. I belatedly realized this call had ruined her day before it even started.

Twenty-Three

Whatever Brian needed me to be in Lexington to help him do was going to happen in two days' time no matter what I did. I was out of leads, and I saw no reason to hope that Hank Grainger returning my call would give me enough new information to understand what was going on any more than I presently did.

My process of elimination left the FBI as my only potential source of information on the manhunt for Brian Hollis, and perhaps some background on the crime itself. Sami's presence indicated there were far more pieces to the puzzle than I initially understood.

There was absolutely no reason to believe the FBI would be forthcoming with what they knew. It was still worth the drive to Kansas City to speak with the SAC. I did some hasty research to locate the address of the FBI's office in Kansas City and to study the agency's website's biography of Special Agent in Charge Harold Rogers for anything I could use to my advantage.

I put on the suit I had packed as an afterthought, and clipped my detective shield to my belt and holstered the .45 caliber handgun on my right hip. I looked at myself in the mirror and practiced looking like a competent investigator for a couple of minutes before I went downstairs.

I took a few minutes to feel around the car for any tracking devices Sami's men might have installed while he had me distracted upstairs. I found nothing but noticed that the gas gauge indicated I was nearly out of gasoline. I knew I had gone to bed with over half a tank. Someone had intentionally drained the gasoline from the car to force me to refuel before I left Lexington. This meant I was either about to be ambushed or they wanted to force me to stop for fuel so they could track me from the filling station. I had to admire their plan. I had to refuel even though I knew there was a trap involved.

I bought gasoline and a cold drink at one of the new filling stations on the south end of town. A Ford Explorer left the shopping plaza across Highway 13 as I left the station. It was green and looked brand new. The color told me that it was not a police vehicle and that suggested it was a rental car, which implied the driver and his passenger worked for Sami Habib.

This was the first time I had noticed a tail. I had my doubts that it was the first time I had been followed since I arrived. The sheriff was unlikely to be keeping tabs on me. The FBI would use one of their own vehicles. The Missouri State Patrol had so far ignored my presence.

I pulled into the parking lot where the black Crown Vic was still parked and honked to get the attention of Agents Bennett and Kinsey before I circled their car and headed back into town. The Explorer confirmed it was following me when it made a U-turn in the same parking lot. The driver stayed six car lengths behind me as I began to drive around town. I spotted one of Sheriff Franks's deputies parked on Fifteenth Street with a radar gun aimed down Main Street. I slowed well below the speed limit and waved as I passed him by. He waved back uncertainly, and then turned to face south again.

I waited until I was three car lengths past the deputy and pressed my foot to the floorboard. The Cadillac's supercharger whined as the speedometer needle passed one hundred miles an hour. The driver in the Ford Explorer reacted by doing the same thing lest he lose me, but this meant he was driving recklessly above the speed limit when he passed the radar trap.

I saw the deputy's flashing lights behind the big SUV as I passed the Casey's convenience store at the edge of town. I could have turned left as I crested the slope leading out of town and crossed the new Missouri River bridge, but that road led me away from where I wanted to go. I sped past that turnoff and entered westbound Highway 24 barely a quarter of a mile further on. I exited this highway almost immediately to resume my original course on Highway 13. The men in the Ford Explorer undoubtedly knew I was headed back to the city, but they would have no idea what route I chose. They also had to know that they had just drawn the attention of the local sheriff, which was probably no more of a deterrent to them than my own interaction with him was to me.

The trip into Kansas City was uneventful despite the driving skills of Missouri drivers. I checked my rear-view mirror three times but never spotted a second tail. I passed two state patrol cruisers and neither of them showed interest in me, or my license plates. I exited the interstate at 12th Street after negotiating the bottleneck where Interstates 35 and 70 meet.

The FBI office in Kansas City is one of the downtown skyline's newer buildings. It sits on a virtual peninsula, flanked by interstate on its north and south sides and a steep bluff on its west side. Nobody can get close to the building without permission or a fight. I used my badge to talk my way past the armed security manning the heavy rolling gate. I parked in the visitor lot and smoothed my hair and clothes before I made my way to the front door.

The security guard that greeted me at the metal detector just inside the front door seemed disinterested in my Louisiana identification and badge, but he allowed me to pass with my handgun all the same. He directed me to the counter nearby, where I presented myself again and asked to speak with the Special Agent in Charge. I hoped using the ranking agent's name would imply we were acquainted.

"What is the nature of your visit?" the agent manning the reception desk asked.

"The Brian Hollis case," I stated as I signed my name in the daily visitor log. His eyes narrowed just enough to betray that I was the first non-FBI investigator requesting an audience with SAC Rogers to discuss Brian Hollis.

The agent gave my name and expressed my interest in speaking with his boss to someone at the other end of the phone. He repeatedly glanced at me as he waited for a response. I backed away from the desk and paced casually, trying to suggest I knew this was all a formality before I would be allowed to speak with SAC Rogers.

Two middle-aged agents came through a side door and approached me. One checked out my identification and the other relieved me of my sidearm.

"Can I get a receipt for that?" I tried to joke with him. He did not smile and avoided making eye contact the entire time.

"Come with me, Detective Holland," the first agent finally said and turned to lead the way to an elevator. We rode in silence until we reached the floor he had selected. I silently followed the humorless agent until he opened the door to a conference room and ushered me inside. He closed the door behind me and stood guard outside the room in case I decided to wander. The small conference room was paneled, and every window faced west. The door and interior wall were solid, and kept my presence masked to agents working in the cubicles on the floor.

A surprisingly young man in a well-tailored suit arrived ten minutes later, with an agent and a female who immediately sat down at the far end of the table and opened her notepad. That there was going to be a transcript of our conversation was a positive sign. It indicated that SAC Rogers might not consider me to be an obstruction to the manhunt. I knew better than to hope that he might share everything he knew. The best he was likely to agree to would be an information swap at an exchange rate favorable to the FBI.

"Good morning, Detective Holland," SAC Rogers said and shook my hand. He was taller than I anticipated, with meticulously groomed black hair and a pair of wire-framed glasses. "I am Special Agent in Charge Harold Rogers. Thank you for coming by. It saves us sending a car for you."

"That has already been done once," I pointed out. I liked the way he frowned at this comment. He waved to a chair and took a seat at the head of the table.

"I am aware of the meeting," he said.

"Can I assume that was an unofficial visit?" I asked. "Perhaps unauthorized?"

"Feel free to assume anything you wish, detective," Rogers firmly dismissed the topic. "I do not believe last evening's encounter is why you are here. Would you mind explaining your interest in Brian Hollis?"

"He called me at about two thirty Monday morning and asked me to meet him in Lexington this Saturday. He said he was in legal trouble, but he did not tell me what sort of trouble it was. I told him I was not going to do so, and he hung up. That was the extent of our call," I shared.

"If you told him no at the time, then why are you here now?" Rogers asked.

"Because his sister paid me a visit later that same day. I had not seen her in twenty years, so I was more than a little surprised that she knew where to find me. She told me she was an antiquities expert and was in town to provide provenance on a large collection of Persian artifacts. The combination of those two reaching out to me made me reconsider Brian's plea for help."

"How did you know Brian Hollis was involved with those artifacts?" Rogers skeptically asked.

"I didn't know when we spoke. I learned about his being suspected of the theft from a different source than his sister," I explained but left out Ralph Easter's being the source.

"Do you believe looking for Brian Hollis is considered to be light desk duty by your supervisors?" SAC Rogers asked. He must have had an agent make inquiries about me back in Louisiana. I was probably in trouble if they spoke with the SAC in New Orleans or my captain at the state patrol.

"I imagine not. For the record, I took vacation time rather than sit at that desk. I am not here in an official capacity. Unless you ask for my help," I informed him.

"You will want to keep that in mind, detective," Rogers told me. "You are out of your jurisdiction, and you are not going to be any part of our investigation. Your actions will be considered those of a normal citizen, and that means you should avoid presenting yourself as a member of law enforcement while you are here."

He was trying to make a point, but I was going to ignore the implied threat. "I will keep that in mind."

"You won't have a badge to hide behind if you shoot someone," he clarified his warning. "You will have a hard time making a good case for self-defense with your background."

"Good to know," I acknowledged. This was a serious problem. I doubted I was going to get through this without shots being fired, but I could not let him see he had created a wrinkle in my plans.

"Perhaps you should reconsider being here," SAC Rogers suggested.

"Perhaps," I sighed. "The thing is, Brian was my high school roommate. We have not been close friends in years, but I do not believe he has gone into the truck hijacking business. I came here to see if I could track him down and get his side of the story, and then convince him to turn himself in. Hopefully that can be done without bloodshed or unnecessary drama."

"You are not his partner here to turn yourself in?" Rogers was joking but he sounded disappointed.

"You know I am not," I challenged him. "You have been tracking him for some time and would have intercepted any calls between us or found signs that I was giving him material support by now."

"You're right," Rogers admitted and shook his head. "What you are is a joker. You're that extra card in the deck that nobody knows what to do with."

"I came here hoping you might help me decide between staying and leaving. I thought this was just about stolen artifacts, but now I think the container is the key to a larger investigation you aren't going to discuss with me," I told him. "That means I have to stick around until I know what is really going on."

"What do you think is going on?" he asked and locked eyes with me.

"I had a visit from Sami Habib a couple of hours ago. He told me he intends to personally extradite Brian and me to Iraq after he recovers the container," I told him. "It does not occur me that Sami is doing either of those things under any authority from the Iraqi Ruling Council."

"He is not," Rogers confirmed but did not offer anything further.

"I have dealt with the Habib family in the past. I see no reason to believe his true intentions are to return the shipment and become a national hero. The family tends to have its fingers into a lot of things nobody seems to notice, and national treasures are maybe the best bargaining chip on the planet." I did my best to open as many topics as possible for SAC Rogers to share what he knew.

"I am better versed in your past with the Habib family than you might imagine," SAC Rogers unexpectedly informed me.

"I read your biography before I came here," I let him know.

"I know we were in Iraq at the same time."

"I sat in on the interrogations of the members of Operation Stoplight the Iraqis rounded up in the aftermath of the ambush that ended with the disappearance of Colonel Habib," Rogers said and leaned towards me. "SAC Conroy in New Orleans provided me with an unredacted copy of the after-action report that he claims a Deputy Director of Homeland Security attempted to use to compromise your sister to get your cooperation in some sort of crazy plan he had."

"Nothing worked out as he planned. If you read the report, then you know our operation in Iraq began as an effort to interdict the attacks on our troops. What we found was that the attacks were orchestrated by Colonel Habib. The colonel had begun siphoning money from Iraq's treasury while Saddam was still in office. Our government sending that much cash to the Iraqi's treasury with no controls in place made it easy for Colonel Habib to steal even more money. He literally backed a truck up and drove away with an entire pallet of hundred-dollar bills in American currency he used to destabilize the interim government," I touched on the report's high points. Its four hundred pages held more low points than high points.

"Yeah, I noted that the report claims that same pallet went missing during the ambush intended to free Colonel Habib from your custody," Rogers reminded me. "I do not suppose you know where it went."

"Sorry, I was busy having my skull caved in at the time," I snarled. I had not asked for this interview to become a re-hashing of my failures.

"That's right. You died," Rogers said and sat back in his chair. "How was that?"

"Dying?" I asked him. "Involuntary, but fortunately brief. I barely missed the whole bright light and talking to a dead relative thing. I was in pain, then I wasn't, and then I woke up in enough pain to make me wish I was dead."

"One of the plates they put in your head saved you in that last shooting, right?" he asked. I could not tell if he was morbidly curious or still trying to show me how much thicker his file was on me than mine was on him.

"Yep," I confirmed. "And that is why I have the time to be here."

"In case you have missed it, what I am saying is that I know how you operate. Try any of your usual nonsense around here and you will end up dead or in prison. Are we clear?" the Special Agent resorted to explaining his choice of topics in plain English. "And for the record, the FBI still shares the Iraqi government's interest in what became of Colonel Habib and the family's bank accounts that were emptied the day after the ambush."

"I suggest asking Colonel Habib about them when you find him," I shrugged. It was a practiced shrug. Most of the money redirected from the colonel's offshore accounts became Tony's bankroll when he opened our bistro and the colonel most likely died at the hands of the Iranians. I have always assumed the truck with the cash wound up in the hands of whoever was paid to ambush us.

"Nice answer," SAC Rogers snorted. "You are not going to be allowed to interfere in our investigation or to take part in Brian Hollis's apprehension. I will confirm that Sami Habib's interest in the missing container has nothing to do with returning it to the Iraqi National Museum. Do with that information what you will."

"What I hear is a warning to watch my flank and to trust the FBI to handle things because you guys have such a great track record with situations like this," I said as I pressed my forearms on the table and interlaced my fingers. "I also suspect that you intend to use me to distract Sami Habib. I already know to watch my ass, but I do not trust you to arrest Brian without getting him killed."

"That will be Brian's decision when the time comes," the Special Agent in Charge said and gave a dismissive shrug. "I hope he surrenders and leads us to the container without a fight. I honestly do."

"Well, thank you for validating my decision," I told him and stood up.

"For what it's worth, have you ever stopped to consider what your big mistake was in Iraq?" SAC Rogers told me and stood up as well.

"Mistake? What mistake do you think I made?" I asked in a mixture of challenge and confusion. The truth is, I stopped re-hashing Operation Stoplight before I was out of the hospital.

"You telegraphed your next move," Rogers said and smiled just a bit at the thought he had outsmarted me. "You were ambushed because you told the wrong guy what you were about to do. You would have gotten away with grabbing the colonel, who I agree was dirty, if you had kept quiet about doing so."

I started to respond to his analyses, but all I managed to do was move my lips a couple of times before I realized he was right. Everything would have gone to plan had I not informed our handler what we planned to do and refused to stand down.

"Agent Evans will escort you out. The security officer at the door has your handgun. I suggest you refrain from carrying it."

"Until we meet again," I said and refused to extend my hand before I spun and left.

I walked to my car replaying the last exchange the FBI leader and I had before I left. I wondered if he was sending me another message. I had told him why I was there and what I hoped to accomplish, much the same as I had done with my handler that fateful day in Baghdad. Was he telling me to keep him out of the loop in the future, or was he telling me I was digging my own grave yet again?

Twenty-Four

It was barely eleven o'clock and my day had already involved being threatened with rendition to Iraq and a stern reminder that the FBI did not consider me to be a law enforcement officer while I was outside of the state of Louisiana.

What I had not accomplished that morning was to contact Hank Grainger or to track down Brian Hollis. I was running out of time for background interviews. Whatever Brian was doing would happen whether Hank Grainger returned my calls. Considering the minimal actionable information Sean and Peter had provided, speaking with Hank was no longer high on my list of things to do. I turned my attention to the second problem, which was really the only problem.

Brian had asked me to meet him in Lexington on Saturday, now only two days away. I had a day and a half to convince him to hand the stolen goods over to the FBI and surrender on his own terms. I needed to figure out a way to insinuate myself into whatever Brian was doing, at the risk of being viewed as a co-conspirator.

I left the FBI's parking lot and drove to the nearest parking garage. I chose a spot on one of the upper decks where I could back in and watch the vehicles entering that level of the garage. I was sure I had thwarted the men in the rental SUV, but that didn't mean Sami did not have someone waiting to take their place when I was closer to Kansas City. I imagined SAC Rogers planned to keep a very close eye on me as well. I set my handgun on the console between the seats and opened my messenger bag to remove my iPad.

I booted up the tablet and opened the case file I was building based on my interviews. I added my notes from my conversation with SAC Rogers and reviewed the handful of things I had come to accept, then began reviewing what my conversations with Alexis, Sean, and Peter added or detracted from these points. I did the same with my conversation with Agent Bennett, Sami Habib, and my brief discussion with Special Agent in Charge Rogers.

I found only two things each conversation had in common. The first was their certainty that Brian had absconded with a twenty-foot-long shipping container loaded with antiquities previously stolen from the Iraqi National Museum. I remained skeptical that Brian had stolen the container with the intention to illegally transfer the contents to someone in exchange for something of value. The second thing was that Brian intended to emerge in Lexington on Saturday at an unspecified time and place. Neither of these items gave me anything to work with and I did not believe waiting until Saturday was a viable option if I was going to learn and perhaps change Brian's plans.

Everyone I had spoken with had developed their own suppositions about Brian's motive for taking the antiquities and his possible intentions when it came to getting rid of them, but their disparate ideas amounted to the equivalent of blind men describing an elephant based on what they felt in front of them.

Peter Yoder claimed the antiquities were in a twenty-foot-long steel shipping container, which made it closer to the size of a large U-Haul moving van than a regular sixty-foot-long aluminum-sided box trailer that would require a semi to move. Referring to it as a shipping container also suggested it was not limited to being moved on the highways. Shipping containers are designed to be put on ships or trains for transport, and then transferred onto special carriers in a port or rail yard for final delivery by truck. I imagined that the value of the cargo had dictated the extra security of using a steel sided container even though its original destination was only a few hours from Peter Yoder's shipping yard.

I reread my notes on my conversation with Peter Yoder. He claimed to have a shipping manifest that showed the cargo container was sent to Baltimore on a container vessel that left Kuwait nearly a month ago. Peter also seemed convinced that Brian had changed the numbers on the container and the cargo manifest after he slipped it aboard a ship loaded with hundreds of other trailers in P-Y International's inventory. Using the original container number on the ship's list of containers was a deliberate attempt to let Peter Yoder know the container was on its way to the United States.

I looked forward to learning what Brian had called the antiquities to get the container past Customs. I suspected that Brian was moving the container from railyard to railyard like the ball in a shell game to keep it from being located by the authorities before he could do whatever he planned to do with it.

This suggested to me that Brian would be hiding not far from the final railyard. Ideally, he would have found a place that overlooked the tracks so he could watch for the container's arrival. He would want to be close to the container's destination because he needed to monitor the railyard for a few days to detect any change in activity that would indicate the FBI was lying in wait to arrest him.

I looked up Peter Yoder's company in an online phone directory and called P-Y International's local shipping office. I claimed to be a truck driver trying to drop off a container but was frustrated with Kansas City's unfamiliar layout. The city has multiple rail yards, so I used this ruse to find the one Yoder's company used to process their containers rather than canvas every yard.

I brought up a map of Kansas City on the iPad. Yoder's preferred railyard was located just across the state line in Kansas. I ran a search for motels in the area and then used a satellite image in one of my map applications to research the lodging possibilities in the Rosedale neighborhood. I located one chain hotel which appeared to have a clear line of sight to the railyard, though from a considerable distance. There were half a dozen other hotels and motels close to the railyard, but all these other possibilities lacked a clear view of the railyard.

The hotel I zeroed in was located near the KU Medical Center, and it likely did the bulk of its business with patients and the families of patients at the sprawling medical facility. Someone booking a week or two stay there would not appear unusual to the hotel desk clerks. The hotel also had access to a half dozen expressways and Interstate 35 if Brian needed to make a hasty exit.

The tricky part of confirming Brian's presence was approaching the hotel without being followed, and then to find a place to watch the parking lot long enough to determine if the hotel was already under surveillance and whether someone was stationed to protect Brian from anyone approaching his room. Brian owned a private security company of his own, so he had men on his payroll with the experience to handle protecting him. He was not able to drive the container off Peter Yoder's lot in Iraq by himself, so the men who helped him were also on the run. It was likely that Brian had evacuated the remaining staff before he stole the container if he had thought things through, and doing so made it hard to know who was with him and who was on the sidelines. Tony and I had run Operation Stoplight using a dozen handpicked operatives doing the raids while Tony and two other men handled the interrogations. I converted any information they extracted into action plans for the next raids. I never counted the technical crew from D-Tech because they were never in the field with us and only interacted with us by encrypted emails. It would have taken less than a dozen men to move the container off Peter Yoder's lot in Iraq; a truck driver and armed passenger and at least two vehicles worth of security detail. Brian would probably need fewer men to accomplish his goals on Saturday than he needed to hijack the container. Even a small group of single men staying in a hotel without a clear purpose for doing so would eventually draw the attention of the desk clerks and housekeepers.

I could not approach the hotel where I suspected Brian was holed up in a bright red Cadillac convertible with COP CAR license plates. Anyone protecting Brian would notice the vanity plates before they realized they were Louisiana plates and could satisfy themselves that I was not a threat. I locked my car and took the elevator down to street level and spent the next twenty minutes trying to get a taxi driver's attention.

I had the cab driver take me to the hotel and told them to wait for me. I passed him a fifty-dollar bill to incentivize his patience. It was more than enough to pay the fare on the meter, but he understood this tip was over and above that amount. He smiled and nodded his agreement to wait for me.

"Good afternoon," the cheerful woman on the front desk greeted me. I glanced up at the clock behind her and noticed that it was barely past noon. She was a very aware person, and that was who I wanted to speak with if possible. "Early check-in, sir?"

"I don't know," I said and tried to give the impression of a confused traveler. "I am supposed to meet members of my sales team here, but I do not know if this is the right hotel. I left my reservation information on the plane."

"No problem, I can look that reservation up for you," she responded.

"Well, the reservation is not in my name," I apologized. "I am supposed to share a room with one of the other salespeople. Can you check out a couple of names for me, to see if they have already checked in?"

"Sure," she said, but with a faint tone of suspicion. Giving out the names of her registered guests was probably against a whole range of company policies. I was not asking her to give me any names, only to confirm whether the names I gave her were in her registration system.

Brian would not be checked in under his own name. I had no idea of the names of any of his men or an alias that he might be using. That was less of a problem than it seemed because Peter Yoder or the FBI did know, and they might have been through here looking for anyone with those names by now. I found myself at a loss.

"Try Alexis Paradis," I suggested out of desperation. Maybe Brian's sister was footing the bill for his rooms and was pretending not to be involved in his actions.

The desk clerk clicked away on her keyboard and we both held our breath until the computer gave her an answer.

"Sorry, sir, nobody by that name is registered here," she said with a comforting frown. "You're sure the reservation is not under your name?"

"I'm all but positive of it," I assured her, but then decided to spin the wheel. "But let's go ahead and try."

She entered Cooter Holland into the reservation system and broke into an unexpected smile.

"There you are," she said and swiveled the screen so I could see my name where it absolutely did not belong. "Three nights. Check-out on Sunday. Is that right?"

"Yes, I guess it is," I said in a state of mild shock.

"Let me get you a key and you are on your way," she told me.

"Is the room paid for?" I asked. I truly hoped someone had not hacked my card and linked me to Brian's crime by charging a hotel room to my account.

"Yes, sir. Your company has prepaid all the rooms," she told me. I could not hide the confusion I was having at that moment. "We get a lot of business from D-Tech."

My heart missed two beats and I felt my face flush at the very mention of the company. I placed a hand on the counter to steady myself while I did my best to act as though there was nothing wrong.

"Can you tell me when the reservation as made?" I croaked.

"This morning. I made the reservation myself about an hour ago," she said after checking the reservation details on her computer. The clerk paused what she was doing when she noticed my reaction to something she considered to be perfectly normal.

"Sorry, something I ate at the airport is catching up to me," I said and forced a grin.

"Eww, I understand," she said and hurried a little more. She produced a single room key and a pair of complimentary drink tickets but spared me the spiel about the pool and breakfast times so I could get to my room.

"Thank you," I said in what probably came out as a mumble. I picked up the key and returned to the safety of the taxicab.

"Where to?" the driver asked. I had to pause to consider my answer. I had a room waiting for me on the top floor of the hotel. I could check it out and then call another taxicab to take me back to my car. I chose to have the driver return to the parking garage while I considered the multiple explanations for, and problems posed by, my unexpected lodging arrangement.

Somebody had anticipated my approaching the hotel before I thought Brian might be lodged there. At the very least this meant whoever arranged for the hotel room was aware of our telephone call. Brian and I were the only ones who should have known about his call, but I was all too aware of D-Tech's capacity to monitor telephone calls without being detected. They were likely tracking Brian's phone, which meant they were on his trail and already miles closer to catching him than I was. It also meant they were very likely tracking my own movements.

My having a room at the hotel, under my own name no less, was no assurance that Brian had a room there as well. If anything, it contraindicated his being anywhere near the hotel. There was a possibility that Brian had booked the room using a company name he knew I would see as a red flag. I was torn between checking in and seeing if there was a clue waiting for me and staying as far from the hotel as humanly possible because it struck me as being a trap designed to be as obvious as possible. I looked at the room key. The room number indicated that the room was on the side of the hotel facing the railroad yard, and it was close to the elevator. Neither was a coincidence of booking. Someone specifically requested that room for me, and I had no idea why that was.

My darkest fear, and the one that made me retreat for the moment, was that D-Tech played some role in the theft of the container. I had survived the ambush they arranged in Iraq, and I had recently dismantled the operation they were running in New Orleans at the behest of Deputy Director of Homeland Security Bradford Kinkaid. The now former Deputy Director was currently awaiting trial on a slew of corruption and malfeasance charges related to D-Tech's unauthorized deployment in New Orleans. I had absolutely no interest in facing off against the shadowy company a third time. I had a winning record and understood the stakes involved in playing against them a third time. Sooner or later, they would win, and I would likely be dead.

But...

Curiosity has killed more than cats. I needed to understand the extent of D–Tech's involvement in Brian's actions or their role in affecting his eventual capture. Knowing which side of the law D-tech had chosen to be on this time would be a huge leap forward in figuring out what was going to transpire on Saturday.

I smelled barbecue as we pulled away from the hotel. I asked my driver if he knew where the unmistakable odor was coming from and he broke into a broad grin.

"That is Rosedale Barbecue," he said. "Good stuff."

"How good?" I asked. I could not miss that the car was slowing down in anticipation of a turn at the foot of the hill.

"My grandfather told me about the place. They have been at it that long," the driver made his best sales pitch.

"Have you had lunch?" I asked.

"I could eat," he let me know. He may have just eaten lunch, but the prospect of a free meal made room in his belly.

The hour of working my way through a Belt Buster meal of pork, beef, and ribs with a side of macaroni and cheese satisfied my appetite and left me envious of my driver's experience with his grandfather. It did not calm the queasiness I still felt about the hotel room in my name or the knowledge that D–Tech played any role at all in the matter of the purloined container.

Twenty-Five

I dared not test the FBI's resolve to charge me with something if I interfered in their investigation into Brian Hollis. Considering the sort of weapons that I had in my arsenal, such as a Class-3 fully automatic carbine with a stack of thirty round clips and a suppresser, they would not need to work very hard to get a conviction.

I needed someone to do my shooting for me.

I chose not to involve Lexington's city police because their authority was especially limited, and I was unlikely to convince any small-town police chief to get involved in anything as complicated and potentially violent as Brian's situation was shaping up to be.

The county sheriff had already demonstrated an interest in what was going on. He would not have established a rolling roadblock if he did not sense something was amiss in his jurisdiction. I needed to come up with a convincing argument for Sheriff Franks to get involved in Brian's drama because the sheriff and his deputies were my only hope for armed reinforcements the FBI would not arrest.

The sheriff's office was located behind the courthouse. I parked on Eleventh Street and looked both ways before crossing the street. Nobody appeared to take notice of my presence as I made my way to the front door and approached the young male deputy behind the front desk.

"I would like a moment of the sheriff's time," I informed the uniformed gatekeeper. I presented him with my badge and ID despite SAC Rogers' admonition.

"He is on patrol. Would you care to leave your name and number? I will have the dispatcher relay the information and the sheriff will contact you when he has a moment to do so," the deputy suggested.

"I'm afraid this is too important for that," I said with as authority as I could and glared without making him flinch. "I believe we are presently working against a clock."

"Would you care to elaborate on that?" the sheriff's deputy

asked.

"Not with you," I said and took one step forward. "Perhaps you could let me know where Sheriff Franks is patrolling. I can intercept him so we can have this conversation in private."

"I realize you are a detective, and I imagine whatever you wish to discuss seems very important to you, but Sheriff Franks prefers to handle things in his own time," the young deputy politely thwarted me again.

"Tell me, deputy, how fast would Sheriff Franks respond to an active shooter in this building?" I asked him and unsnapped my holster. The stunned deputy looked from my stern face to my hand on the butt of my pistol and swallowed hard.

"I imagine he would be here as fast as he could," he said. "But he would come in with his own guns blazing."

I admired the nervous deputy's determination to dissuade me from testing Sherriff Frank's patience.

"That might get innocent people injured," I agreed with his point. "Wouldn't it make more sense for the sheriff and I to meet somewhere that is less likely to happen?"

"Give me a moment," the now terrified deputy stammered. He noticed that I had not removed my hand or snapped the holster. "Let me raise him on the radio."

A pair of other deputies had witnessed our conversation and had their hands on their own sidearms. I turned towards them and smiled. We were thirty feet apart. Statistically, neither of them was likely to hit me with their first shot. I was confident I could place a pair of ninety grain jacketed hollow point bullets squarely on the chest plates of their body armor if either of them chose to intervene. A shootout would land me in a jail cell until long after Saturday. They mistakenly sensed a mismatch in their own favor and satisfied themselves with watching me.

"Sheriff? I have a detective from Louisiana wanting to speak with you," the deputy nervously spoke into the radio on his desk. The female dispatcher turned towards us to figure out why she had been cut out of this loop.

"Tall guy. Kind of cocky?" I overheard Sheriff Franks's inquiry.

I nodded my head and smiled just a bit.

"That's him, sir," the deputy confirmed. "He wants to know where you are so he can drive out and see you. He is very insistent about speaking with you."

"Instruct him to cool his heels at McDonald's. I will be there in ten minutes," Sheriff Franks instructed the deputy.

"Thanks for your cooperation," I said and calmly snapped the holster. "See, that wasn't so hard, was it?"

"Have a nice day, detective," the still shaken deputy managed to say as I turned towards the door.

Twenty-Six

Sheriff Franks arrived at the McDonald's restaurant in barely half the time he had quoted his deputy. I heard his siren approaching from several blocks away and spotted the flashing lights atop his cruiser as he made his way towards me on Main Street. Another cruiser entered the parking lot from the opposite direction at the same time. It narrowly missed a minivan pulling away from the drive-up window.

The two deputies I had seen at the station came through one set of doors as their boss stormed in through the other door. All three had their guns drawn and converged on the table where I sat calmly enjoying a cup of black coffee. It was fresher than expected, and I had passed the time watching as the town went about its normal business through the large plate glass windows. Every citizen was unaware of the potential mayhem and menace Brian Hollis might bring to their weekend.

"Hands on the table," Sheriff Franks shouted as he aimed his revolver in my general direction.

I did as he instructed.

"Take his gun," Sheriff Franks ordered the deputies.

"I am unarmed. My handgun is under the seat of my car over there," I told them and pointed a cocked finger at my sleek red sportscar in the parking lot.

"Search him anyway," Franks snarled and holstered his heavy pistol. I slowly rose and extended my arms to allow his deputies easy access to my body for their pat down. The deputy doing the search failed to reach low enough on my ankle to have found a holster if I had carried a second gun. He also failed to touch my crotch, where I could have concealed a variety of secondary weapons as well. The sheriff did not look interested in hearing my critique.

I thanked the deputy for his massage and sat down without the sheriff saying I was permitted to do so. I watched the anger and fear on his face morph into a state of exasperation as he tried to decide how to deal with me.

"Get me a coffee and head back on patrol. I have this," he instructed his still anxious deputies. We waited in silence while one of the deputies rushed to bring him a tall cup of coffee and the two creamers that he knew the sheriff would use.

"What the hell was that stunt in my office, detective?" he demanded.

"Your desk sergeant was being uncooperative," I told him. "I am sure he was just following your orders, but he needed to learn about showing initiative."

"I will initiative your butt into a cell the next time you threaten to shoot up my building," Franks snapped at me as he emptied the second creamer into his coffee and tossed the empty container on the table between us.

"I never threatened to do any such thing," I protested. "I merely asked whether you would return to the office if you learned there was an active shooter present."

"Don't get cute with me," Franks growled and gave me his most menacing facial expression. It wasn't half bad. "Now that you have my attention, what the heck do you want?"

"I want to know everything you know about what is going on around here," I said. "And before you tell me nothing is going on, let me remind you that you were stopping every vehicle with out-of-state plates when I got here. You are also aware of the FBI surveillance of the motels on the far end of town. They may have told you they were here, but I am guessing you figured it out for yourself and raised hell with them. I imagine the Special Agent in Charge won't tell you anything and that is why you decided to lock down the highways in and out of town."

"Is this how you investigate things in Louisiana?" Franks asked, calmer but no less angry with me.

"You mean by kicking cans over until I find the one with the worms under it?" I asked him. "Yeah, pretty much."

"What worms are you looking for?" Franks asked. He clearly hoped I might be able to answer his own questions about what was happening in his county.

"Do you remember the Hollis family? The father owned a trucking company. His son went off to war and his daughter was something of a local slut," I asked. He looked about forty. Brian and Alexis would have been a little older, but the sheriff likely heard gossip about both siblings when he was younger.

"My uncle worked for the old man's trucking company," Franks informed me and paused. "Both of my older brothers knew Alexis. In the Biblical sense if you know what I mean."

"Oh, I do," I said and laughed. Franks loosened up enough to laugh as well. The things men can find to bond over.

"Well Brian Hollis stole a shipment of antiquities recovered from the thieves who stole them from the Iraqi National Museum in the first place. It is worth millions of dollars and now there is an international manhunt for Brian and the container. The search is focused on Lexington. Does any of this sound familiar?"

"We received an APB about Brian last week. The instructions were to call the FBI office in Kansas City but to not approach him. I have been wondering what the story is," Franks informed me. "So, you're saying Brian is a truck hijacker?"

"Not in those words, no," I told the sheriff. I borrowed his pen and unfolded a napkin on the tabletop between us. I began diagramming what I knew. "His taking the Iraqi's national treasures has set off a diplomatic and law enforcement mess beyond your wildest dreams. The Iraqis think there was a big conspiracy because the men responsible for moving and protecting that shipment attended Wentworth with Brian. I was his roommate. The FBI thinks the antiquities are somewhere in this country, but they have no idea where Brian is. Brian asked me to meet him here on Saturday, but I told him I was not coming before I learned what he had done. His sister is an antiquities expert, and she has a contract to do the provenance for a collection that seems to match what Brian stole. I want to stop Brian from doing anything stupider than he already has and to convince him to turn himself in to the FBI. I was confronted by a man this morning who claims to represent the Iraqi government, which means agents from two countries are after Brian."

"What does any of this have to do with me?" Franks

asked. He was clearly a happier sheriff when he was completely unaware of the events unfolding in his jurisdiction. The napkin he could not stop touching was filled with occasionally intersecting lines shooting out from the box representing the missing container.

"Well, my guess is that everyone is already working around you instead of with you," I told him. "The FBI historically distrusts local law enforcement. They think small town cops cannot keep a secret and that your men are not trained well enough to help their agents with anything but manning roadblocks and making coffee runs. The Iraqis won't trust you because their own local cops are all corrupt. Brian won't approach you because he knows he is a wanted man, and he knows your jail is not a safe place to be considering the people after him."

"And what about you, detective?" Franks wondered. "You are a long way from Louisiana, and it sounds like none of the other players want you on their team, either."

"What I do depends on what needs done to help my friend," I said.

"Are you sure you are not planning to help Brian Hollis escape?" he asked.

"Oh, hell no. We stopped being that kind of friend years ago," I said without cracking a smile. "I would like to see Brian surrender rather than be hunted down and for the antiquities to be safely returned to where they belong. I just don't think I have the full, or honest, story behind the theft. That makes planning my next move very difficult."

"How so?" the sheriff asked. He motioned for an employee wandering the dining room with a pot of coffee to top off both of our cups. She pulled two creamers from her apron and set them beside his cup. It seemed that everyone in town knew how the sheriff drinks his coffee. There was a certain charm in that.

"Brian Hollis owns a successful and respected private security company with very lucrative government contracts. His services will be needed elsewhere after his contracts run out in Iraq. Why screw that up over a high-profile hijacking? I do not imagine he knows where to fence something as hot as artifacts from a national museum. They would be so easily traced that nobody in their right mind would want to own them, which leaves people not in their right minds."

"And who might that be?" Franks almost begged me to keep going.

"The container Brian took off with belongs to a company one of our classmates owns. His name is Peter Yoder, and he got his start by buying Hollis Trucking. The company does a lot of business with the Pentagon. That means his trucks move military materials all over the Middle East, and probably for our military bases in Europe as well as NATO. Those contracts will disappear if the container is not returned intact. That could make him do some crazy things to stay in business. The son of Iraq's Deputy Interior Minister is on Brian's tail and plans to forcibly return Brian to Iraq despite the sort of international legal furor doing so might cause. He also threatened to add me to his list."

"I can see why nobody wanted me to get involved," Franks said and sat back. "I do not think I would know who to arrest if I walked in on that deal going down."

"I was sort of hoping the two of us might work together on doing exactly that." The sheriff did not seem to like this idea nearly as much as I had hoped.

"Exactly what?" he asked.

"Arrest Brian Hollis and secure the container," I said. I tried to hide my fear that the sheriff was too overwhelmed with all of this to be of any help.

"Do you really expect me to jump into the middle of all this?" he demanded incredulously.

"It would look good on your posters come election time," I suggested. "You can be the sheriff that solved an international art theft. Who wouldn't want that guy as their sheriff?"

"My wife and kids, for one," Franks shook his head. "This sounds suicidal. I assume all these people are armed and ready to kill to get the container, right?"

"Doing a routine traffic stop is the most dangerous thing any cop does if you look at the statistics," I argued. "At least doing this means you will see the risk up front and be prepared for whatever happens."

"What would you want me to do?" he sighed and finally warmed to the idea. It was undoubtedly the most exciting thing anyone had ever asked him to do, and having any edge in an election is a good thing.

"Just be available on very short notice. You may not need to do any more than close the roads to keep someone from escaping. Your department has AR-15s, right?" My request for the sheriff's cooperation escalated dramatically when I asked about the assault-style rifles.

"We have a dozen Army surplus M-4s we got a grant to buy right after 9/11," he said and shook his head. "I just never thought we would get to use them. The FBI has been sending us bulletins lately warning us about the rise of white supremacist and secessionist movements, and their local agent in charge keeps referencing groups that have not been around these parts for fifty years. I think the FBI believes we are still a simmering pot of right-wing rebellion."

"Give it time," I sighed. "He may prove to be right. These things go in cycles."

"We take them out to the range once a month just for fun," Sheriff Franks said and ignored my comments. "I suppose it is better to be prepared for a fight than it is to be surprised by one."

"Roger that," I agreed. I overcame a momentary urge to show him the arsenal in the trunk of my Cadillac. "Do you think your men can defend themselves, if need be?"

"Sure, we can," Sheriff Franks assured me. I had not seen anything to convince myself that the sheriff's young deputies constituted any sort of highly trained tactical response team, but I was satisfied to leave the McDonald's with Sheriff Frank's reluctant assurance of the support I needed and that was a good day's work.

Twenty-Seven

I looked for the green Ford Explorer as I left McDonald's and headed for my lodging rental. I wondered but what having the names of those two operatives noted in Sheriff Frank's database might have caused Sami to swap out the agents and reassign the pair I had exposed somewhere deeper in the background. I briefly considered asking the sheriff about the traffic stop but had decided not to raise any more hairs on the back of Sheriff Franks's neck than necessary to get through the weekend.

Sheriff Franks was going to spend the next day and a half thinking about, and reconsidering, involving his department in the high-profile arrest of an international art thief with local ties. Sure, there was positive publicity and prestige to consider. There was also a near certainty that his men were outgunned and outclassed by the sort of criminals involved. Keeping the sheriff on board was going to come down to what movies about major crime capers gone wrong he and his deputies had watched.

I checked the water glass behind the door to my rental and scanned the room before I pulled a cold bottle of water from the refrigerator. I hung my suit on the wooden valet and donned my running shorts and a clean t-shirt before lacing up my New Balance running shoes for a long jog. I usually run a few miles every other day to stay in shape, despite my doctor's concern for my replacement kneecap. I needed to scout Lexington for where Brian might do his cargo swap.

I had already driven the small town's perimeter and mentally marked a half-dozen parking lots where a truck could pull over long enough to make an exchange without attracting a lot of attention. Not one of these locations was totally private. They all risked a passerby taking an interest and contacting the sheriff's office or the local police about something shady happening. The later in the evening Brian made his move, the more likely it was that someone would call the police. I needed to find a location offering a higher degree of privacy in the dark which would not place more civilians in danger than necessary if there was an exchange of gunfire. Those are hard to find spots in towns as small as Lexington.

I made an ever-expanding circle around Wentworth. I had convinced myself that whatever Brian did was going to occur not too far from the school. Asking me to be part of his crime by returning to Lexington meant he would use landmarks that someone with as limited a knowledge of the town as I have could find them without too much trouble. I was equally certain that he would not use anywhere on the school grounds to further his criminal act.

Wentworth sits closer to the edge of town than it does to its center. The campus is bounded by Seventeenth Street and Twenty Fourth Street. The latter street ends at a baseball field. The parking lot for this field was secluded enough to fit Brian's needs, but the street leading to it is lined with homes whose residents would take an interest in an unfamiliar truck headed to the ballpark at any time of day. I also had to consider that the field might be in use on a weekend night because it had the lights necessary for night games. I turned around and ran back the way I had just come. I chose to ignore the blocks on the opposite side of Main Street because all of those are densely residential.

Trucks and semis pass through Lexington every day, especially small to medium sized delivery trucks and moving vans. A heavy steel cargo container hauled behind a large truck was likely to draw someone's attention. That thought encouraged me to get back in my car and scout for additional locations in the commercial strip on the south side of town, but knowing there was a concerted search for the container in Lexington made me discount the possibility of Brian heading there. That part of town was certain to be the focus of the FBI's search because they like to pursue the most obvious solutions to problems like this. They would also pull the state police and sheriff in that direction to seal off the roadways when they sprag their trap.

Brian would be smart to circle the town and approach it from the north rather than the west or south as he was expected to do.

I had the impression that the FBI believed Brian would approach Lexington from Kansas City, either because it was how they imagined Brian would do things or because someone like D-Tech had fed the FBI information which would lead them to believe he would. A truck crossing the Missouri River bridge and approaching Lexington from the north could be in downtown Lexington in under five minutes, which was fast enough to do a hand-off before the FBI was able to respond to their miscalculations.

I was across the street from Maid-Rite when I glanced to my right. I had missed seeing the deep ravine below me when I drove through town because of the steep angle to its bottom. The former quarry's towering rocky sides were the perfect backstop for its playing field. I turned around and approached the field from Sixteenth Street. I passed only two businesses and a radio tower before I turned to my left onto Lafayette Street and finished circling the ravine. Nobody was likely to be working night shifts in either of the commercial buildings over the weekend.

I noted that there were only a handful of homes on Lafayette Street where it backed onto the ravine. All of them faced the street and their backyards ended at an angle that denied the occupants a good view of the playing field. Other than being on the very edge of downtown, this was an ideal place to do a shady deal.

It was also a kill box as there was only the single road in and no secondary path for a vehicle to exit. There were some trees well to my right as I stepped onto the ballfield. The slope behind the houses on Lafayette was not as steep as the rock faces on the opposite side of the ravine, but it was a tough slope to tackle if someone sought to escape on foot.

The woods provided cover for a strike team. There was a line of parking spaces directly above the ravine on Main Street, so a SWAT team could line that area to close the trap and have clear shots into the ravine. I could use the sheriff's deputies as that SWAT team when the time came. It kept them safe but allowed clear shots at anyone firing from the open field below them.

My gut told me that this was the place to encourage Brian to do his trade, but I had no way to communicate this conclusion to him. It would only work if he and I were the ones to spring the trap. It would be disastrous for Brian if he pulled onto the ballfield with that container of antiquities and a strike team of the FBI's well-armed HRT agents stormed out of the dark tree line with SAC Rogers bringing up the rear, so I needed a plan for distracting them.

This mental exercise only managed to underscore the importance of my finding Brian while there was time left to mitigate the damage done to himself and those around him. I did not believe Brian grasped that taking the container was going to lead the Iraqis to suspend their contracts with Peter Yoder and Hank Grainger, or that it would increase the level of stress on the already fraying relationship between the United States and the Iraqi government. Returning the antiquities unharmed was not going to be enough to make things right for the Iraqis. They would insist on putting Brian Hollis through a sham trial before executing him for all the world to see. That was an entirely different problem, and not one I had any idea how to handle.

Twenty-Eight

I took a nap when I returned to the rental space. I needed to escape the sense of dread that came with knowing my name was on the list of paid reservations at a hotel barely an hour away thanks to a company whose operatives had ambushed me on two continents.

I woke up shortly after five o'clock. I checked my phone for any messages which may have been left while I was asleep, but nobody had seen any need to discuss their roles in what was happening with me. Tulip was unusually silent as well.

I dialed Hank Grainger's number again. I decided to call him the next morning if this attempt failed and then to abandon trying to contact him because he clearly intended to stonewall me. I did not have a long list of pertinent questions for Hank, anyway. I wanted to confirm that his men were the ones assigned to protect the container during its delivery to the Iraqi National Museum. The only other question I needed answered was why they did such an inadequate job of securing the cargo while it was parked in Peter Yoder's shipping yard.

I impulsively dialed the cellphone number Alexis Hollis had written on the back of her business card. I wanted to formally inform her that I was in Lexington and that I believed I was close to locating her brother, if measured by proximity alone. I was curious how she would react to this news.

"Good evening, Cooter," Alexis cooed after she answered the call on the second ring. "How are you enjoying your homecoming?"

"Lexington is your hometown not mine," I reminded her. The greeting was obviously her way of letting me know that she was already aware of my location, and that made me even more curious about the source of everyone's information about my activities. "I would be interested to know why your Kansas City apartment is not listed on your business card."

"A girl needs a place to hide every so often," she informed me.

"And to peddle your wares to my old classmates," I suggested. I wanted her to know that I had spoken with at least one of the men she had foisted her lukewarm antiquities off on after screwing them senseless.

"What's wrong with mixing business and pleasure?" she purred.

"Like the Beatles said, happiness is a warm gun," I played along.

"You don't need to be so dark," she commented sourly and dropped the word game we had barely begun playing. "Who has been crying on your shoulder? I will bet it is Peter Yoder. He is preoccupied with his public image."

"Then why is he having an affair with someone like you?" I wondered.

"What can I say? Most men find me irresistible, and I am discreet," Alexis said and laughed in a way that suggested she had been drinking.

"Discreet hardly describes your showing up at Strada in that outfit," I said to bring the topic I called to discuss into focus.

"Would you have taken my call if I had phoned you instead?" she challenged.

"Probably not," I admitted.

"Is that why you called me?" she asked. "To scold me for doing business with your old classmates?"

"No," I answered honestly. "I called because you never told me who your client is. You said you were going to do provenance on a large collection of Persian antiquities that were coming on the market, but you never told me who you were working for."

"Because I am discreet," she repeated in case I missed it the first time.

"Surely every collector on the planet knows there is a fresh infusion of very hot stuff on the market, but nobody respectable will want to get anywhere near them. There must be a good reason for you to destroy your reputation to work for a real scumbag," I said. I hoped Alexis's being drunk would help my abrasive approach to loosen her tongue.

"He is as big of a scumbag as they come," Alexis laughed hollowly. There was a pause and then I thought I heard her beginning to cry.

"Does he have a name?" I pressed.

"Daniel Logan," Alexis finally divulged. "But he is just the buyer's attorney."

"Do you know who Logan's client is?" I asked and hoped she did not catch that I knew the answer before I asked the question.

"Yes." Her response surprised me. "He is some Russian oligarch. He agreed to take possession of the collection here."

"Why here?" I asked. I seriously doubted that Daniel Logan was encouraging Dudiyn Alekhin to leave the legal sanctuary of Russia to finalize such a clearly criminal transaction in a country where there were outstanding arrest warrants for his client. It made me wonder but what Logan was finally making his power move against Dudiyn Alekhin. I had already experienced firsthand how ruthless Daniel Logan could be. "Was meeting here your idea or Logan's?"

"Dan suggested they make their transfer here. He said nobody would expect his client to be in Kansas City," she explained.

"Alexis, listen to me," I insisted. "You need to call Dan Logan and tell him the deal is off. You can tell him I told you to call, or you can make up any excuse you want, but you cannot go through with this."

"Why not?" she demanded. Her slurring was getting worse.

"Because Daniel Logan's client has his hands in everything nice people do not touch. He sells guns to both sides of any fight, he sells dope to children, and he sells women like they are cattle. There is no way he will not try to double cross your brother," I tried to warn her.

"Why would a man like that worry whether any antiquities he buys are legal to own or sell?" Alexis asked. Something in what I had just told her sobered her up enough to take me seriously.

"He wouldn't," I stated flatly. "He must have a very

specific reason for wanting to meet your brother here."

"Should I worry about going to the meeting?" she asked in drunken confusion. "Dan said his client insists that I be at the meeting."

"You and Brian will die if you go to that meeting," I burst her balloon.

I allowed her a couple of moments of expletive filled rants and visceral screaming before I attempted to refocus our conversation.

"How were you intending to give provenance for things the entire art world can recognize?" I demanded.

"I never intended to have to," she told me.

"That response begs elaboration," I stated. It was a very loaded statement, and my initial interpretation of it was that she was about to commit far more than professional suicide.

"Can you meet me for breakfast tomorrow? I promise to explain everything, and hopefully you can tell me what to do next." She was sober enough to grasp that these details were best not shared over unsecured phone lines, or maybe she knew she would need a few hours to fully explain her mess.

"Let me check my calendar," I joked to lighten the mood. "Sure, where and when?"

"There is a restaurant on the ground floor of my apartment. You know where it is, right?" she asked. Her tone let me know she was fully aware that I knew the address, and the sharpness of her question implied she knew I had already toured the place in her absence. "Can you be here at ten o'clock?"

"Ten it is," I agreed and let her be the one to hang up.

I got dressed and went looking for a bar. I needed a glass of bourbon in my left hand and to be able to watch the front door with my right hand on my pistol. A crowded pub offered more safety than the room I was renting or driving aimlessly in my neon sign of a Cadillac.

Friday

June 25, 2010

Good friends help you find important things when you have lost them...your smile, your hope, and your courage.

-   Doe Zamata

Twenty-Nine

I parked a block away from Alexis's building just after seven o'clock with my back to a newly built apartment building on Second Street, making sure I had a clear view forward to Alexis's building a long block away. The traffic on Second Street seemed to be limited to the tenants of the sprawling apartment complex, so my choice of locations minimized the likelihood of anyone else who might be watching her building noticing me or driving past my location.

I used a pair of twenty power binoculars to study the few people I suspected of not belonging in the neighborhood. This included the dog walker who walked their German Shepard back and forth across the street from Alexis's apartment for thirty minutes and what appeared to be a vagrant curled up inside a ratty blanket on the sidewalk in front of the building. The dog walker was not focused on his dog, though he did pick up after it, and the homeless guy blew his cover by failing to ask the dog walker for money even one time as he passed back and forth.

The prep cooks and chef arrived at the restaurant just after I parked. A produce truck unloaded the restaurant's order shortly after the chef arrived. There was another flurry of foot traffic just ahead of eight o'clock as the manager, line cooks, and servers arrived for their day shifts at the restaurant. The manager tried to shoo the homeless guy away but lost the verbal sparring match with the belligerent false vagrant.

The restaurant opened at nine o'clock and the dog walker moved on, turning to his left at the corner of Fourth Street, as the homeless guy shuffled into a new position on the opposite side of the street. Fifteen minutes before I was due for breakfast a silver Jeep Wagoneer with tinted windows turned the corner and parked in front of the door to Alexis's building just long enough for three men to pile into the back seat before the top-heavy vehicle zoomed away and crossed the Interstate 70 overpass at a reckless speed. I did not have time to get a good look at the faces of the men, but I did notice that the rear license plate on the Wagoneer was from Kansas and that the vehicle bore no bumper stickers or other identifying markings. The tight phalanx and vehicle's exit looked like bodyguards protecting a high value asset. The supposed vagrant rolled up his blanket and walked away after the Jeep departed. I lost sight of him after he turned to his left at the same corner as the dog walker.

Seeing all of this changed my mind about going into the meeting unarmed. I retrieved my compact .45 from under my seat and holstered it in the small of my back. I also clipped a folding knife inside my trousers along my right hip before I locked my car and started walking towards the restaurant.

A new dog walker approached the restaurant as I locked my car and started in that direction. It was the same man, now alone, walking the same albino pit-bull I had encountered the day before. Whoever staffed this surveillance either had too few people to work with or they hoped my seeing a familiar face would make me discount their potential threat. Alexis and an unexpected red haired female companion left her building at a quarter to ten and they paused to pet the albino pit bull. Any conversation they had with its master was brief as they proceeded to the restaurant's entrance after only a moment.

My PTSD chose this moment to kick in and I had to stop and take deep breaths until I convinced myself that I was not walking into an ambush. I accepted that I was going to be blindsided by whatever Alexis would not discuss over the phone, but it was unlikely that I would need to shoot my way out of brunch. I stepped inside the restaurant and gave the hostess Alexis's name. The young woman checked her reservation book and picked up a menu before she motioned for me to follow to her onto the patio where Alexis and the red-haired woman were seated.

"Good morning." Alexis stood up to welcome me with a quick hug before she stepped aside to let me sit down. Alexis mixed a mimosa for me from the chilled bottle of champagne and carafe of orange juice in the middle of the table while I began studying the menu.

The attractive redhead in business attire Alexis had invited to join us was seated to my right with a glass of iced tea in her hand. She wore a green dress that accented the color of her blue eyes.

The way she sat close to the edge of the table seemed to indicate it was not worn to emphasize the slim figure or shapely legs she used the table to conceal. Her copper-hued hair was pulled into a tight ponytail, and she wore minimal makeup. She was clearly there on business and not to share a pleasant meal among new friends. I noticed that she seemed to be mildly worried about something, and that her eyes repeatedly locked on Alexis.

"Cooter, this is my new friend Meghan Bridges," Alexis handled introducing the two of us.

"I hope it proves to be a pleasure to meet you," Meghan said without smiling. She remained seated but leaned forward to set her glass on the table.

"I am not sure how to take that," I told her and glanced at Alexis.

"Alexis tells me that you have a reputation for being something of a Lone Ranger and that you are as likely to create new problems as to solve existing ones," Meghan clarified her statement.

"I have not seen Alexis in over twenty years, but I can assure you that any reputation I have of being a bull in the china shop is exaggerated," I countered and flashed Alexis an angry look. She did not know me well enough to judge me this accurately.

"Exaggerated but not entirely wrong, perhaps?" Meghan attempted to soften her unintentionally inflammatory comment.

"Well, this has been unpleasant. Thank you for inviting me to this nonsense," I told Alexis and pushed my chair back to stand up. I had no idea who Meghan was, but her opinion of me did not seem to leave much room to work with her if that was why I had been invited there.

"Hank Grainger told me about you," Meghan abruptly gave up her source to keep me there.

"I have no idea what Hank Grainger thinks he knows about me. I have not spoken to him or even seen him in over twenty years either," I informed her as I scooted my chair back in place and reclaimed my cocktail.

"I don't know how, but he does know a great deal about you," Alexis confirmed Meghan's statement.

"Like what?" I asked her.

"You'll need to ask him about that yourself," she cryptically sidestepped answering my question. At least now I had an idea of who had left in the SUV just before I arrived and who was most likely paying the men watching the building.

"Putting that aside, why did you want to see me this morning?" I decided to refocus my attention on Alexis.

"I am hoping you might have some suggestions for how to handle the mess I am in," Alexis explained.

"And how does Meghan fit into this conversation?" I asked and nodded towards the silently defiant redhead across from me. She decided to speak for herself.

"I work for CPAA, Cultural Properties, Art, and Antiquities. We are a new agency within Homeland Security. We work directly with local law enforcement and are assisted in our mission by the State Department and the Smithsonian Institution. Our mandate is to locate and retrieve stolen antiquities and works of art and to prosecute those responsible for taking them. Our mission is to return stolen artworks to their rightful owners."

"That's commendable," I stated. I was being serious, but the two women looked at me as though I were dismissing Meghan's endeavors. "Really, it is. It just does not explain how your presence meshes with Alexis's problem."

"There is a twofold answer to that," Meghan began. "I received evidence of an imminent threat to a container filled with antiquities scheduled to be returned to the Iraqi National Museum. CPAA and the Iraqi National Police have slowly been recovering those artifacts since they were looted after Baghdad fell in 2003. The recovered antiquities are collected in a secure compound until they are repatriated to the museum in an armed convoy. The wrinkle is that the Deputy Interior Minister oversees the National Police. The Deputy Minister directed that his son be placed in charge of transferring the next shipment of antiquities to the museum. I was provided with proof that the Deputy Minister placed his son in charge because they planned to allow the caliphate who overran Basra to hijack the container to pay a ransom for members of their family the caliphate captured."

"What was the evidence?" I asked.

"I received an audiotape from a member of the German

Foreign Intelligence Office. The recording captured a phone conversation of the Deputy Minister finalizing the deal with the leader of the caliphate. The caliphate leader claimed to have a buyer for the contents of the container. My source told me that he had received the taped discussion from the Director of the Iraqi National Museum. The Director's hands were tied because he dared not upset the minister involved, so he reached out to this German agent because the agent had helped set up the task force recovering the museum's antiquities," Meghan told me. It was a good example of the interagency cooperation she had just mentioned.

"And what was the original source of that audiotape?" I asked her.

"The museum official said he had promised not to divulge the source. We took that to mean it was someone outside of the Iraqi government," Meghan told me.

"But you are positive the tape is real?" I asked. It seemed too perfect.

"The NSA has confirmed both voices on the tape," Meghan said with conviction. I was becoming impressed with how many established agencies would work with this new one.

"When did the caliphate begin selling antiquities to fund their jihad?" I asked Meghan. I noticed that Alexis was mixing herself a fresh mimosa and that the champagne bottle was nearly empty.

"Every radical caliphate must do two things to exist. They need to find a way to finance themselves and they must denigrate any existing Muslim authority. We first started hearing about this happening after the civil war broke out in Syria. Someone must have taught the Iraqi caliphate to declare the religious cultural sites that they overrun to be heretical to justify confiscating any antiquities they come across to secretly trade them for the cash and weapons necessary to sustain their campaign," Meghan patiently educated me.

"Bad men with a solid business plan," I quipped to my unamused audience. "And the Habib family trusts the caliphate to hold up their end of the deal?"

"I did not mention the Habib family's name," Meghan

balked.

"Sami Habib paid me a visit yesterday and told me he intends to recover the container to free his family in Basra. Now it makes much more sense," I said.

"Sami Habib will do anything to recover the container," Meghan warned me. "The caliphate has threatened to marry the women in the Habib family they are holding to members of their following and to murder the male family members unless they receive the antiquities as ransom. The Habibs's situation is not my problem."

"What is to keep the caliphate from doing both of those things once they get what they want?" I rephrased my question rather than comment on her callous dismissal of the Habib family's conundrum, not that I was any more concerned.

"Not a damn thing," Meghan agreed with my own skepticism. "They *are* going to double cross the Habibs as they did everyone else that they have extorted."

Our waitress interrupted our conversation to recite the daily specials and to take our food order. I did not burden her with my usual rant that restaurants should stop calling anything they hide under a skim coat of hollandaise Eggs Benedict. It is a specific recipe, and the myriad alternative meats and weird bread combinations deserve names of their own. I quietly ordered a chorizo omelet with a side of fried potatoes and a biscuit.

"How did you get involved in all of this?" I asked Alexis after the waitress left.

"I work with the FBI's Art Crimes division. They have used me as an informant on stings aimed at traffickers in stolen paintings and antiquities," she responded and paused to allow the surprised expression to leave my face. I was stunned to learn that Alexis was doing anything so serious, so grown up. "I have intentionally cultivated a reputation for flexibility in my provenance because doing so attracts propositions to whitewash private collections, and occasional museum acquisitions, involving stolen artwork and antiques. I report any that I come across to the FBI and they find a way to make an arrest that does not require my testifying so I can continue working with them."

"I never would have guessed," I said without making the

apology she deserved.

"The FBI informed me that nearly four hundred pieces of Persian antiquities that were supposed to have been delivered to the Iraqi National Museum were expected to hit the black market, and the seller would be a Russian gangster named Dudiyn Alekhin. They sent me to New Orleans to renew an acquaintanceship I have with the Russian's attorney and to make it clear that I was prepared to provide fraudulent provenance to make the container's contents appear to be a private collection that was legal to transfer to his client," Alexis explained. "The FBI did not inform me they had lost track of the container until after I had already made my pitch to the attorney. They insisted on going through with the transfer because they hoped to arrest Daniel Logan and Dudiyn Alekhin at the meet. When I saw you in New Orleans, I had just come from meeting Daniel Logan to tell him the seller had one demand, which was that Alekhin had to personally take delivery. Logan agreed to these terms and the FBI began working with Meghan on the best way to make the arrest. The FBI sees this as their best chance in a decade to put Alekhin in an American prison for the rest of his life."

"You cringed when Alexis said Daniel Logan's name," Meghan interjected. "How do you know him?"

"Logan has been a thorn in the side of prosecutors in New Orleans ever since Hurricane Katrina. I didn't know who Daniel Logan's principal client is until very recently. Daniel Logan is also the guy who shot me in the head to keep me from blocking Dudiyn Alekhin's plans to be the new organized crime boss in New Orleans. Alekhin is considerably more ruthless than the caliphate when it comes to getting what he wants, but his attorney is the one to watch. I think Logan has been planning a coup against his client," I informed the pair. Both women's eyes went wide at the mention of Logan's attempt on my life.

"Dan Logan shot you?" Alexis asked breathlessly.

"Obviously he did not kill me. You realize that you are nothing but bait in the FBI's trap, don't you?" I asked Alexis.

"Bait," Alexis repeated. "That's a nasty way to put it."

"Maybe not bait, but you are definitely the goat the FBI tied to its stake to draw the wolves," I insisted.

"Can you protect her?" Meghan asked in hopes of hearing some good news.

"I have no idea," I disappointed them. "What I can tell you is that the way to tackle problems like this is to break them down into ones that are easier to solve. I see four problems needing to be addressed. The Habib family needs to rescue their family from the caliphate, Alexis needs to survive dealing with Dudiyn Alekhin, and the container full of antiquities need to wind up back at the museum."

"And that means outsmarting the caliphate, the FBI, and the Russian," Meghan said and followed her summation with a forced laugh that Alexis did not appreciate.

"That's only three problems," Alexis pointed out. "What is the fourth one?"

"Sami has threatened to extradite me to Iraq on his own if I do not help him locate the container," I let them know. "I am sure that he will deliver the container to the caliphate if he gets ahold of it. He will also drag your brother back to Iraq if he can."

"Why does he think you know where the container is?" Alexis wondered.

I paused before I answered her question.

"I believe our classmates at Wentworth conspired with your brother to take it. Your brother is the one being held personally responsible, but I doubt he could have pulled it off without Peter Yoder and Hank Grainger allowing him to do so," I told her.

"Brian must have had a good reason for taking it," Alexis lamely protested. She was not denying that he had done so.

Our food arrived at that moment and the shuffling of plates and refilling of drinks allowed us some time to adjust to what the three of us had shared with one another. The waitress offered to bring a fresh bottle of champagne and Alexis agreed before I could discourage the idea.

"You knew your brother was involved in this when you approached me in New Orleans," I said and waved a finger at Alexis. She bit her lip and nodded guiltily.

"Brian is not the problem," Meghan tried to play down Alexis' withholding information. "Recovering the antiquities is the only thing that is important."

Alexis finally told me what sounded like the truth, "I was questioned by the local FBI office after Brian was accused of taking the container. They wanted to be sure that I was not involved in the theft, and that I would agree to help with the recovery. They claimed that Brian had already agreed to cooperate with them in a sting operation to arrest Dudiyn Alekhin."

"What is the FBI's plan?" I asked Meghan because she was the only member of law enforcement involved in making the arrest sitting at the table. Alexis was a barely willing bit player in the FBI's operation. I was a total outsider and grateful for anything either of them would share about the plan Harold Rogers refused to discuss with me.

"Logan called me yesterday to let me know that the container is being delivered to a warehouse near the international airport at ten o'clock tomorrow night. Logan has insisted that Alexis be there to confirm the authenticity of the container's contents and to provide the new provenance she promised to deliver. He told me that Dudiyn Alekhin will be present to confirm the antiquities are real. Alekhin plans to fly out of the country after I confirm the antiquities are real and to leave Dan Logan to handle the details," Meghan informed me. Alexis silently nodded to confirm what Meghan told me. "The FBI intends to arrest Alekhin and Logan when the container arrives at the warehouse."

"Are you taking part in the arrest?" I wanted Meghan to explain her own role.

"I will be the agent who makes the arrests because my agency brought the case to the FBI. Rogers will get his name in the headlines because people still want the FBI to be the hero," Meghan informed me. Her displeasure with this was obvious.

"Alekhin will want to kill whoever set him up and the cop who puts the cuffs on him. The FBI's plan places a bullseye on both of you, and on Brian," I let them know. "Dudiyn Alekhin will not forget any of your names and there is no place to hide you from the men he will send after you."

"You are just trying to scare us," Meghan scoffed.

"Look him up," I said and put a fork in the last bite of my omelet. I knew I was right.

"Is there anything you can do?" Alexis asked now that the three of us had a clearer picture of the situation.

"I can try to muck things up as best I can," I said with little enthusiasm for doing so. I saw no way to convince SAC Rogers and the FBI honchos he wanted to impress that their plan was deeply flawed. SAC Rogers saw himself as being hours away from parading a major Russian gangster into the federal courthouse, and the Sunday morning headlines he was already imagining inside his thick skull blinded him to the retribution Alekhin was almost certain to seek against the CPAA's lead investigator, whom Rogers would be quick to blame if this high-profile arrest fell through. Neither of my companions admitted whether they were currently in touch with Brian and that left me baffled about what he intended to do, which made disrupting whatever plan the FBI had for the container even more difficult.

"I will do what I can to help you, Detective Holland," Meghan promised. Apparently, she had developed a sudden willingness to set a bull loose in her china shop.

"I do not have a plan right now, but I will by tomorrow," I told her. "Is there anything else anyone would like to confess or share with group?"

"Funny," Alexis angrily snapped at me. "It's not your life on the line, is it?"

"Everyone at this table has their life and livelihood at stake," I corrected her. "You are in the line of fire even if the FBI gets what they want, which is Dudiyn Alekhin's head on a silver platter. He will certainly put both of yours on one if he is arrested. I am going to be in trouble with the FBI for meddling in their plans even if everything works out. Meghan seems willing to work against the FBI and that won't sit well with her bosses. Our choice of poisons might come down to the FBI arresting us or the Russian killing us, but we will have to face the wrath of whichever of those two we cross. I see no winning move to make."

"You are just one big ray of sunshine this morning, aren't you?" Meghan said and smiled ruefully as she poured herself a mimosa.

"She invited me here," I said and tipped my glass towards Alexis. She was openly crying and barely able to staunch the flow of her tears with her napkin.

Meghan and I washed the last bites of our meals down with long gulps of warm champagne, forgoing the use of orange juice to conceal our day drinking. I asked Meghan about herself and her background to keep the conversation going. She was Alexis' age and came from a family of cops in a town near Savanah, Georgia. There was only a little more of that accent in her voice than there was New Orleans in my own. We had both spent too much time away from home. She had joined the Drug Enforcement Agency straight out of college and had then switched to her current assignment when CPAA began looking for agents. The idea of any nation's heritage being sold off upset her more than the drugs being smuggled from some of those same countries.

One part of my brain was maintaining this banter with Meghan, but the larger part was already looking for solutions to each of the problems I had defined for them. A tiny part of my mind was waiting for the right moment to make my next request.

"I need to meet with Hank," I declared and looked to Alexis.

"Why?" she asked in a challenging tone. "How do you think he can help?"

"The only reason I can imagine that he is avoiding me is that he knows more of what is going on than either of you or the FBI does. Hank had been responsible for guarding the container in Peter's supposedly secure container compound. I was certain that Brian had not tricked anyone into allowing him to leave with the container. An inside man must have helped Brian, and it was more likely to be Hank Grainger than Peter Yoder or any of their employees.

"I will call him right now," Alexis consented with obvious reluctance. Meghan nibbled at the melon on her plate and did her best to look like she was thinking of her own solutions to their dilemma.

Thirty

The gatekeeper was expecting me when I arrived at Sean's club. The heavy gate was opening even before I turned into the driveway. The valet waved me past the front door and pointed towards the carriage house. I guessed correctly that Hank would want to talk in the same pagoda where Sean and I had met. Sean was standing in the middle of the shaded space, and I spotted two other heads over the stone knee wall. I parked to block the driveway to the carriage house. There were no vehicles parked anywhere in sight, so either everyone else had their driver leave them here or their vehicles were in the carriage house.

"Good morning, Cooter," Sean hailed as I approached the pagoda. "Is it too early to offer you a drink?"

"I just came from having brunch with Alexis Hollis, so I could use a drink, yeah," I told him as we shook hands. Neither of my other former classmates made any effort to stand and shake my hand.

Peter Yoder had let his hair grow. It hung past his shoulders in a thick ponytail. His blonde locks included a few strands of gray. He was tanned and looked like a retired surfer. He wore jeans and an open collared button-front shirt. I almost asked what brand of cowboy boot he was wearing, but I did not really care to know and doing so would have implied I was impressed by his curated look.

Hank Grainger looked older than any of us. He was also the only one of us wearing a suit and tie. The suit was not off anyone's rack and the soles on his Italian loafers were lightly scuffed. Tony wears the same brand of shoes, and I knew they were not cheap. Hank's dark hair was thinning and turning gray. I thought to myself that he might be bald before the last strand of hair turned silver. His dark brown eyes looked tired behind his tortoise shell framed eyeglasses, and he had a loose belly, although he was not entirely out of shape. Hank may have exercised at home every other time he thought about his weight, or he might have had a trainer who cashed his checks without making Hank raise a sweat.

The same tuxedoed waiter who had waited on Sean and me on my first visit arrived with an Old Fashioned and I thanked him before I lifted it from his silver tray and took a seat in the only available chair. Sean had positioned me once again to be blind to the movements of the handful of security guards watching us from the mansion. I was likely to be the only one of us who was armed, but I did not believe that waving my pistol was going to prove helpful in questioning these men.

"Shall we begin?" Peter opened the conversation once I settled into my chair. I shrugged, and Sean and Hank both nodded their heads. My companions were all drinking beer. This allowed them to control the pace of our conversation by taking their time leaning forward to place or retrieve their pilsner glasses each time they took a drink. I studied the dampness of the thick paper coasters beneath their glasses and estimated they were finishing their second or third round. It confirmed my suspicion that Hank had called the others here for a strategy meeting while I was dining with Alexis and had expected her phone call. It also suggested that he was the man in the Jeep.

"Tell us what you know," Peter casually suggested. The trio were clearly here to learn what I knew, not to explain their own actions.

"I do not know a thing. In fact, I know less than I thought I did when I arrived in town," I disappointed them and twirled my cocktail glass on the arm of my rattan chair. "I have heard a lot of things, but I do not know what to consider to be fact or fiction. Why don't one of you find a good starting point?"

This was not the answer any of the three anticipated or wanted to hear.

"I probably got the ball rolling," Hank finally broke the uncomfortable silence. "I was informed that one of our call monitors had intercepted a cellphone call between Iraq's Deputy Interior Minister, a guy named Rashid Habib, and the leader of the caliphate who has seized control of Basra. The caliph informed Habib that everything his family owned in Basra was under the caliphate's control and they were holding a dozen members of his immediate family who had not fled in time for ransom. It is a seven-figure ransom. Rashid tried to explain that his family was unable to pay any ransom because all their assets were in Basra and the caliphate had likely drained their accounts. The caliph informed Rashid that he knew the Interior Ministry was responsible for making sure a container full of antiquities was returned to the Iraqi National Museum and suggested that Rashid pay the ransom by allowing the caliphate to hijack these antiquities when they were being transported back to the museum. Rashid agreed to the offer and placed his son in charge of returning the container. Sami Habib intended to allow the caliphate to steal the container while it was on the way to the museum."

"A call was intercepted." I focused on the first thing that I wanted to discuss. "I know of only one private contractor in Iraq capable of doing such a thing. I am going to assume D–Tech was the source of the intercept."

"That's right," Hank casually confirmed my suspicion. He also flashed me a frustrated look, as though this sort of needless interruption threatened to derail the pressing concerns everyone agreed to gather here to discuss. I finally understood Alexis's comment about Hank having the answers to my questions.

"D–Tech is still tapping the phone lines of Iraq's political shakers and movers," I persisted. "What is your relationship with D–Tech?"

"I own the company, if you must know," Hank said dismissively, as though this were common knowledge. "I own a lot of companies."

"Screw me," I sighed. "How many agencies are you sharing your intelligence intercepts with these days?"

"I don't understand your question. Are you assuming our government asked us to illegally wiretap an Iraqi official?" Hank pushed back as though I had insulted him.

"If you are not listening in on behalf of the CIA or the State Department, then why are you wiretapping anyone at all? Whoever you are keeping such close tabs on must fall outside of the parameters the NSA needs to conduct its own electronic surveillance in Iraq," I snapped at him. His outraged reaction did not mean he was not doing the things I was claiming he had.

"We are not routinely sharing what our call monitors collect with any agency. As a foreign contractor, I find it prudent to know where my company stands with the Iraqi government. I have, though, occasionally shared useful information from these intercepts with Peter and with Brian because they also own companies which are doing business with the Iraqi government. Iraq's Ruling Council is at a critical point in establishing their new authority, so it is prudent to know what their intentions are," Hank tried to justify his actions one more time.

"Control of the country will always be a problem for the Iraqis until their next dictator stages a coup," I challenged his justification. "Why don't you simply admit that you have been using your intercepts to blackmail members of the Iraqi government to make sure all of your contracts get renewed?"

"What's your point?" Peter Yoder interrupted. Was I the only one upset by this?

"My point is that I unwittingly worked for Hank's nosy little business for two years after I was led to believe the black-ops I was doing were done at the State Department's request, and it got me killed. Then I discovered that his company tried to start a gang war in New Orleans between the El Camino drug cartel and a street gang of teenagers. You do not care about obeying the law in this or any other country, and I don't think you even care about what the rest of us consider to be decent behavior," I accused Hank and managed to explain my history with his company to our classmates without raising my voice.

"I did not approve the ambush you were wounded in, and I was not at all pleased when I heard you had died," Hank let me know. "I was unaware that you had survived the attack until two days ago."

"What about New Orleans?" I demanded. My intervention in his grand scheme there cost the lives of multiple D-Tech operatives and resulted in the indictment of a lucrative client.

"Jack said you were the one causing him problems, but I thought he was using your name as some sort of metaphor," Hank shared. He was clearly discussing things he never spoke about with these friends of ours, and he gave me a look that bordered on begging me to stop talking about the past. "Would you prefer to see terrorists run off with the museum's antiquities because we allowed criminals to plot in private?" Hank tried to persuade me. My expression remained disdainful, but arguing was a waste of time neither of us seemed to have. "We do not have the manpower or resources to listen to every phone call made in Iraq. We focus on the handful of influencers we know to be working against the new Iraqi government. The State Department and the CIA never question the source or quality of the intelligence we share, so why should you have a problem with our collecting it?"

"The ambush you sent my way in Baghdad turned me into a reborn fan of civil liberties," I told him. "That's why I tore apart your operation in New Orleans."

"That you did," Hank said with a faint chuckle and leaned forward to address me. "I owe you apologies for D-Tech doing wrong by you. D-Tech is one of a half dozen divisions within the security operation that I have built, and I leave the day-to-day workings of those divisions to other people. What happened in New Orleans was not a project I was aware of until you brought about that gunfight at the airport. It took a lot to keep that quiet and now I am monitoring things much more closely. I promise you that I intend to avoid that sort of messy operation in the future. The projects you were involved with were run by my sister-in-law. I think she was influenced by her former fiancé. He was the cowboy who served as your contact in Baghdad, and he was also the person who paid the men who attacked your convoy when you disobeyed his order to stand down. The two of them made another bad decision when they allowed Deputy Director Kinkaid to utilize our services in New Orleans."

"Jill Bledsoe is your sister-in law?" I asked to be sure we were talking about the same person. Hank's aggravating lack of names and specifics was meant to shield the full extent of D-Tech's transgressions from our former classmates.

"She left the company after her fiancé disappeared in New Orleans," Hank informed me.

"Jack Hill didn't disappear. You know damn good and well that his body went into the incinerator D-Tech bought in Mississippi to dispose of any evidence of their activities in New Orleans, including that shootout." I could not imagine Hank was unaware of such major operations by his company's managers. The expressions on Peter's and Sean's faces told me they were unaware of the full extent of Hank's clandestine activities.

"Disappeared sounds better," Hank insisted in a huff and sat back with his beer in his hand.

It was time to change the subject. "Will you at least explain why you made a hotel reservation for me?"

"I was impressed that you found that," Hank said and grinned broadly. "I won fifty bucks betting that you would think to watch for the container to be delivered by rail. I told our call center to notify me if they got a suspicious call. We only use our own drivers so, when you called to say you were lost, I had them send you to Rosedale. Our actual railyard is elsewhere, but it let me know how hard you were looking. I admit that I also hoped knowing D–Tech was involved might be enough to make you leave town."

"You came close," I admitted.

"I understand that you are staying at Alexis's place."

"Her childhood home in Lexington," I set him straight.

"Can we get back to work?" Peter was exasperated with how far off topic our conversation had become.

"What do you think we are going to accomplish here?" I asked Peter.

"We need to find a way to return the container because Hank and I are losing money every day the Iraqis refuse to do business with us," my millionaire friend lamented.

"The Iraqis would have ordered both of your companies out of the country by now if they were not looking for a solution to this situation as well. We share a mutual problem with the Habib family with the Ruling Council," I offered my view.

"How so?" Peter wondered.

"The Ruling Council must know about the Habib family's situation in Basra. I imagine the Deputy Minister asked for help from his boss before he decided to take matters into his own hands. The Iraqis are aware of how corrupt the Habib family is, but the Habibs are powerful enough that nobody on the Ruling Council would have sought to have Rashid and his son arrested if they had delivered the container to the caliphate. Brian taking the container outraged the Habib family more than the Ruling Council because it jeopardized the agreement between the family and the caliphate in Basra. The Interior Minister allowed Rashid Habib to cast Brian as some sort of genius international art thief rather than confront his deputy about his agreement to hand the container over to the caliphate. Your businesses got rolled into the mess because both of you are friends with their designated culprit. The Ruling Council and Habib are hoping you will put your own interests ahead of childhood friendships."

"You understand this better than I expected," Hank let me know.

"Whatever," I dismissed his attempt to praise me. "What we need to do is to find someone else to blame for the container's theft besides Brian or the Habib family. The Iraqis will lose interest in Brian if you give them someone else to hold accountable. That means finding someone who is politically acceptable to the Ruling Council to make into the new bad guy, because they dare not move against Rashid Habib. But first, can one of you explain why Brian was the one who took the container?"

Peter answered my question after a moment of head bobbing and nodding back and forth with Hank to decide whether either of them were going to give me a straight answer. "Brian drove off with it after the three of us decided to hide it from Sami Habib. My plan was to fill a container with sandbags and trick Rashid into hijacking it while the real one was taken to the museum. Brian ran off with the container holding the antiquities on his own because he did not think things through. He failed to consider the Deputy Interior Minister would convince the Ruling Council that the three of us conspired to steal the antiquities and then declare that my company should be held responsible for the container's theft and Hank's company responsible for the lapse in security that made it possible for Brian to steal the container. The Ruling Council cannot shut Brian's company down because it would mean sidelining the Ruling Council's best trained bodyguards, but the Iraqis now believe the State Department was behind Brian's plan to take the container. The Interior Minister is pressuring them to assist in capturing Brian to prove our government did not sanction the theft. Sharing Hank's audiotape with the Ruling Council would prove that Sami planned on surrendering the container to the caliphate, but sharing the tape would expose that we are listening to their Deputy Interior Minister's phone calls. They would assume that we are listening to everyone's calls, and we are."

"So, you two decided that keeping your ability to wiretap the Ruling Council is worth more than Brian's life," I sneered at the dilemma my classmates had brought upon themselves. "The Iraqis would much rather have bemoaned the loss of so much of their national heritage after the caliphate swiped the container than address any proof you could have put forth about the involvement of the Habib family in the theft. I will bet that the Deputy Interior Minister has already contacted one or both of you to solicit a bribe large enough to pay the caliphate's ransom in exchange for restoring your contracts."

"No comment," Peter snapped before Hank could open his mouth.

"If I am not mistaken, the position of Deputy Interior Minister runs the Mukhabarat. That means Rashid would have investigated his son's crime if anyone had the guts to suggest Sami allowed the caliphate to steal the container. As it is, Rashid Habib is positioned to continue to make your lives miserable and to keep Brian on the run for the rest of his life," I pressed on with my conjectures about their situation.

"What the heck is the Muckborat?" Sean finally found something to say to take part in the discussion, though he mangled the pronunciation of Mukhabarat.

"It is the FBI and CIA all rolled into one agency, but without any rights for their prisoners or limits on their activities. Think of them as D-Tech in Iraqi uniforms," I offered, much to Hank's displeasure. He was clearly close to standing and demanding satisfaction, though I felt certain I would have to duel his second rather than Hank. "They were the secret police under Saddam Hussein. My partner in Hank's thing in Iraq worked for them before our country invaded Iraq and I watched him do some incredibly horrible things to the suspects he interrogated that still make me sick to remember."

"Which brings us back to what we should do," Hank set his empty glass on the teakwood coffee table and interrupted my insults and memories of Iraqi justice in action.

"Bribery is off the table. None of us has that much money lying around, and our own government would arrest us for paying a bribe anyway. The Iraqis want the container returned intact and they are determined to punish Brian," Peter summed up their situation.

"Like I said ten minutes ago, we need to find someone else for them to blame," I repeated.

"Why can't you simply deliver the container to the museum?" Sean suggested.

"The Iraqis are going to accuse whichever of them delivers the container of having stolen it in the first place. They will hang anyone who is caught hiding it or tries to give it back. It is a lose-lose situation no matter what," I argued against the idea and echoed Sami Habib's statement about Brian's fate at the hands of the Iraqis if they captured him. "By the way, where is the container?"

"I believe it is in Kuwait," Peter said after a moment's hesitation. "Brian told me that he planned to stash it in our port facilities with a new number and a fake shipping manifest. Brian is the only one of us who knows where it is for sure."

"You do not know whether it is there or if Brian placed the antiquities on the container ship headed to Baltimore. You are not about to admit that you cannot tell me for certain that Brian still has control of the container," I surmised and turned to directly address Peter. "You blew smoke up my ass when we talked on the phone yesterday."

"And I blew it up the ass of anyone who might have been listening to our call. The FBI is convinced the container is in this country, so it seems reasonable to think they are tapping my calls in case I let slip where it is," Peter half-apologized.

"I do not think that they care about the container as much as you want to believe they do. They are after the guy wanting to buy it," I surprised everyone by stating the opinion I was left with after my meeting with SAC Rogers. "The FBI is convinced Brian intends to deliver the container to a Russian gangster named

Dudiyn Alekhin. Their plan to arrest Brian and Alekhin is going to fail and likely get Alexis Hollis killed, along with the federal agent they have chosen to spearhead making the arrest."

"I gave them the audiotape between Brian and Alekhin's attorney about setting up the meeting," Hank informed us. "I did so anonymously."

"Then you know where Brian is, right?" I demanded to know.

"We are tracking the attorney. He will lead the FBI to the meeting between the Russian and Brian," Hank said. His cavalier attitude about wiretapping was beginning to bother me.

"Too bad for the federal agent," Peter interrupted us and began laughing. "I do not think any of us care whether Alexis takes a bullet or not. Sean told us that you think she sold us hot antiquities, so now we have to worry about that as well."

"I do not know for sure that anything Alexis sold you is illegal to possess. In fact, it is all probably fine," I backtracked on my conversation with Sean. Learning Alexis's relationship with the FBI made me reconsider whether she intentionally placed her brother's classmates in legal jeopardy by making those transactions. I also did not know about her work with the FBI when I shared my suspicions about her ethics with the museum curator. "Alexis can find buyers for anything you think she screwed you on if you want to play it safe and get rid of them."

"Sure, she can," Sean mocked my assurance. "She set us up to be arrested on charges of trafficking in stolen antiquities when she sold these things to us. It cannot be any more legal for us to sell to them someone else."

"We are getting off the subject again," Peter said and held up his hand to get our attention. I chose not to share that Alexis was an FBI informant. Let it be a surprise.

"The subject seems to be how to bail yourselves out of the mess you made when you allowed Brian to swipe the container. We also need to find a way to return the antiquities to the museum without them being hijacked by the caliphate," I repeated myself a third time. I knew the trio heard me, but Peter and Hank seemed preoccupied with protecting their own interests rather than solving the larger problem.

"Okay, smart guy," Peter huffed. "What do you propose we

do?"

"The three of you need to do absolutely nothing further," I demanded with considerable conviction. "The things you have already done led to this situation. I think I finally have enough understanding of what happened, and the players involved, to find a solution that works for everyone."

"But you are not a police officer here," Peter objected.

"I said nothing about arresting anyone," I pointed out. "The solution involves pitting everyone against one another and then forging temporary alliances to achieve a goal."

"I have no idea what any of that means," Peter complained.

"You don't have to," I told him and stood up. It was a strategy I learned from watching Uncle Felix manipulate situations to his politician clients' favor. I swallowed the last of my cocktail and started to walk out of the pagoda. "Just take my call when your phone rings."

Thirty-One

I left the meeting still reeling from Hank Grainger's casual disclosure that his sister-in-law and her dead boyfriend had conspired to kill me.

If I were in New Orleans, I would have locked myself in my apartment and begun scrawling on the floor-to-ceiling whiteboards mounted on the walls of my windowless home office until everything made sense. I was getting a headache trying to do this strictly in my head and decided to see what bouncing ideas off someone else would accomplish.

I made a telephone call to Alexis to check on her mental well-being and to get Meghan's phone number. Alexis asked if I wanted to speak with Meghan instead of calling because Meghan was still at her apartment. I asked her to tell Meghan to stay put because I was on my way and needed to speak with both of them.

Alexis buzzed me into the building and greeted me at her door. She looked much more composed than when I had left the restaurant. Meghan was sitting on the sofa and offered barely a nod to acknowledge my arrival. She looked relaxed now, with her hair hanging loose and her shoeless feet curled under her on the sofa. Her guarded expression suggested that the opinion she had of me before we had even met had not changed significantly over our cold eggs and warm champagne.

"What do you want to ask me?" Meghan got straight to business as soon as I had settled into the low chair across the coffee table from her. Alexis waved a bottle of beer and a bottle of water in the air from her position beside her open refrigerator. I tilted my head in the direction of the water. She opened the bottle and placed it on the coffee table before she sat on the sofa, almost touching Meghan.

"A number of things, actually," I said and took a quick gulp of water before I began unspooling the questions that had come to mind after I met with my former classmates and heard their version of how things had reached this point. I believed most of what they said, but I also realized they had shared as little as possible.

"Go ahead and ask," Meghan said a bit impatiently.

"Can you confirm you entered this investigation after an official at the Iraqi National Museum provided a German intelligence officer you know with the audiotape of the conversation between Deputy Interior Minister Habib and the leader of the caliphate?" The audiotape seemed to be what initiated this mess.

"Yes. I was contacted by an Interpol agent who had received their copy from German Intelligence. Interpol contacted CPAA because the presumptive thief was an American citizen and the companies involved in the disappearance of the container are American owned. It made sense to Interpol to hand the case over to an American law enforcement agency," Meghan told me.

"Have you interviewed Peter Yoder and Hank Grainger?" I continued. I was sure she had, but my purpose was to be sure I had each fact block in place before I stacked the next one upon it.

"Yes," Meghan said. "They were forthcoming and misleading at the same time. They never lied to me, but they were careful not to say more than necessary to answer my questions. Their lawyers coached them through the interview."

"No doubt," I told her. Neither of them would have known how to answer the pointed questions either of us asked without eventually spilling their guts had they handled things on their own. Peter and Hank knew more than we were likely to find out in the next twenty-four hours. "So, you came into this believing Brian Hollis swiped the container without anyone's consent."

"Without consent but probably not without foreknowledge. Brian hid the container after he and your friends spoke about Sami Habib's intention to allow the container to fall into the wrong hands. There was apparently no plan about what they should do after Brian took the container. I believe they thought hiding the container would be enough to keep the antiquities safe, but they seriously underestimated the Habib family's capacity for protecting their own interests. Deputy Interior Minister Habib is using his position to squeeze Peter Yoder and Hank Grainger to force them to turn Brian over and to surrender the container to Sami," Meghan shared.

"Brian's call to me was possibly an indication that he no

longer trusts Peter or Hank not to give him up," I belatedly realized. "Brian has buried himself deep enough to not be found but too deep to pop his head out to try to clear his name."

"That sounds right to me," Meghan agreed and smiled for the first time.

"How did you get involved?" I asked Alexis.

"Like I said before, the local FBI office contacted me and asked if I would be willing to help them arrest Dudiyn Alekhin. It sounded like an adventure and more of a challenge than the usual stings they involve me in, so I said yes. They did not inform me of Brian's involvement until I had agreed to help them, but then it was too late to back out," Alexis answered.

"They never mentioned your brother's involvement when they recruited you to take down the Russian?" I asked her.

"Not until I agreed to help," she angrily confirmed. "They interrogated me until they were convinced that I was not involved in the theft and then told me they have a plan to lure Dudiyn Alekhin to this country so he can be arrested."

"Did the FBI ever explain why they chose to target Dudiyn Alekhin?" I asked.

"I know the answer to that one," Meghan interrupted. "Alekhin has been stealing from the heavy weapons stockpiles the United States provided to the puppet armies they trained in Afghanistan and Iraq. The caliphate has been using the antiquities they confiscate to pay him for those weapons. The caliphate intended to trade the container with Alekhin for a large shipment of mortars and enough money to pay their men."

"You gave me the impression that the FBI sent you to New Orleans to cold call Daniel Logan about handling the provenance on the antiquities. It sounds like sending you into the lion's den, but that wasn't the case at all, was it?" I bluntly accused her.

Alexis could tell I would challenge everything but what I believed was true.

"I have known both of them for a few years," Alexis finally admitted. "Alekhin was just a bit player in the antiquities black market until he got involved with the caliphates in Syria and Iraq. The FBI originally asked me to give Alekhin bad provenance on a few stolen artifacts, but they abandoned making that case when they realized indicting Alekhin over a few pieces of stolen art was not going to compel the Russians to extradite him to stand trial. Their interest returned when they learned that the quantity of antiquities Alekhin is buying had increased fiftyfold. The FBI sent me to New Orleans to convince Dan Logan that I was prepared to provide the paperwork to make it look like Dudiyn had acquired the antiquities on the container from a small museum. I have no idea what Dudiyn planned to do with them."

"Do you know?" I asked Meghan. She nodded her head but remained silent rather than interrupt my increasingly hostile interrogation of Alexis.

"I think you are lying to me. I believe it was your brother who told Alekhin or Logan that he had the antiquities and wanted to make a deal. I think the FBI used you to seal the deal so they could arrest Logan and Alekhin along with your brother. Why did you really make a point of finding me the last time you were in New Orleans?"

"Because I was going to ask you to be my bodyguard when I met Alekhin to do the provenance work," she admitted.

"Why did you think you needed a bodyguard? Do you always have one when you deal with Alekhin?" I asked her.

"No, not usually," she sighed. "I was scared about the number of antiquities that were involved. I was afraid that Alekhin had found out Brian is my brother and that he'd kill us both after I gave him the paperwork."

"Good hunch on your part. At least you learned something useful from dealing with Daniel Logan in the past," I tried to get her to laugh. I had a much clearer picture of several things, including Alexis's reaction to my story about Logan shooting me. "And you swear you have not been in touch with your brother about this?"

"I swear," Alexis said. She sounded convincing, but the circumstances made me doubt her honesty.

"I think I know how to get the two of you out of this without upsetting the FBI," I said after a giving everything they had shared careful consideration.

"What's your idea?" Meghan asked.

"I cannot tell you. It is not entirely legal, and it might

backfire," I told her honestly. "There are other things to discuss, anyway."

"Such as?" Alexis asked. She did not want to be left out of the conversation because her life was on the line.

"Like what Brian is up to," I continued to focus my attention on Alexis. "He must have a specific reason to have asked me to meet him in Lexington, but you told me that the trade is supposed to happen at the airport here."

"Do you believe the container is in this country?" Meghan asked.

"I suspect Brian stashed it somewhere overseas. Brian probably lacks the wiles and connections necessary to get four hundred and something Iraqi antiquities across the Kuwait border, much less to sneak them through customs in Baltimore. I think he found a place to hide the container in Iraq and is looking for a way to get it to the museum without getting himself killed."

"Why not negotiate returning the container with the Iraqis?" Meghan asked.

"He doesn't trust them not to let the caliphate have them, and admitting he has the container is the same as admitting he stole it in the first place. He also knows Dudiyn Alekhin is deadlier than the Iraqis and the caliphate combined," I guessed.

"How would my brother know a man like Dudiyn Alekhin?" Alexis asked.

"He might not know him personally, but he has been close enough to the Ruling Council and the State Department's intelligence apparatus to know about Alekhin trading weapons to the caliphate for stolen antiquities. I am confident that Brian figured out a way to get in touch with the Russian," I replied.

"You are positive that you have not spoken to your brother in the last thirty days?" Meghan unexpectedly challenged Alexis. It was not a good thing for her to begin doubting Alexis as much as I did. Alexis needed someone on her side.

"No!" Alexis insisted. "I am tired of everyone asking me that question."

"It would help if you had a way to get in touch with Brian," I said to encourage Alexis to be honest about this. I was relieved that Meghan also doubted her denials about the siblings being in contact. "There are far too many variables right now to know the right approach to end this without anyone getting killed."

"What else can we tell you?" Meghan asked me. "If you expect me to trash my career then I need to be sure your plan is better than the FBI's."

"Who set the meeting place for tomorrow night?" I asked Alexis. This question was not as innocuous as it sounded. "Did you suggest the warehouse because you have used it before?"

"No. Daniel Logan told me where the meeting is going to be," Alexis angrily told us. Meghan and I locked eyes.

"Text me the address," I ordered Alexis.

I dialed Tulip's number once I received Alexis's text, and she answered immediately. I set the phone on speaker and set it on the coffee table.

"Do you need bail money yet?" my sister asked by way of hello. Alexis and Meghan laughed at Tulip's comment without grasping that she was not joking.

"I am good so far, but I need your ability to dig into things," I told her. "I am texting you an address. Can you find out who owns the building by the end of today?"

"I can try, but I have maybe three hours before every county records office in the country closes for the weekend," Tulip admonished me even as she agreed to help. "What am I looking for?"

"Dudiyn Alekhin is flying into this country to take delivery of a shipping container full of stolen antiquities," I informed Tulip. "I need to know why Dan Logan chose this address. He must know whoever owns the warehouse."

"You need to stay away from whatever they are doing," Tulip immediately advised me. She hung up and I noticed the shocked expression on the faces of the two women on the sofa across from me.

"Does this give you any ideas about how to keep Alexis and her brother alive?" Meghan asked.

"The best idea is to dissuade Dudiyn Alekhin's interest in the container. That is going to be tough. He probably thinks he will be able to get the container for free and still collect payment from the caliphate. A sweet deal like that may be why the FBI thinks he will let his guard down."

"What do you mean he is getting the antiquities for free?" Alexis asked.

"Are they supposed to pay you for the container?" I asked her.

"No," she confirmed.

"Alekhin knows the caliphate does not control the container, right?" I directed my question to Meghan.

"Correct," she said.

"Alekhin most likely intends to murder your brother rather than pay him a dime for the container. Alekhin will also want to execute Alexis after she hands over her paperwork. He will not want to risk Alexis recanting her provenance if she is arrested or risk her growing a conscience and going to the authorities. He probably already suspects she is working with the police."

"The FBI plans to arrest everyone in the warehouse as soon as the container's doors are opened," Meghan informed me. "I will arrest Alexis to protect her cover."

"The FBI is going to have to settle for prosecuting anyone left alive after the shootout Alekhin will use to escape," I said. I could see this scenario in my head because the FBI's plan mirrored the situation that I had created to spark the shootout between Jack Hill's D-Tech shooters and the El Camino cartel's sicarios.

"That is not an ideal outcome," Meghan needlessly declared.

"I would also prefer things not happen that way," I assured them. "I will do my best to make sure the two of you are alive when the smoke clears and to be sure you will not spend the rest of your lives looking over your shoulders."

"That's a better deal than the FBI is offering me." Alexis began crying again.

"I have this," Meghan waved me away when I stood up and moved towards Alexis. Alexis muffled her sobs by burying her face on Meghan's shoulder. "Call me if there is anything else I need to know or do."

"I will," I assured her. This was the only promise I was sure I could keep.

Thirty-Two

I made one stop on my way back to Lexington. I called Special Agent in Charge Rogers's office and informed his secretary that I was five minutes away and wanted to meet with her boss or they could both could read my version of what I knew about the FBI's plan to arrest Dudiyn Alekhin in the Kansas City Star over Saturday's breakfast, along with the target of their operation.

Rogers was waiting for me as I entered the FBI building. I was not at all surprised to see the chilly expression on the supervising agent's face, but I was more than a bit concerned that he was not accompanied by the usual witnesses he kept in tow to verify what was said. He might be planning to throw me through a plate glass window or waterboard me about what I had threatened to spill to the newspaper.

"You have some balls, detective," the supervising agent snarled at me.

"I was born with two, but I learned how to use them from an expert," I said to test his sense of humor. He blinked, smiled for an instant, and then motioned for me to follow him. I did so but kept my distance even though he allowed me to retain my handgun.

Rogers led me to a ground floor conference room. It was the one his office used to hold press conferences and public receptions, so the space dwarfed the two of us. The room's folding chairs were arranged in a dozen rows facing a podium with the FBI emblem prominently displayed on its front. The SAC stood behind the podium and glared at me. I took a stand beside the plate glass window and did my best to keep the sun in his eyes. I saw no need to sit down. This would be brief.

"You are on thin ice threatening to go to the press," he informed me.

"You have placed Alexis Hollis on thinner ice by using her to go after Dudiyn Alekhin." I spoke to him far more bluntly than anyone had in a long time. I saw his jaw go slack and his eyes widen. He pulled his glasses off and began to wipe them with a cloth he pulled from inside his jacket. It was a way to channel his anger and it kept his glasses from steaming. "You are putting an informant's life at risk to make an arrest that will look good to your bosses but won't stand up in court."

"Explain," he demanded.

"You plan to arrest Alekhin and Daniel Logan when they take possession of the container you believe Brian Hollis is bringing to Kansas City," I began. He did not contradict me or bother to shake his head to suggest that I had this wrong. "You will get a moment in the spotlight and the FBI Director will see your name in his Sunday morning newspaper. Then Monday will roll around and Daniel Logan will pay whatever bail the prosecutor demands for someone with Alekhin's criminal record and flight risk, but Alekhin has no intention of fleeing. He will stay right here, in your own backyard, and spend the months until he goes on trial making friends with what is left of Nick Civella's outfit. Daniel Logan will eventually humiliate you in court when he files a discovery motion demanding that you produce the audiotapes that led to his client's arrest. You are not going to be able to produce those audiotapes because doing so would expose an illegal wiretapping operation our intelligence agencies need. Your prosecutor might try to salvage the arrest by filing a conspiracy charge. You will not be able to hold Alekhin on any of the other charges you have against him once the antiquities trafficking charge is dismissed."

"Sounds like you have it all figured out," Rogers scoffed at my argument. He still looked defiant, but the anger and cockiness he had when he entered the room was gone. I had struck a nerve with something I had just told him. "What makes you so sure Logan can beat the charges we bring against Dudiyn Alekhin?"

"Because Daniel Logan came to New Orleans after Hurricane Katrina as part of Dudiyn Alekhin's plans to build a criminal enterprise before anyone local could do so. Logan established legal precedents about evidentiary handling and production that he will use to beat you at trial. He will convince the jury to laugh you out of court," I told him in one long breath. I paused to allow him to make a rebuttal and to absorb the fact that I knew so much about the FBI's plan to arrest Dudiyn Alekhin.

"What if I told you the prosecutor has already anticipated that and has a plan to beat it?" Rogers responded. This sounded much more like a bluff than a fact.

"I would say you need to get a second opinion and that you should find yourself a less ambitious prosecutor," I told him. He sighed a little too deeply to maintain his façade of control. "You have already done the first thing and you know I am right about the second, haven't you?"

"This is still our best chance to place Alekhin on American soil," Rogers declared. "That's all I have to say."

"Are you honestly prepared to make Alexis Paradis spend the rest of her life looking over her shoulder for Russian assassins and to humiliate yourself in court just to get your name in one glorious headline about his arrest, or are you open to an alternative plan of attack that does not risk Alexis' life and will severely damage Alekhin's operation? You won't get to make the big arrest or headlines you want, but it might spare you the sort of career suicide that is sure to follow Dudiyn Alekhin walking out of the courtroom a free man." I did my best to sound rational.

"Come up with something better and we can talk," Rogers semi-agreed. "But tomorrow night the plan we have goes forward if you cannot produce a better idea."

"Fair enough," I said and extended my hand. Rogers looked at it and shook his head before he turned and left me standing alone in the room where he still hoped to announce Alekhin's arrest in less than thirty-six hours.

Thirty-Three

I ran scenarios for how the FBI's arrest of Dudiyn Alekhin would play out by varying the factors involved. There was a scenario for Alekhin sending gunmen into the warehouse, or already having them staged there, to kill everyone the moment the container arrived. It was dramatic and drastic, but also plausible. There was a scenario in which the FBI's hostage rescue team neutralized Alekhin's men before they could kill anyone and Alekhin surrendered peacefully. This was SAC Rogers's fantasy. It was also the outcome least likely to happen. Rogers had probably not pondered a scenario in which nobody showed up at all. Rogers would interrogate everyone on his team and beat the bushes until he learned who compromised the operation, because he would never credit Alekhin with seeing the trap in advance.

I was passing through Blue Springs when an unasked but obvious question came to mind. Why did Alekhin consider it necessary to finalize this transaction in person rather than simply allow Daniel Logan to serve as his proxy? Was there a personal connection between Dudiyn Alekhin and Brian Hollis that nobody was aware of? No one I had spoken with had suggested that this might be the case, but it was also true that nobody I had spoken with had denied that the two men somehow knew one another. I concluded that this was a lead nobody had pursued or had dismissed as being too outlandish rather than investigate. A shared history or misplaced trust might explain why Dudiyn Alekhin was committing a crime on American soil that could see him imprisoned for the rest of his life.

I had only one way to find out. I pulled off the interstate in Odessa and checked every filling station and convenience store in town until I found a payphone. I gave the store clerk ten dollars for a roll of quarters and stacked half of the loose coins on the shelf beneath the phone. I did not care if the call I was about to make was traced to this phone, but I certainly did not want it traced to my own.

I had memorized the number rather than keep it in my phone

contacts. I could not afford for anyone to ever know the two of us spoke to one another in private.

"Who is this?" Daniel Logan demanded after the third ring. I had no idea how the number came up on his phone ID. An unknown caller was not out of the ordinary for a defense attorney. An unknown caller with a Missouri area code should have given Logan pause considering his primary client would be there the following evening.

"Answer one question and I will leave you alone." I wanted him to recognize my voice before I asked my question. "How well do your client and Brian Hollis know one another?"

"Who is Brian Hollis?" Logan immediately asked. He did not say my name but the tension in his voice indicated he knew who he was speaking with.

"Seriously," I said.

"I do not believe either of us know anyone by that name," Logan expanded his denial. I caught that he saw reason to distance himself from Brian as well.

"You might want to check your memory one more time and call me back if you learn anything different than what you are telling me," I firmly suggested.

"I will be sure to do that," Logan said and disconnected the call.

Thirty-Four

I passed Agent Bennett and Agent Kinsey in their Crown Victoria as I drove into Lexington. They were still parked in the same gravel lot where I had noticed them the first time I had driven past the hotel entrance. I knew more now than I did then and had a clearer idea of who they were watching. I had the top down on the Cadillac coupe, which undoubtedly annoyed Bennett even more than my driving a car he could not afford as a police cruiser. I parked so close to the driver's side door that Bennett could do nothing but roll his window down to speak with me.

"What are you up to, Holland?" Bennett snapped at me.

"Are you guarding Sami Habib and his daddy's henchmen or are you watching them?" I was fishing without much bait. I only felt certain about the fishing hole.

"What makes you think we'd be guarding them?" Bennett asked indignantly.

"Sami would already be under arrest or on his way home if someone did not have a good reason for letting him still be here," I told them. "Using Sami to scare me into leaving town did not work."

"Speculate all you want," Bennett snapped. His nephew managed to keep his lips sealed for once.

"Oh, I will certainly be doing that," I assured him and drove away. This question only came to me when I spotted them still watching the motel. It was now one that I needed answered as soon as possible.

Thirty-Five

I had difficulty getting to sleep. My mind continued to generate scenarios which incorporated everyone I knew with any interest in the whereabouts or recovery of the missing container. I was at a loss because even the connections which were clearly fantasies made nearly as much sense as the interpersonal links which I considered to be highly probable. I was confounded by my inability to find any sign of coordination between the disparate interests.

Brian was likely in hiding because he held our classmates responsible for his predicament and he apparently no longer trusted them not to protect their business interests. Everyone I spoke with swore they had not heard from Brian since the container went missing, or that they did not know who Brian was. Both claims struck me as untruthful in the mouths which spoke the words. I also could not convince myself that I was the only person Brian had reached out to for help, but everyone I had spoken with since my arrival seemed oddly prepared to see Brian arrested, either for his crime or for his own good.

Alexis could have contacted her brother after she learned the FBI intended to arrest him, but she continued to swear to me that she had not. Either she was scared about her reputation being damaged by her brother's actions or she believed SAC Rogers when he promised to take Brian into custody alive.

Meghan was supposed to be working with the FBI to secure the missing container, but she was aware that the FBI was no longer focused on recovering it. They were focusing their efforts on arresting Dudiyn Alekhin, which was something she did not care about. Sending him to prison was unlikely to put much of a dent in the illicit trade of antiquities.

The FBI and the Habib family were inconvenienced by Brian's continuing to elude them, but they both seemed unusually confident about their ability to secure the missing container.

Alekhin might be prepared to drop his guard because he believed he had an opportunity to obtain a fortune in antiquities without having to honor a deal with the caliphate's leader, who would pay for whatever the antiquities were meant to buy with the cash he stole from the Habib family's bank accounts. I remained reluctant to believe that Alekhin and Brian had some sort of prior relationship nobody else knew existed.

I gave up getting any sleep and pulled my iPad from my messenger bag just after one in the morning and opened a blank Excel page. I segmented the page into as many columns as there were parties interested in recovering the antiquities.

It proved to be an extensive list. The Iraqi National Museum received the first column because they were the intended recipients of the container. They were not suspected of any involvement in the container's hijacking but they were also powerless to effect its return. Brian Hollis was given the second column, because he alone knew the container's location. I lumped Peter Yoder and Hank Grainger together in the third column. Their businesses were suffering unsustainable financial losses because of the theft of the container. The FBI was given the fourth position and Alekhin the fifth. Alexis earned a column, as did Meghan. I decided to allow Sami Habib a column of his own and put his father's name atop the ninth and final column. I stopped at that point and fought off the urge to create a column for myself. Seeing nine interested parties who were either working alone, working together, or conspiring in small groups despite having opposite goals, created far too many moving parts to assess any one part as clearly as I wished to.

I had suggested that Alexis break her problems down into their smallest parts, and now I needed to do the same to find one common thing, besides the container, in each column to find a solution.

The sound of my car alarm startled me out of my trance-like state shortly after three in the morning. I grabbed my handgun and stormed down the stairs and through the wooden gate to the alley as fast as I could, but all I found was a handful of gravel lying beside the driver's side door. It matched the gravel in the parking lot of the small single-story apartment building a few dozen yards away. I looked that way but saw no sign of movement and the lights were off in every apartment.

The alarm sounded a second time barely fifteen minutes after

I returned to my seat at the kitchen table. This time I opened the windows above the sink and looked out, but I still failed to catch sight of the culprit. I knew for certain that I was being tested but was unclear if this was happening because someone wanted to check my response time or if they were trying to distract me from my work.

I quietly stepped out of the rental and stood at the top of the stairway to wait for the third time my car alarm was set off. I was looking forward to confronting the jerk who kept interrupting my strategizing and probably annoying my hosts. The alarm sounded and I dashed down the stairs, turning the alarm off with the key fob in my left hand and holding the large caliber handgun in a firing position with my right. I was prepared to do prison time for shooting this aggravating joker.

The elusive vandal beat me yet again and I trudged up the stairwell for a third time in barely half an hour. The door to the unit had not fully closed behind me but I gave this no thought and pushed the door open. The kitchen light was on when I stepped outside, but the apartment was dark when I returned. My first thought was that whoever was messing with my car was now toying with the fuse box.

I saw movement rising from behind the sofa but was blinded by a hand-held strobe light before I could see who it was. I received a blow to my wrist that was painful enough to make me drop my handgun. The blinking light remained disorienting even after I closed my eyes. I felt a leg slide behind my right leg before it swept forward to knock me off balance just as my assailant's meaty hand shoved against my chest to complete the task of knocking me to the floor. I fumbled for the knife on my hip, but my assailant's booted foot stepped on my elbow and the pain forced me to stop moving.

The light stopped and I opened my eyes and slowly regained my vision. I was looking up at my own pistol, which was aimed at my chest by someone standing just out of my reach. The intruder aimed their flashlight skyward from under their chin, like children do to make spooky faces.

"You're getting soft, Holland," Brian Hollis said and walked over to the kitchen light switch to bring normal light into the abnormal situation. He looked energized rather than afraid or exhausted after having been on the run for so long. His black hair was still cut short, but it was creeping over his ears. He had grown a beard since the last time I saw him. He kept it trimmed to form a narrow line along his sharply chiseled jawline. Brian was inches shorter than myself but carried nearly the same weight and he looked far stronger than I was. He wore black jeans, a lightweight dark pullover, and black sneakers. He also carried a Berretta nine-millimeter handgun in a leather shoulder holster and had a Kabar knife on his hip.

"Nice to see you, too," I retorted. Brian laid my handgun on the kitchen table and turned to reach his hand out to help me stand up. My wrist hurt more than my pride.

"Long time, my friend," Brian said before he sat down in the spare kitchen chair. I returned to the seat where I had been working on the problem he had caused and turned the iPad over. We were nowhere close to sharing my thoughts.

"You asked me to be here," I jogged his memory.

"You said you would not come," he reminded me in turn. "Not that I blamed you. We don't speak for half a decade and then I call you in the middle of the night and ask you to drop everything without any explanation."

"Friends would do that for one another," I said and paused for an instant. "I came because I am curious."

"That has killed quite a few cats," Brian said and laughed. "Tell me you have a bottle of something to drink."

I stood up and reached into the kitchen cabinet where I had placed a bottle of Weller bourbon. I poured tall shots into two juice glasses and handed him one as I sat back down.

"So, how have you been?" Brian asked as he swirled the liquor in his glass.

"We're really going to do this, huh?" I asked without hiding my annoyance.

"I haven't seen you in quite a while. I'm curious about what happened to you in Baghdad," he calmly avoided the elephant in the room, his alleged crime. "What became of that maniac Iraqi intelligence guy you hired as your number two? I heard he had killed a bunch of his bosses right after we took Baghdad."

"He is marrying my sister in September. The operation that you recommended me for, and that he and I ran, ended very badly and we had to leave the country in a hurry," I told him. "I wound up returning to New Orleans to try to find my father. He had disappeared right after Hurricane Katrina. My uncle hooked me up with a position in the state police so I could use their resources in my search. I have been working for my dad's old partner in the New Orleans Police Department since I left the police academy. Tony opened the restaurant he was always talking about. I think he used money he stole from the Habib family's offshore bank accounts to do so, but I really don't care."

"Well, you don't have to worry about anyone messing with your sister then. You were always the best intelligence officer in my experience. Playing cops and robbers seems to have kept your edge sharp. You seem about as capable as when we served in the Rangers together," Brian may not have realized that he had just let slip why he had asked he for my help. He needed someone who could see the whole game board and make smart moves. He also needed someone with combat skills. Brian had emptied his glass and poured himself another while I was speaking. "Did you find your father?"

"I am satisfied I know what happened," I replied because I did not want to get into the longer version of that story.

"Are you married?" Brian continued to stall. Not wearing a wedding ring did not preclude my being married. We were both trained not to wear anything that might give an opponent any insight into who we are outside of work.

"I was working on it, but no," I shared. It sounded accurate. "Are you?"

"Nah," he said and chuckled. "I always imagine myself telling my kids that they do not need to fear imaginary monsters because there are real ones all around them in real life."

"Just as well then." I shared in his laughter and took a sip of bourbon and tried to change topics.

"Now that we have that out of the way," I said as I refilled my own glass. "Did you really steal a container full of antiquities?"

"I don't even know what the beginning of that story is anymore. You know how long I have been in Baghdad," Brian started his explanation. "My company handles close protection for State Department and Defense Department honchos. It puts my operators in the room during some very sensitive discussions among the brass, and one of those discussions involved the Habib family. I know that you had Rashid Habib's brother in custody when you were ambushed."

"Old news," I said because I did not want to interrupt his story. I was not going to discuss what happened because I saw no reason to confirm who Tony and I had arrested the night we were ambushed.

"The Interior Minister does not want to know what it takes to keep the country in line, so he closes his eyes to what his Deputy Ministers are doing most of the time. Deputy Interior Minister Rashid Habib controls the national security and domestic intelligence operations in Iraq. The State Department has substantiated evidence that Habib is active in the black market. Habib's source of goods is a Russian gangster named Dudiyn Alekhin. The Russian is also known to be stealing weapons that we stockpiled in Afghanistan and Iraq and exchanging them for any antiquities the local jihadists steal."

"I know Alekhin. Don't let me interrupt your story." I stopped talking before I told him more than he shared with me.

"There is an international team of investigators in Iraq recovering the artifacts stolen from their national museum. Any items they recover are placed under tight security in locked containers at Peter Yoder's transportation compound outside of Kut. Hank Grainger's company is responsible for securing the lot and protecting the convoys with the containers while they are transported to the museum."

"Sorry," I interrupted again. "Did you say containers, as in multiple?"

"Yes," Brian replied. He sounded confused by my confusion.

"So, there are usually more than one there at a time?" I

asked.

"Right. They use the shorter containers because it puts fewer of the contents at risk if someone lights one up with an RPG," Brian elaborated. "Shall I continue?"

I pressed a finger to my lips to encourage him to finish his story.

"The caliphate hit paydirt when they overran Basra last month. Rashid Habib is from Basra, and the caliphate made certain to capture as many members of Habib's family as they could. Their leader offered to ransom these hostages for what he thought was the only container of antiquities on Peter's lot. Peter, Hank, and I saw the writing on the wall when Rashid placed his son Sami in charge and moved up the date of the next convoy."

"That's when you guys decided to hide the container." I wanted Brian to have a chance to rest his voice and to know I was aware of much of what had happened.

"Sort of," Brian said. He rocked his empty glass to let me know he wanted more to drink. This pour was less generous than the first. I needed him to be sober enough to finish his version of the disappearing container story. "Peter and Hank asked me to help them think of a way to protect the containers from Sami without causing a bloodbath or crossing Rashid. The three of us hashed out bad ideas for hours before I stepped outside for a cigarette. I was full on drunk, and the next thing I knew I had lined up a driver and headed off with the container Sami was supposed to pick up the next morning. I never said a word to Peter or Hank. I just drove off with the container."

"Where is the container?" I asked in hopes it was miles away from us.

"It is in a garage a few miles from where I took it. My guys are guarding it, and the seal is still intact." Brian sounded unusually casual about what he had done, but he also failed to give me an exact location to prevent me from betraying him.

"Why didn't you let Peter and Hank know what you were doing or where the container wound up?" I wondered.

"Because they needed plausible deniability and things went crazier than I expected after Sami found out that the container was gone. He called his father, and his father notified the Interior Minister, and he notified their Prime Minister. The entire Ruling Council was already raising hell with our ambassador by the time I sobered up enough to take stock of what I had done. The Ruling Council has refused to allow Peter or Hank to conduct any business whatsoever until they deliver the missing container to Sami Habib. The two of them are also expected to personally deliver me to Rashid Habib to face trial for stealing the cultural treasures he planned to let someone else steal. That right there is a deal breaker for me," Brian declared. He had begun slurring his words.

"Do you really think Peter and Hank would turn you in?" I asked. He knew them better than I did, and I trusted his opinion over my gut feeling.

"In a heartbeat," he assured me. "Friendship does not pay their bills. The three of us had even discussed making the container disappear that night, but they were both more concerned with avoiding exactly what I caused than they were about doing the right thing."

"The right thing in a place like Iraq does not always equate to what we see as being the right thing in this country. You have been over there long enough to know you have to step aside and bite your tongue every so often," I chastised him. He frowned deeply at my comment. "But I would have done exactly what you did."

"We always were a bad influence on each other," Brian laughed. It was a relieved laugh, and I could see the stress of the last month fall from his shoulders.

"Do you have any idea what sort of trouble your stunt caused Alexis?' I asked.

"I know that that she is helping the FBI capture Alekhin. Getting him out of the picture will weaken the caliphate considerably," Brian said.

"How do you think Alekhin is going to respond when he gets arrested and finds out Alexis works for the FBI, or that you two are related?" I gave Brian the fuller picture of what his actions had brought about.

"We cannot let that happen," he declared. This level of

anxiety was more than the bourbon talking.

"There are a lot of things that need to not happen tomorrow," I pointed out. Saving Alexis was distressingly low on my personal list of priorities. "Tell me this, why did you decide to draw everyone's attention here?"

"I never intended for things to get this complicated. I only intended to ambush Dudiyn Alekhin," Brian replied. His answer only brought more questions to mind.

"Ambush him how?" I wondered. The ambush idea had a very nice sound to it.

"I still come back to Lexington for the holidays. My cousins live here. My father used to pay a guy Nick Civella sent around to shake him down because my old man refused to let his drivers join the Teamsters union. Apparently trucking companies are low hanging fruit for gangsters everywhere on the planet. Who knew? My father told me it was a lot easier to pay Civella than to deal with the union. The Mob guy had a teenaged son who he would drag along with him. Maybe he wanted to teach the kid the ropes. My cousin Jerry used to play catch with the kid out on the lot while the grownups did their thing. A few years later that kid wound up doing eighteen months for embezzlement and his dad was shot dead in some sort of mini-gang war that sprang up after Civella died in prison. My father got tired of coming home smelling like diesel fumes and dealing with so much drama. He sold out to Peter and took my mom to live in Arizona about ten years ago."

"If there is a point being made, I missed it," I told him.

"My cousin used to visit his pal in prison. The three of us still have dinner whenever I am in town. The guy is just a two-bit hood, but he tells great Mob stories," Brian said, as though his friendship with a low-level mobster explained everything. "The last time we met, he mentioned that some Russian was trying to get a toehold in Kansas City. He told us that the local guys made it clear that they were not interested in sharing their turf, and they have been keeping an eye out for the Russians ever since because everyone knows they are looking for another way in."

"And the Russian was named Dudiyn Alekhin," I stated more than guessed.

"Yeah, the Russian used this attorney called Daniel Logan to make his case with the locals and they kicked him out of town. I came up with a plan to use a fake container to eliminate Alekhin for the local Mob and to solve a lot of problems in Iraq. I called the lawyer guy to see if he would be interested in buying a container full of Iraqi antiquities. I wanted to let Alekhin know that I had the container the caliphate was supposed to deliver to him," Brian said and lightly slapped the table with his left hand. The last portion of bourbon I intended to pour for him was in the glass he gripped in his right one. "I told the lawyer that I would only close the deal in Kansas City and his boss had to meet me here. It took a lot to convince Alekhin that this was the only way he would ever get his hands on the container. I bribed a captain sailing out of Kuwait to add a shipping invoice to his records and to add the container number to his cargo inventory. That way it would look like the container was headed for the States in case Alekhin had a way to check. Peter Yoder agreed to dummy up a container to look like the one I stole and gave it to Robbie. Robbie had lined up a warehouse out by the airport where we can close the deal. Our plan is to eliminate Alekhin when he shows up. I will return the container to the museum after Alekhin is dead, and the Iraqis should forgive me because they will get their antiquities back and because I killed the caliphate's weapons dealer."

"It looks good on paper, but it is not likely to work like you hoped," I poured a little water on his plan. I also did not mention that Alexis had given me a similar, but notably different, story about how Dudiyn Alekhin was being drawn into a trap. "In fact, it has already spiraled out of your control."

"No, this was a good plan" Brian angrily insisted and waved his empty glass.

"Was?" I immediately interrupted Brian's drunken account.

"I thought I had a deal with the FBI to help them arrest Dudiyn Alekhin in exchange for them not arresting me. I told them I planned to return the container as soon as Alekhin was arrested," Brian elaborated. My suspicions about his sister were replaced with a certainty that SAC Harold Rogers had completely blocked me from knowing the details of the sting.

"The FBI wants to be the hero. They want to be the ones to

recover and return the container to the Iraqi Ruling Council. They also hope to arrest Alekhin, and to extradite you to appease the Iraqi Ruling Council," I informed Brian. He was potentially walking into his own trap. I was not certain that the FBI intended to hand Brian over to Sami, but I did know they were not very concerned about his safety. "The FBI sees a perfect opportunity to trap Alekhin in a crime too controversial for his protectors to shield him from. The FBI is overjoyed at the prospect of arresting Alekhin in this country and being able to tie Robbie's bosses into the scheme is icing on the cake. You are expendable because they only see a nearly perfect opportunity to eliminate the threat of a guy like Dudiyn Alekhin ever getting a toehold in this country."

"I don't believe you," Brian snapped at me.

"I think your sister ruined your plan. Maybe she tipped off the FBI that you were luring Alekhin here so they could arrest him and not you," I suggested. This made more sense to me than her story about the FBI approaching her. They would not recruit an outsider with any connection to their suspects and then make them privy to their plans to take them down.

"It wasn't her," Brian immediately defended his sister against the accusation.

"I believe you," I told him, though I felt certain she was their source. "It was probably your pal Robbie."

"Why would he call the FBI on me?" Brian wondered aloud.

"Because he has a different plan," I surmised. "You have managed to find a way to put Dudiyn Alekhin and the FBI's top guy in Kansas City in the same place. SAC Rogers will absolutely want to be the guy who takes Alekhin into custody."

"Do you really think Robbie would double-cross me?" Brian demanded.

"He won't see it as double-crossing you. You do not matter to him. You are not part of his Familia. He would have needed his capo's permission to help you. Robbie's capo's may have seen an opportunity to disrupt the FBI for at least two or three years. He likely put your name on Robbie's kill list to keep you from ever testifying about Robbie's involvement," I suggested.

"Well, hell," Brian mumbled and collapsed in his chair. The bourbon had fueled his pride in his grand scheme. I had finally managed to convince him that his plan was nothing but a death warrant for his sister as well as himself.

"You said you have a dummy container, right?" I resumed critiquing Brian's grand plan. There were a lot of good parts to it. I needed to figure out a way to write a new plan that made the most of the handful of things I saw were usable, and which did not involve Robbie killing Brian.

"Yeah," Brian rejoined the conversation.

"I assume Robbie built a bomb into it," I suggested.

"Why would he do that? All he needs is for the Russian to be arrested," Brian scoffed at my conclusion.

"The guys who Robbie works for have a long history of blowing things up, and a bomb means putting fewer of their men in the line of fire. They are not concerned with any collateral deaths. The best part is that you will take all the blame, not them." The singular flaw in Brian's elaborate plan was his choice of partners.

"What a bastard," Brian yelled and reached for the bourbon. I moved the bottle out of his reach. "I will kill him if he hurts Alexis!"

"Keep in mind you are supposed to be there as well," I pointed out.

"Do you have a better plan?" Brian sighed deeply before he challenged me.

"No, but the two of us need to come up with one," I said and opened the bottle of bourbon. I poured us each another shot.

It was going to be a long night.

Saturday

June 26, 2010

The trouble in not dying for a friend, but in finding a friend worth dying for.

-   Mark Twain

Thirty-Six

Tulip called just as I left the carriage house early the next morning. I was making a coffee and donut run while Brian caught some much-needed rest.

"Good morning," I said with much more gusto than I felt in person.

"I have an answer for you about that warehouse," Tulip said. I had almost forgotten that I asked her to check into its ownership. "A gangster named George Berdella owns it through about six different holding companies. He is connected to the local mob family. What have you gotten yourself into?"

"I will tell you over dinner when I get back," I told her. "Brian Hollis showed up at my place late last night. His cousin is pals with some low-level hood who must work for Berdella. I had to convince Brian that this guy planned to take out Dudiyn Alekhin and the local FBI SAC and to pin the blame on him."

"I would tell you to be careful, but you are clearly back on your roller coaster," Tulip said and hung up before I could respond. It was good to hear that Brian had not lied to me about his local mobster connection. It meant I could trust the rest of his story a little bit more than I dared.

I had managed to get barely three hours sleep and was not going to see a bed until very late that night. I stopped at the Casey's convenience store and paid cash for two large black coffees and a dozen assorted donuts. I stepped back outside and stacked the remaining quarters from the day before on the shelf of the payphone by the bagged ice freezer at one end of the building.

Seven o'clock in the morning in America's heartland translates into two o'clock in the afternoon in Moscow. Alekhin's jet should have already been airborne if he intended to be at the warehouse on time. I estimated Alekhin's jet was entering Norwegian airspace about then.

I dialed Daniel Logan's cellphone. The phone rang once before he answered. I must not have been the only one who was losing sleep.

"We need to meet," I told him without identifying myself.

"You aren't afraid to be seen with me?" Logan challenged me.

"Not in public, no., but I will not meet you anywhere in private," I insisted. "I think you have a good idea why that is."

"So paranoid," he laughed out loud. "Sure, let's have lunch somewhere public. I am interested to know what you think there is to discuss."

"We can start with talking about a meeting in a mobster's warehouse by the airport at ten o'clock tonight," I offered. It was a reason Logan could not possibly ignore. I wanted him to understand that there was no longer any secrecy if I knew the time and location where Alekhin and Brian were supposed to meet.

"Where would you like to have lunch, Detective?" Logan asked. He managed not to allow the sense of panic I knew he was feeling to affect his voice.

"The Harvey Restaurant in Union Station. It's nothing fancy but I am a big fan of irony and neither of us are going to feel very hungry," I instructed him. My choice of locations also informed Logan that I was aware he was in Kansas City, and my call had just informed him that I was there as well if he did not already know. "I picked the place. You get to pick the time."

"Noon?" Logan offered. He needed to leave plenty of time to formulate a new plan for Alekhin to obtain the container.

"High noon it is," I agreed and disconnected the call.

I did not bother to wipe the payphone receiver this time. It looked like there were already as many fingerprints on the receiver as there were germs.

Thirty-Seven

Informing the FBI of my lunch plans with Dudiyn Alekhin's attorney did not seem like a particularly good idea. I would not deny that I had requested the sit down if SAC Rogers confronted me with a phone intercept that recorded my invitation. Having lunch with a criminal's attorney cannot legally be interpreted as my conspiring with their client. I was proposing any sort of cooperation between us, anyway. I invited Daniel Logan to lunch because I planned to spring a far cleverer trap than SAC Rogers's straightforward, but doomed, plan to arrest Dudiyn Alekhin or Brian's ill-considered intention to murder Alekhin.

Brian was asleep on the sofa when I returned to my rental unit. He had his face still hidden under the light coverlet. He also had a firm hold on my Tavor carbine beneath the blanket. I set the donuts on the kitchen table and divided the coffee between the two largest mugs I could find in the cupboard before I woke Brian. I placed one hand on the carbine and used the other hand to gently press on his arm until he stirred. You never want to surprise a former Ranger sleeping with a loaded firearm in their hand. Waking him by shaking him risked triggering an instinctive defensive reaction.

"I called Alekhin's attorney and set up the lunch meeting. I also let him know the meeting at the airport is no longer a secret," I informed Brian once he was sitting upright and appeared to be able to focus. He left the carbine on the sofa and padded over to the coffee and donuts in his stocking feet. He wore the light blanket like a shroud.

"How did that go over?" he asked as he raised the mug of coffee to his lips.

"Hard to tell," I admitted. "Logan is not much of a history buff. He agreed to meet me at Union Station."

"That's funny," Brian laughed and returned to the sofa to devour the chocolate frosted Bismark he chose from the box.

Union Station is a landmark in Kansas City's long history with violent criminals. The building's stone façade still bears pockmarks from the machine guns used in what the newspapers at the time called a 'massacre.' The shoot-out was an attempt by Pretty Boy Floyd, Verne Miller, and Adam Richetti to free a fellow bank robber named Frank Nash from the FBI agents assigned to return their comrade to the penitentiary in Leavenworth, Kansas in 1933. The shootout left four agents and local law enforcement officers and Frank Nash dead on the ground.

"Should I set my meeting with Rogers now or wait until I know I have sold our idea to Logan?" I asked Brian. We had multiple chess pieces to rearrange on our imaginary board. We finally had a plan, but it would result in disrupting everything the people involved expected was going to happen that evening.

"Rogers is going to be a busy man. I suggest getting your name on his to-do list if you can. You can cancel if things go sideways at lunch," Brian suggested.

"Everything falls apart if I cannot sell Logan on our new plan," I said. "Rogers will have my badge if we mess up his bust and don't find a way to make him still look good."

"Rogers sounds like a man whose ego has a big appetite," Brian offered his own thought on the subject. "He is not going to be happy after tonight no matter what we do."

I silently nodded my head in agreement and picked up my phone.

"This is Harold Rogers's office," his administrative assistant answered after the main switchboard transferred me to the SAC's office. She sounded as cheerfully efficient as the woman who worked for the retiring Special Agent in Charge in New Orleans. Perhaps every Special Agent in Charge's administrative assistant is trained to sound helpful despite having their guard up to protect their boss.

"This is Detective Holland. I need a moment of Harold's time if he is available," I politely introduced myself. She had no verbal reaction to my being so familiar with her boss.

"Special Agent Rogers has left specific instructions not to put your calls through," she informed me, sounding neither happy nor confused by such orders. "I can take a message if you like. I do not guarantee that he will return your call."

"That will be fine. Are you ready?" I asked and pulled my notepad close. I had a contingency plan for this. She said she was ready, so I recited the message I had laboriously edited in the wee hours of the morning. "Harold needs to call Jerry Ingram at the Kansas City Star and give him a statement about his failed attempt to lure a Russian gangster to Kansas City to frame him for trafficking in antiquities. I have already given Ingram my version of things. The reporter's number is 234-4310. Do you need me to repeat any of that?"

I swear I heard her gulp.

"No, Detective Holland, I have it all. If you can wait for a moment, I will pass this message to Special Agent Rogers. I am sure he will have a response," his assistant suggested before the line went dead.

"I will charge you with obstruction of justice if I read one negative word about my arresting Dudiyn Alekhin in tomorrow morning's newspaper. Am I clear, Holland?" the Special Agent in charge bellowed into the phone only seconds later. Brian was so startled by the sound and volume of the FBI agent's voice on the speakerphone that he spilled his coffee.

"So, you are available to talk to me," I deflected the threat. I had no intention of contacting any reporter from the newspaper. I had pulled the name from an article byline in the only copy of the paper I had read while in town and the phone number from an online phone directory.

"Make this quick," Rogers sighed in frustration and calmed down.

"I need ten minutes of your time around four o'clock this afternoon. There is about to be a major development in the case," I politely requested.

"What sort of development are we talking about?" Rogers asked. He was not going to allow me to string him along with these games much longer.

"Like I said, a major one," I repeated but emphasized the word 'major.' It was up to him to recall Brian Hollis retired from the Army Rangers as a Major.

"Four fifteen. My office," SAC Rogers relented. "Bring a good attorney if you intend to pull any more stunts."

"I am done playing, Agent Rogers. I can assure you of that," I promised. Brian and I burst into laughter as soon as I hung up the phone.

Thirty-Eight

Brian and I toured the statues in Penn Valley Park, located across the street from Union Station, until eleven thirty. The restaurant where I would be meeting Daniel Logan was on a mezzanine-style platform on the east side of the old train station's towering lobby. It was named after a famous restauranteur named Fred Harvey, whose waitresses left more of an inedible image on the history of America's westward expansion than Harvey did. 'Harvey Girls waited tables in the cafes Harvey opened in railroad terminals just after the first transcontinental railroad was completed. They set a standard for service that became legendary, and they provided a steady source of wives for the men who settled the desolate western plains. Daniel Logan was no more likely to appreciate this trivia than he was to recognize my inside joke of our meeting at the scene of a shoot-out involving far more notorious criminals than his client.

The former railroad station was now a natural science museum, and the place was packed with kids of all ages and parents doing their best to keep up with them. The problem with having so much activity in a small space is that it makes not moving into an artform. Brian left the park thirty minutes before I was supposed to sit down with Daniel Logan so he could find a place to both hide and to watch my back. I was counting on Brian to provide any necessary intervention if my luncheon with Logan took a violent turn. Brian was one of the few individuals in the lobby full of families and summer school groups, but he still managed to blend into the background and position himself with a good view of our table. We were going to rely on hand signals to communicate in case Logan took my phone.

I anticipated Logan would arrive with no more than two bodyguards of his own. He might station others in the parking lot, but I have never known him to surround himself with enough men to attract any notice.

I arrived at eleven forty-five and requested a table at the western edge of the dining room and overlooking the lobby below. I did not spot Brian, but assumed he saw me.

Logan arrived two minutes early. Two of his men remained on the lobby level while the largest of the three joined us at the table. I noticed that the pair beneath us were scouting the main floor for any surveillance or other threats to their boss. I saw the need to move our meeting along as rapidly as possible. This pair recognizing Brian would change everything.

"What a surprise to hear from you, Detective Holland," Logan said as he sat down and calmly spread his napkin across his lap. He was trying to act like my presence was not a surprise.

"I am sure it was," I smiled. "I wish I could say I was surprised about your being in Kansas City as well."

"But you are not surprised, are you?" he asked and gave me a hard stare.

"Not at all," I told him and then paused to give our waitress my order for a cup of hot tea along with my order for the prime rib dip sandwich and onion rings. It was nearly ninety degrees outside, so she gave me a brief questioning look, but she did not ask me to repeat myself. The cup of tea was my only weapon against Logan's bodyguard. Throwing it in his face might buy me five seconds to leave the table and escape.

"You should not be surprised I am here," I said once we were alone again.

"Oh, I am not. I just did not expect to have to deal with you directly," he said. Our forced cordiality was becoming painful for both of us. "And yet here we are."

"I will be brief," I said. "I am here to protect Alexis Paradis, not to threaten your client. I received a tip that the FBI was setting her up and came here to help her get out of the trap they have set for Dudiyn."

I made a point of using Alexis' married name to avoid providing Logan with a connection between Brian and Alexis.

"And what trap is that?" Logan asked. He ignored everything else I said.

"Alexis has been known to be, how shall I put this, overly generous in her reviews of the records of antiquities. She went to good schools and has done work for prestigious museums. She even consulted for the one here at one time. Then she discovered the money to be made by selling her reputation to people like your client. Alexis has caught the FBI's attention, and they think they can flip her on her clients if they arrest her on serious enough charges. They know she is supposed to be at a sale out by the airport tonight, but they don't know the name of her client," I began weaving my web.

"You're telling me that the FBI knows about the meeting but not that Mister Alekhin will be there? You want me to believe that they only seek to arrest Alexis?" Logan was never going to believe Alexis was the FBI's primary target in the evening's meeting, or that they were unaware of Alekhin's intention to be at the meeting. I just wanted him to know the meeting was compromised and that I was working against the FBI for the umpteenth time. *That* he would believe.

"Don't be silly," I laughed. The waitress returned with our drinks and food orders. Logan had chosen a spinach salad for lunch, while his bodyguard ordered nothing to eat. I turned to him after the waitress left. "You really need to keep your strength up."

"Back to what you were saying," Logan snarled and gave the bodyguard a glare that wiped the very slight smile I had gotten out him off his face.

"If they can arrest Dudiyn at the meeting then it will double their chances of getting a conviction, because they will give her plenty of incentive to testify against your client. She is just a cheap hustler right now, but if she is caught white-washing antiquities stolen from the Iraqi National Museum for a Russian gangster then she becomes a major criminal in her own right. It would be a cake walk to convince a jury to believe her testimony."

"You're saying the FBI wants to prosecute both of them," Logan repeated.

"Something like that. The thing to keep in mind is that Alexis Paradis is their target. I want you to dissuade Alekhin from coming here because it will destroy the FBI's case against my friend if there is no meeting," I continued lying. He seemed to finally be accepting everything I said as fact, but he would do everything he could to verify my story. There was the slimmest hope that Alekhin would be so relieved he dodged arrest that he would choose to distance himself from Alexis but not to harm her. He might think leaving her to the FBI would save him the effort.

"None of which is why I wanted to sit down with you face to face," I told him. His relaxed expression tightened up once again and his bodyguard adjusted his position in his seat. "The FBI supposedly has wiretaps of your calls with the guy who swiped the container you are after. How do you think Alekhin will react to your being indicted for setting up the meeting? Do you really believe he trusts you not to flip on him like Alexis will? You do not look like a man who will do well in a super-max prison."

The long seconds before Logan offered a response suggested that our plan was working.

"I am sure you have a solution," Logan finally spoke. He saw no reason for me to invite him to lunch unless I had an offer or a threat to make.

"I do," I said and prepared to deliver the spiel that Brian and I came up with, but I was interrupted by the waitress checking on our meals. I asked for an iced tea. She smiled and nodded, happy to see I had come to my senses. I opened the bun my sandwich was in and added a thin line of horseradish sauce. I took my time, which enflamed Logan's interest in what I was about to say.

"There is a way to beat the FBI at their own game. It will squash their plans to arrest Alexis and it will negate the calls between you and the hijacker. It should also position your client very favorably in Iraq," I made sure to continue the ruse that my primary interest was keeping Alexis out of prison.

"You are saying a lot of words but not telling me anything," Logan growled. He looked down from the mezzanine and made eye contact with the two men assigned to be sure he had not already walked into a trap.

"Alekhin needs to personally return the container to the museum," I told him. His eyebrows shot up and he nearly choked on a bite of food. "The container he was coming here to buy is a fake. The one he wants is still on the other side of the ocean."

"In Iraq?" Logan asked me to confirm.

"I did not say where," I pointed out.

"How could Dudiyn return the container to the museum if he does not have the container?" Logan thought he had found the fatal flaw in my suggestion.

"The container is going to be delivered to the museum this Tuesday morning with or without him," I told Logan in a firm but not belligerent tone of voice. "I am simply suggesting that there are benefits for your client if he is credited for arranging its return."

"What kind of benefits?" Logan was clearly interested, but my suggestion was going to look like the steel trap it was unless I could make it sound like a publicity stunt.

"Good will," I said.

"What can one buy with good will?" I could tell he was looking for a downside.

"It buys power, that's what. But we are talking about expanding your client's influence in Iraq and not in New Orleans, right?" I said to make my own interest in this matter crystal clear. He would not believe sparing Alexis was the only thing I wanted to gain from disrupting everyone's evening.

Logan nodded his head and let a small grin form at the edge of his mouth as he chewed on another bite of spinach and considered my proposition. "You just want my client to find somewhere else to set up shop than New Orleans."

"That and to forget and forgive Alexis," I reminded him. "Dudiyn is probably capable of convincing the caliphate to release its hostages, which will put Rashid Habib personally into his debt. Rashid is positioned to help Alekhin drain the Iraqi treasury from within because the Habib family has been doing so for years."

"I see what you are saying," Logan finally swallowed my hook. "I do not believe Dudiyn has fully considered his options."

"Kipling warned Westerners against trying to hustle the East, but he failed to mention that the East occasionally hustles itself," I blathered because I had prepared nothing else to convince Daniel Logan to persuade Dudiyn Alekhin to reconsider his options in Iraq.

"I will call him. Thank you for tipping me off about the FBI," Logan said and tossed his napkin in the middle of his plate.

"I only warned you that your client was being induced to commit a crime in order to worsen the charge against a much smaller fish," I reminded him. "I trust Dudiyn will distance himself from Alexis in the future. She is no risk to him and is as much of a patsy in this as your client."

"I believe he will find many other things to worry about once we speak," Logan stated. This was as much of a guarantee that Alexis was safe from the Russian's wrath as I was going to get. It would still be worth the effort for her to find that deep hole I recommended for a while.

I remained seated until the attorney and his bodyguards left the restaurant and then I paid for our meal in cash. I had just tipped off an international criminal to the FBI's plan to arrest him, which made me the only person involved in recovering the container who was committing a crime. There was nothing to be gained by having a receipt to prove what I had done.

Thirty-Nine

Brian needed to remain hidden from anyone looking for him. We were unclear how many people would arrest him on sight, who would let slip that they had seen him to those who sought to arrest him, and who among them would attempt to force him to tell them where the missing container was located. I dropped him off at the Kansas City Public Library's downtown branch because nobody thinks to search for a fugitive from justice in a public library. I called Peter Yoder once Brian was safely hidden in the library's stacks.

"We need to meet as soon as possible," I told him.

"I am free right now. Where are you?" he asked.

"Driving around downtown. Tell me where to find you," I suggested.

"I am playing golf at the Leawood Country Club," he informed me. "Do you need directions?"

"I have GPS," I said. "Can you meet me in the pro shop in half an hour?"

"Would you prefer to meet in the clubhouse?" Peter wondered.

"How many people do you want to know your business?" I asked as a means of explaining my odd choice of meeting places.

Being seen together in the clubhouse would look like our paths crossing was planned. Happening upon one another in the pro shop would appear coincidental.

Nobody questioned whether I was a club member when I parked my expensive Cadillac near the pro shop. It received more than a few envious looks from the members who were loading their clubs into chunky sedans and SUVs. I was under-dressed, wearing loose dungarees and a rumpled polo shirt, but I sensed this only burnished my image of being a fellow member slumming for the day.

Peter intercepted me before I entered the pro shop. I suggested we take a spin on his golf cart, which he correctly guessed meant I wanted to speak to him in absolute privacy.

He drove the electric powered four-seater to a spot in the

rough of the eighteenth green. Members continued to play through around us but very few of them seemed to notice that Peter and I had no golf clubs and never stepped out of the cart.

"I need for you to do something that might not make much sense," I told him.

"You have my full attention," Peter assured me.

"I need for you to deliver every container with antiquities in it that you have to the Iraqi National Museum as early as possible this Tuesday morning," I told him.

"I do not think I can do that," Peter objected. "It is not that I am not willing to do so. It is because my trucks and containers are banned from moving."

"Do you think anyone is going to challenge a fast-moving convoy traveling under heavy guard?" I argued. "You will need to get Hank involved, and I can arrange for reinforcements from Brian's company."

"Are you in touch with Brian?" Peter immediately asked.

"I can use his men. That is all I can tell you right now," I replied without giving him an answer.

"Why would I do this?" Peter asked. He did not sound unwilling.

"For one thing, handing the antiquities over to the national museum will stop them being your responsibility. For another, returning the container gives the Ruling Council a reason to allow you to get back to business and to lose interest in prosecuting Brian. The container Brian ran off with will join your convoy en route to the museum."

"That sounds good," Peter sighed in relief.

"Dudiyn Alekhin is going to take the credit for its return. I am trying to lead him to believe it will enhance his own position inside Iraq, but returning it implies that he has had the container all along and Rashid Habib will waste no time arresting him, if only because returning the container might doom his family members being held by the caliphate. At the very least, arresting the Russian should give the Iraqis a good reason to lose interest in prosecuting Brian. They will have their stuff back and a bigger fish will have accidently implicated himself in stealing it."

"I like this," Peter said and grinned. I was not entirely sure how much he heard that did not pertain to his being able to get back to work in Iraq. "If you want my convoy of trucks to deliver those containers to the museum Tuesday morning, we should move the convoy in the dark."

"That was my thought," I said.

"I will get with Hank. We will get this done, alright?" Peter assured me.

"Everything else I am putting in motion is based on you doing this," I told him. "Your life will become more of a living hell if you let me down."

"I believe you," Peter said. The look on his face when he saw my expression confirmed that he understood that I was making a promise that was worse than any threat.

Forty

The next piece of my puzzle required the cooperation of Meghan Bridges. I felt certain she was no longer on board with the FBI's plan after my dissection of everything that was likely to go wrong with arresting Alekhin. I was not entirely confident of my ability to persuade her to mutiny and take part in a trap a pair of bourbon-soaked Special Forces veterans concocted in the dead of night. I knew better than to use that detail about formulating our plan in my sales pitch.

"Do you have a few minutes to meet with me?" I asked her over the phone. I was polite but I made sure to add an undertone of urgency.

"How about right now?" she asked. "I am staying at the President. Come meet me in the lobby. I will find us a quiet table on the mezzanine."

"Let's go for a drive instead," I countered. "You will want to hear what I have to say away from other people."

"Are you afraid I might start screaming?" she laughed.

"This might involve a little of that," I confessed.

It took me five minutes to sort out the maze of one-way streets in the central business district to locate Meghan's hotel. Hilton had recently remodeled the time-worn hotel but retained the landmark's name, and their updates avoided destroying its 1920s ambiance. The hotel's original neon-lit letters still spelled out PRESIDENT in red letters atop its roofline.

I initially missed seeing Meghan because she was standing a few yards past the hotel's entrance. I waited until she was buckled in before I sped away from the curb and made a hard right-hand turn at the first corner. I checked my rear-view mirrors for any sign that we were being followed.

"What is so important that we need to speak?" she asked. She had one hand on the dashboard to steady herself as I continued to make a half-dozen similar sharp turns. My last turn put us headed northbound on Broadway Boulevard.

"I have set some things in motion which I need you to see

the rest of the way through," I told her but focused more on my driving than on explaining myself. I crossed above Interstate 70 and headed to the city's downtown airport.

"I am all ears," she said and waited for me to park. The other cars in the old airport's terminal parking lot probably belonged to employees. I had the top up on the coupe and rolled the windows down before I turned the engine off rather than lower the convertible's top and leave the two of us exposed. FAA regulations prevented anyone from using a drone or helicopter to track or surveil us within the airport property, but I was taking no chances.

"Dudiyn Alekhin is not coming," I informed her. Her expression ran the gamut from confused to relieved before settling on a look of deep concern.

"What have you done?" she demanded.

"I proposed a different arrangement for the container to Alekhin's attorney," I informed her.

"What was your suggestion?" she asked. She visibly tensed in anticipation of my response.

"I recommended that Alekhin personally return the container to the Iraqi National Museum. I have not heard back from Logan that Alekhin has agreed to do so, but I made a strong case," I informed her. She could barely form the words to respond to this audacious proposal so I went ahead and answered the question she could not ask. "Giving the museum the container negates the FBI's case against Alekhin and, if Alekhin agrees to return the container, the Russian will no longer have a need for Alexis' services. He should see no reason to suspect or punish her as she played no obvious role in the theft or recovery of the container."

"Okay, that is a good thing for Alexis," Meghan understood. "But why would Dudiyn Alekhin agree to give the container to the museum?"

"My pitch was about exploiting public perceptions. Alekhin should understand by now that he will never get his hands on the antiquities in that container. He can, though, be the Ruling Council's hero for returning something he never even had. I am sure he can convince the caliphate to release Rashid Habib's family with the promise of continuing to do business with them. That will put Rashid in his debt. Alekhin can use Habib to open the doors of other corrupt members of the council. Daniel Logan has agreed to encourage Alekhin not to ignore the benefits of trading a container he never had for the chance to establish a lucrative presence in Iraq rather than New Orleans. Logan was easy to get on board because he is intent on building his own empire in my back yard. I can handle him easier than I can Alekhin."

"Is keeping Dudiyn Alekhin out of New Orleans the only thing you want to do?" Meghan asked in a tone tinged with disappointment.

"It is not the only thing, no. This plan will clear Brian Hollis's name and save Alexis and yourself from Dudiyn Alekhin's vengeance were he to be arrested. Those things are important to me as well," I told her. I did not share that these matters all ranked well behind protecting New Orleans.

"You said there was something you need me to do," she prodded me.

"Actually, there are a couple of things," I amended my original request. "The first is that you need to coordinate with Peter Yoder to deliver every full and partial container of antiquities he has to the museum. I spoke with him before I called you and gave him a Tuesday morning deadline. The more time that passes, the more likely Alekhin will reconsider forfeiting any hope of hijacking the container."

"And the second thing?" she asked. She had not objected to doing what I asked for the first part, so I did not imagine she would have any trouble with the second.

"You need to contact the museum and tell them the missing container has been located and that it will be returned at whatever time Peter tells you he can deliver it. You also need to tell them the container was recovered in Mosul," I told her.

"What will that accomplish?" she asked.

"It will misdirect the attention of anyone who hears about the plan to return the container. There will be a quick reaction force ready to interdict any attempt to hijack the container a second time. With a little luck, the caliphate will attempt to do so and some of their senior leadership will get killed in the process."

"You have given this a lot of thought, haven't you?" she asked with what sounded like grudging admiration. "Yesterday you had no idea what to do, and now you have this huge international plot to ruin every bad guy's day."

"I had a long night."

"Have you presented this to the FBI?" she asked.

"I will in a couple of hours," I told her. "I hope to have heard back from Daniel Logan by then."

"I might have to find a way to be in the room with Rogers for that meeting," Alexis said and laughed. "The fireworks are going to be impressive."

Forty-One

Daniel Logan called me barely half an hour before I was supposed to meet with Special Agent in Charge Harold Rogers. I was working on an explanation for my interference in the FBI's plans which I hoped would temper the agent's anger and reduce the odds of his charging me with obstruction of justice in retaliation.

"I will not lie to you," Logan prefaced his announcement. "Dudiyn is not a happy man, but he is a grateful one. He already believed the reason he was told to come to this country was that there was a trap with the container as its bait, and you have confirmed that this was true. He will not forget this."

"It might be best for both of us if he did," I said. I would have a hard time explaining why a member of the state police was owed a favor by a Russian gangster if this ever came to light.

"He sees your vision for how to trade the container for a seat at the table with members of Iraq's Ruling Council. The container is worth a small fortune, but you have made him understand that returning it might be worth a larger fortune," Logan said the magic words I wanted to hear.

"The most powerful family in Iraq will be in his debt if he can persuade the caliphate to release the hostages they are holding in Basra," I reminded him. "The Habib family are among the most corrupt families in the country, so they can teach Dudiyn how to steal from their countrymen in ways that they will not notice."

"Dudiyn and I both want to know what you get from helping him. I believe your plan involves more than using the Iraqis to distract Dudiyn from his interest in New Orleans," Logan guessed correctly. His boss would want a better reason.

"It will help friends of mine get back to their normal lives. Maybe coming this close to prison will convince Alexis to go straight. Also, Brian Hollis was impulsive about taking the container, but he does not deserve to have the Iraqis breathing down his neck for keeping their cultural treasures out of the hands of the caliphate. Granted, he did screw your client in doing so. This plan should more than make up for that loss," I offered. Surely the Russian would accept such altruistic motivations. It sounded like something an honest cop would say.

"What does Dudiyn need to do?" Logan asked. The trap was set.

"He just needs to arrive at the Iraqi National Museum in time for a press conference at eleven o'clock on Tuesday morning. The Iraqi Prime Minister will probably give him their equivalent to a key to the city," I instructed Logan.

"You know what is going to happen if something goes wrong," Logan warned me. "Dudiyn has a long reach and a short temper."

"I am aware," I assured Logan. I was not about to share with Logan that I still harbored hopes Alekhin would kill his attorney for something else since he was not prepared to do punish Logan for murdering the nephew Alekhin was grooming to one day become his replacement. Logan had managed to convince Alekhin that the nephew died at the hands of the Dixie Mafia because he knew Alekhin was not prepared to go to war with America's redneck moonshine and meth addict version of Chechens.

Forty-Two

"You get ten minutes, Detective," SAC Rogers informed me after I had made myself comfortable on the leather sofa in his office. His witnesses were back on the job, with the junior agent silently trying to intimidate me from his post behind his boss and the stenographer seated in a chair to the left of Rogers's uncluttered desk. Her neck swiveled as though she were watching a tennis match between Rogers and myself.

"I only need ten seconds," I told him. "Dudiyn Alekhin is not coming."

"How do you know this?" SAC Rogers asked without displaying any anger or despair at the news. He was saving that energy for my response.

"His attorney notified me. Dudiyn could smell a rat from half a globe away," I replied.

"Why is Dudiyn Alekhin's attorney speaking to you at all?" Rogers demanded.

"We have history in New Orleans. His client and I understand one another, and our mutual hatred of one another comes in handy at the weirdest times," I explained but baffled the woman taking notes. "Logan called to brag that Alekhin was ruining your plans."

"Did you tell your pal we were setting a trap for him?" Rogers pressed his point.

"I did not have to," I lied. "Like I said, Dudiyn Alekhin is not a dumb gangster. Why else would someone Alekhin has never done business with insist on completing their deal in the middle of a country that wants to put Alekhin in prison for life? Brian's sloppy theft of the container and what amounted to a billboard announcement that the container was headed to Baltimore were not the work of anyone Alekhin is going to trust with his freedom."

"We can still charge him with conspiracy," Rogers consoled himself.

"You might as well send him a parking ticket," I laughed.

"He is not going to even notice a charge like that with everything else he has done illegally. The man has killed people and toppled governments. He makes his money off causing chaos, but he might be trying a new tactic in Iraq."

"How so?" Rogers asked.

"Logan informed me that the reason Alekhin is not coming is that Brian Hollis has decided to return the container to the museum. Brian approached Logan about allowing Dudiyn Alekhin to take credit for its safe return. Brian thinks allowing someone like Alekhin to deliver the container to the museum will take the attention off the hijacking and his involvement in that crime. Alekhin sees the advantage of ingratiating himself with the Ruling Council. Habib could be convinced to repay Alekhin for setting his family free by using his position to legitimize Alekhin's black market operations." I leaned back on the sofa while the Special Agent in Charge ruminated about this unexpected turn of events. I just hoped he did not expect me to offer any proof of what I had just laid out for him, because every word of it was a lie. A plausible lie, but also entirely garbage.

The FBI agent's splashy headline in the Sunday paper was gone, but so was the prospect of someone like Daniel Logan humiliating federal prosecutors in court. I imagined that SAC Rogers considered these two developments to be a wash. He had wasted his office's time and resources, and likely overpromised his own plan to the FBI Director. This turn of events was going to look bad in his file, but it was not going to get him fired.

"I still want to question Brian Hollis," Rogers declared.

"Fine. I will have Sheriff Franks detain Brian when Brian and Sami exchange the container," I offered.

"I know nothing about any such exchange," Rogers was quick to protest.

"You aren't invited," I replied a little too glibly.

"Okay, wise guy, tell me what you know about the two of them making an exchange," Rogers sighed angrily.

"It isn't really an exchange. Brian wants Sami to take it from him." My answer surprised Rogers and he could not catch his eyebrows before they shot skyward.

"Why is that?" he demanded.

"Because the new plan is for Sheriff Franks to arrest Sami on hijacking charges when he does," I informed the SAC.

"Sheriff who?" Rogers wondered.

"Franks. He is the county sheriff of Lafayette County. It is where Lexington is located. He has agreed to help us to stage a sting to arrest Sami," I told the FBI's stunned lead agent.

"Why would you involve this sheriff and not the FBI?" he demanded.

"Because if the FBI arrests the son of an Iraqi Deputy Interior Minister for forcibly recovering a container which he believes contains cultural artifacts belonging to his country it becomes headline gold," I explained. "On the other hand, it will look typically clumsy if a county sheriff does it. The arrest, however, will justify deporting Sami and his entire band of merry men."

"What about the container?" Rogers demanded.

"The one Sami plans to hijack is empty. The one everyone wants never left Iraq and is going to be returned with its seal intact on Tuesday morning."

"How do you know that it never left Iraq?" Rogers asked.

"Because Brian and Peter Yoder worked together to misdirect everyone's attention from Iraq to Baltimore. Even the FBI was convinced that Brian was some sort of criminal genius when he seemingly snuck the container through Customs and disappeared with it. He has been looking for a way to return it without getting arrested. The container, in fact every container of artifacts Yoder Transportation has on their lot, are being delivered to the Iraqi National Museum on Tuesday morning," I assured him. "We wanted to give Daniel Logan enough time to get there and take credit for everything."

"I thought you said Dudiyn Alekhin was doing so," Rogers argued, perhaps just to show he was listening.

"Logan is not going to tell Alekhin that the container is being returned. For one thing, the caliphate still needs to steal it to pay Alekhin for a weapons shipment and he still wants to sell it for millions of dollars on the black market. The last thing Dudiyn Alekhin wants or needs is publicity for doing the right thing. We expect Logan will see an opportunity to make his own points with the Ruling Council by showing up at the museum to say he is the one personally responsible for recovering the container."

"Why would you want Daniel Logan to take credit for the return of the container?" Rogers was clearly skeptical.

"Because Rashid Habib is going to assume that whoever returns the container has had it in his possession this entire time, and that he might have ordered its hijacking in the first place," I explained. "Rashid knows Daniel Logan is Alekhin's attorney and we are betting that Alekhin will react to Logan's betrayal by immediately terminating Logan's contract, because the Russian will have to distance himself from his long-time fixer to protect his black-market dealings with Rashid Habib. It will make more sense to the Ruling Council that a duplicitous lawyer like Logan was behind the theft of the container than it does that someone like Brian Hollis, the respected military veteran whose men are paid bodyguards for the State Department and Depart of Defense would do so."

"Do you really think you can sell this to the Iraqis?" Rogers asked. He was beginning to see the logic and faint brilliance of the scheme Brian and I had hammered out overnight. He would need to find a way to make this his own idea between now and Tuesday morning.

"They already want to believe it," I answered with much more confidence than I felt.

"So, am I supposed to just sit on my hands until this Sheriff Franks calls me to say he has Brian Hollis and Sami Habib in custody?" Rogers asked. We both knew this plan was not going to get him the headlines he craved.

"Well, we will need a little help from your office," I finally broached the subject I had been building towards. Rogers still had the ability to ruin our plan. "I need you to tell the agents you have watching Sami to stand down tonight. I will have the sheriff call them after he makes his arrests and they can call you to come get your face in the news by perp walking Sami Rashid and Brian Hollis," I answered with every bit of disdain I had for his need for accolades.

"I can do that," Rogers agreed. He took my hand in his and gave it a hard squeeze.

"Can you promise tonight will be the last time we see one another?" he asked and grabbed my hand to shake on the deal.

"I promise you that it is the last time I want to as well," I assured him and pulled my shooting hand free. I was going to need it.

Forty-Three

Agent Bennett did not seem very happy to see me when I pulled up next to the dusty Ford sedan. He rolled his window down to speak with me and I pushed my sunglasses up on my head and flashed a smile that annoyed him even more.

"Has your boss called you?" I asked him. Agent Kinsey leaned over the center console to hear our conversation.

"Yeah," Agent Bennett snarled unhappily. "We are supposed to sit right here until we hear from the sheriff."

"That and ignore what I am about to do," I told him.

"And what is that?" Bennett wondered.

"I am going to set up Sami Habib," I told him. "And you are going to tell me his room number."

"Like hell I will," the FBI agent rebuffed me.

"Again, call your boss," I countered. I had not informed SAC Rogers that I had any intention of engaging with Sami Habib on my return to Lexington. I doubted that he would approve of my doing so if he was asked. He might very well see that keeping me from speaking with Sami would punch a large hole in the scheme I had laid out for him earlier. Keeping Brian and I from succeeding might seem like a better idea than allowing the two of us to take credit for anything.

"Room 263," Bennett relented.

I drove to the motel and parked across the parking lot from the building, so Sami's men would have a clear view of my presence. I needed to be as careful approaching Sami's room as I would be walking towards a caged tiger, more like a rabid caged tiger.

I removed my handgun from its holster and held it over my head for all to see, and every Iraqi eyeball was certainly tracking my movements as I dropped it on the seat of my coupe and used the remote to lock the door. I wanted them to hear the car alarm confirm that I could not retrieve the pistol.

One of the men patted me down at the foot of the exterior steps to the second floor. A second one repeated the process, with a lot more vigor, at the top of the steps.

"I want to speak with Sami," I told them both. They had to have already deduced my purpose in being there.

The second bodyguard escorted me to Sami's room. He knocked on the door and placed himself between me and Sami.

"You may enter," Sami said from inside the starkly utilitarian motel room. I was curious why he chose to base his barely legal recovery operation out of a place with not much more to offer than free internet and a mini fridge. He could afford the sort of suite that Dan Logan was surely enjoying at a place like the Hyatt or Westin hotels in downtown Kansas City.

"I can say what I need to from right here," I told him. There was no way I was going to allow Sami and his men to get me into a cramped motel room with its shades drawn at mid-day when I knew he wanted to extradite me to Iraq.

"So, speak, detective," Sami said. He was clearly amused at my reluctance and distrust, despite my approaching him.

"I want to make a trade," I told him. "I will deliver Brian Hollis to you if you can get your father to agree to drop his plans to put my friend Tony Hussein Al-Majid and myself on trial."

I had to use the name they knew Tony by. My partner in the New Orleans bistro had reinvented himself as Chef Tony Venzo, which is his mother's maiden name, after we returned to New Orleans from the debacle in Iraq that the Habib family was still seeking retribution about.

"You would betray your friend?" Sami asked doubtfully.

"I will give up one friend to save a better friend," I explained. It was the sort of rationality that I knew Sami would understand.

"I will speak with my father," Sami agreed. "Seeing the container of our artifacts returned and having the thief in our custody is better than continuing to demand your government send the two of you to face justice."

"I thought you would think so," I said a little too casually.

"Where can I find Brian Hollis?" Sami demanded. Any anger he felt about my comment was added to the tone of his question.

"He is giving the container to Alekhin Dudiyn at the ballpark across from the Maid-Rite at ten fifteen tonight," I said. "You are going to have to let him get parked before you pounce because there is no place to ambush him until he arrives."

The last thing Brian and I wanted was for the Iraqis to stage an ambush anywhere else than where we planned to ambush them. Sami made a dissatisfied mumble but I took it to mean he agreed to the terms I had set forth.

Forty-Four

Sheriff Franks's desk sergeant directed me to the sheriff's personal office when I asked to speak with his boss. Our previous altercation was behind us, and the young deputy acted as though my presence was both expected and anticipated. I walked down the hall to the sheriff's office and rapped on the frame of the open doorway.

"Detective Holland, to what do I owe today's visit?" Sheriff Franks asked and pushed his rolling chair back from his desk a bit but made no move to stand up.

"Today is Saturday, Sheriff Franks," I prodded his memory. "This is your big day, remember?"

"Oh, Christ, that's right," he frowned and mumbled something under his breath. "Tell me again what you want me to do."

"Very little as it turns out," I said and saw the look of relief on his face. "My partner and I have made sure the Iraqis have been tipped off that Brian plans to close his deal on the container at ten fifteen tonight. I figure the Iraqis will make sure they show up ahead of the intended buyer, so they will only have to fight Brian to get it. The tip we fed them will lead them into that ballpark across the street from the Maid-Rite. It is secluded and easy to secure. All you need to do is make sure no civilians get down there and to arrest whoever drives the container out of there, and anyone with them."

"That sounds unusually simple," the sheriff said and stared at me for a moment as if to confirm some suspicion he had. "What aren't you telling me?"

"You can assume the Iraqis will not surrender peacefully, but we have already had that discussion," I jogged his memory one more time. "The idea is to box them in, with your deputies forming a roadblock ahead of them and Brian Hollis and I blocking their retreat. Peace through superior firepower, as they used to say."

"How many people do you have with you?" Sheriff Franks wondered. "You make it sound like there is just two of you."

"The two of us are enough to hold up our end," I assured him. "We have quite a bit of experience with these things. Our plan is designed to expose your deputies to the least possible risk."

"But there is still risk. In fact, the way you have explained things there seems to be a lot of risk. My deputies are not used to getting into shoot-outs with suspects," he balked more than he had when I approached him about this the first time. "As I remember, you wanted all of them to carry assault rifles. That is a lot of firepower to stop one truck."

"One truck and an unknown number of determined gunmen," I corrected his math. "Look, if you do not want credit for the arrest just say so. The FBI is itching to come in here and do this without you. We both know that it will look bad if you let that happen. The FBI will make your department seem like a bunch of Barney Fifes who were not capable of making a traffic stop."

"You can stop selling me on this," Sheriff Franks snapped. "I said we would help you and we will. Just tell me exactly what you want us to do."

"Put enough vehicles and deputies in the road to stop the container from leaving that ballpark. The truck carrying it will be moving slow and it will be heading uphill so it should be easy to stop. Shoot out the tires or the radiator if that is what it takes to make it stop. Call Special Agent Rogers right before you roll, and he will come and take your prisoners off your hands. He can press federal charges against them come Monday morning."

"You make it sound easier than it is probably going to be," Sheriff Franks sighed and dropped his head back towards his desk. "I hope I do not regret this."

"I hope neither of us has anything to regret," I tried to reassure him. "You will be clearing Brian Hollis's name and likely saving his sister's life. You'll get a good headline for your campaign, and I will be out of your hair for good."

"That last thing you said is good enough for me," the sheriff laughed and waved me out of his office. My reassurances were transparently nonsense. No well-armed foreigners were going to come all the way to Lexington, Missouri surrender peacefully to the county sheriff.

Forty-Five

Brian chose to stage the container at a sizeable truck stop in Concordia. This was nearly twenty miles east of the usual exit for Lexington from Interstate 70. We assumed that half of the men with Sami Habib were already looking for a way to intercept the container after I tipped them off to the location of its supposed sale, and the other half were scouring the countryside for it. Sami and the agents his father sent to help him return the container and Brian to Iraq were almost certain to be anticipating that it would arrive from Kansas City, so their efforts were focused on the exits and backroads west of Lexington. I left to meet Brian just after seven o'clock.

"Cooter, this is Ben. He works for Pete," Brian introduced me to the driver who stepped out of the semi behind him. Ben looked massive and stood well over six feet tall and weighed close to three hundred pounds. His black hair hung nearly to his shoulders, and he had a well-trimmed beard. The desert combat boots he wore caught my attention. Brian noticed how intensely I was appraising his companion.

"I thought your cousin was going to drive the truck," I said to explain my obvious confusion and disappointment that Brian changed our roster without telling me until now.

"He flaked on me at the last minute," Brian said and did his best to not show the same level of concern I had about his cousin disappearing right when he was needed.

"Brian tells me you are a cop," Ben said as he shook my hand in a vice-like grip.

"I am a state police investigator in Louisiana," I confirmed. "That makes me a big fat zero in Missouri."

"We're all friends here," Brian quickly tried to defuse any tension. "Cooter and I served together in Afghanistan and Iraq. He doesn't want to arrest anyone."

"I'd be dumb to anyway," I tried to joke. "Someone has to drive the truck."

"I got that covered," Ben said. I hoped he was not going to be this slow witted when Sami and his men appeared.

"You two look like you are eager for a fight," I tried to start a new conversation. Brian wore a deer hunter's loose camouflage outfit over lighter weight body armor. Ben was wearing an untucked long-sleeved button-front shirt to hide his heavier body armor and any identifying tattoos on his arms. They both had handguns holstered on their belts. The sidearms bulged the fabric of their shirts enough to betray that they were armed, but not one person in the truck stop seemed to care, if they even noticed.

"It's better to prepared for a fight than to be surprised by one," Brian repeated the sheriff's mantra. "Are you armed?"

I showed the pair the pistol shoulder holstered inside the loose button-front shirt I wore. I led the pair to the trunk of my car and opened the trunk. I opened the hidden compartment and offered Brian the Kriss rifle and two spare magazines. I reluctantly offered the Tavor carbine to Ben, but he surprised me by saying he had a carbine of his own in the cab of the truck. I took him at his word and removed the Steyr precision rifle and laid it in the trunk for easy access.

"We have another change in the plan," I blindsided the pair with a late revision to the plan Brian had already briefed Ben about. "The guy leading the Iraqis would like nothing better than to toss Brian and me into the container and deliver both of us to his father. He wants Brian a lot more than he wants me, but it would be especially unwise for either of us to deliver ourselves on a silver platter."

"How does that change things?" Ben asked and gave Brian a nervous glance.

"You and Brian are going to meet Sami Habib. I will take the Steyr and Tavor and be your overwatch. I will shoot anyone who makes a move to grab Brian," I explained. Ben seemed much less displeased with this new arrangement than Brian.

"Brian will drive my car and follow you to the ballpark. Hopefully that will give the two of you a way to escape while the Iraqis sort out the container. Do not put up anything more than a token fight when they take it, but you and I cannot allow them to take Brian from the ballpark in their custody," I stressed to Ben.

"Are you a good shot?" Ben inquired.

"The people who can verify my skills are all dead," I assured him. "I will not hesitate to drop anyone who raises their gun against either of you."

"I trust Cooter to take out as many of them as he can. He is an excellent sniper, but he is using a bolt action rifle," Brian said and laughed as though he had made some sort of joke. My rate of fire would be a third what it might be with a good semi-automatic rifle, so having the fully automatic Tavor to fall back on was no small comfort.

"I think I might just stay in the truck," Ben said.

"Do you want to be a sitting target?" I asked and glanced at Brian again. His companion struck me as the leading candidate for first-to-die in any firefight.

"We should leave here in an hour and circle around to come into Lexington from across the river," Brian said to change the subject. This was the route we chose the night before. I believe we were both surprised that our precariously leveraged plan seemed to be working. "I do not want to arrive too far ahead of the Iraqis because they might get suspicious if they are watching the meeting site and see us sitting around for more than an hour. This needs to look as shady as we can make it."

"All this talk about a gunfight has made me lose my appetite," Ben said as he fell in step when Brian led the way to the truck stop's restaurant. Ben certainly didn't order what might be his last dinner like a man without an appetite.

Forty-Six

We circled Lexington by way of Carrollton and Richmond, with the truck leading the way. Ben accelerated after we drove through Richmond and parked on the north side of the Missouri River bridge. We had one last briefing and checked our radios before we drove the last few miles to the ballpark.

I was concerned that there might be an ambush between the bridge and the ballpark. I would have considered staging one if I were in my opponents' position, but they may have scouted the ballpark and reached the same conclusion as Brian and myself that patience was more than a virtue and the ballpark was the best place to make their move. Brian and the container would be boxed in on three sides and the only road out was easily blocked. I wondered if any of them ever considered what an ideal kill box these same conditions created. Brian would have his back to the steep rock bluff and the arriving deputies could block their exit. This would leave Sami and his gunmen exposed between two fire teams, three if we added my sniper's nest.

Everyone was either nestled snuggly at home or busy at their friends' homes or at the movies. Even Casey's overly bright parking lot was empty at this still early hour of the night. Ben turned right to approach the ballpark and turned off the headlights as he pulled to a stop between the two commercial buildings backed onto the ballpark. Brian jumped out and came to take my place behind the wheel of the Cadillac. Brian was clearly eager to drive my supercharged coupe. He revved the engine a couple of times just to hear its throaty growl. I had to remind him we did not want to attract any attention. "Don't mess with my damn radio," I joked in parting. Brian lowered the retractable roof but left my radio alone.

I grabbed the soft-sided zippered case containing the Steyr rifle and a backpack stuffed with a thin mat and a spotting scope from the trunk before Brian hurried to catch up to Ben and the fake container. I made my way to the commercial building I had already chosen as my overwatch position as Brian parked behind Ben and the truck.

I had selected this building of the two to position my overwatch because anyone not trained in counter-sniper operations would assume I was atop the building which was closest to where Brian intended to hand over the container. The extra distance also provided a wider field of view of the action, and any round I fired would need only a millisecond longer to reach its target.

Ben had parked the truck with its cargo doors facing the steep rock face in the corner of the ballpark. Brian parked my car behind the container but facing my position. We could have looked one another in the face in daylight. I could shoot anyone standing on any of three sides of the truck. Brian and his truck driver would need to handle any gunmen who stood alongside the cargo container's far side.

Hiding behind my car was going to be the duo's last line of defense if things went sour. The thin metal of the coupe's retractable metal roof might add another layer of protection from gunfire. I only needed to provide covering fire until the sheriff arrived.

We had timed the container's arrival to allow fifteen minutes before the sheriff was supposed to arrive like the cavalry in an old Western movie. Everything depended on whether Sami was convinced that Brian intended to transfer the container to Dudiyn Alekhin here at ten o'clock.

Two vehicles approached the ballfield almost as soon as Brian and Ben took their positions in front of the cab of the truck. The two SUVs arrived with their bright headlights on and advanced across the ballpark. I was able to identify the vehicles as the green Ford Explorer which had followed me and a full-size Chevrolet Suburban. The vehicles parked to block the truck from leaving. I watched four men climb out of the Ford and six men exit the Suburban. Four of these gunmen formed a phalanx around Sami as he stepped forward to confront Brian. The remaining members of Sami's team remained behind the glare of the headlights, out of sight of Brian and Ben but perfectly silhouetted for me.

Sami's dividing his men meant I would have to decide which group posed the greater threat if there was a shootout.

My inclination was to focus on the ones Brian and Ben could not see and to leave Sami and his bodyguards to Brian and Ben. It was a four on two fight, which are not bad odds for men as experienced in close quarters combat as Brian and I are. Ben might take one down if he fired first. I focused on Sami because I wanted him to be the first Iraqi to die when the shooting began.

Brian remained calm because any orders Sami might have for his extradition most likely required delivering him to Rashid Habib unharmed. The Deputy Interior Minister would want the personal satisfaction of administering every bruise and broken bone inflicted upon Brian before a kangaroo court sentenced him to hang. There was nothing but me to keep Sami's men from shooting Ben on sight.

Brian tapped his shirt pocket to press redial on his iPhone to connect to my own phone. I would be able to listen to whatever transpired for as long as Brian retained his phone. We would revert to the hand signals we both learned while serving in the Rangers if Sami's men relieved him of the phone.

"Brian Hollis, you are under arrest," Sami called out as he and the heavily armed bodyguards approached Brian and Ben. They stopped roughly ten feet from the pair. Everyone on the ballfield was wearing body armor and had their fingers on their weapons. The Iraqis carried AK-47s, which are plenty accurate at such close range. "I expected to find Detective Holland with you."

"He's around," Brian assured Sami. "Would you like to hear from him?"

"That would be nice, yes," Sami said in an almost playful tone. I had no idea how many men Rashid Habib had dispatched to recover the container. I had a sudden fear that I was not looking at all of them. Perhaps Sami's team included counter-snipers who were waiting for me to expose my position.

I ignored the potential threat and squeezed the trigger. The fully jacketed .308 caliber bullet exploded against the Ford SUV's driver's side mirror and sent it flying to the ground at Sami's feet. Sami's bodyguards jumped at the sound, but Sami did not. Sami seemed to have the misplaced faith that he was immune from death. I have twice learned what a silly notion that is.

The suppressor screwed to the end of the barrel hid my rifle's muzzle flash, but the stillness of our surroundings did not totally muffle the sound of the heavy bullet leaving the Steyr's barrel. A trained counter-sniper would be able to isolate my location by calculating the time between the sound of the round leaving my rifle barrel and when the bullet did its damage. I was praying that this first shot was enough of a surprise that nobody could pinpoint the precise location the shot came from.

"Very funny," Sami said in a clearly unamused tone of voice. "I guess we will have to deal with Detective Holland at another time."

"Let me suggest abandoning that idea," Brian advised him humorlessly. "Shall we discuss why you are here instead?"

"There is nothing to discuss," Sami stated. His men had Brian and Ben boxed in and outnumbered.

"Alekhin will be here in a few minutes," Brian bluffed. He even looked at his watch to sell the idea of his buyer running late. What he was really looking at was the stopwatch he had set on his watch. We were both counting on Sheriff Franks to arrive at exactly ten o'clock.

"My only offer is to let your friend leave here alive if you give me the container and surrender that weapon. I will also promise that no harm comes to you until we arrive in Iraq," Sami said. He sounded firmly convinced he had the upper hand, despite the established menace of my sniper rifle.

"Hmm, I pass on your first offer," Brian told him. There was going to be a brief burst of gunfire in the very near future. I began to select my targets. "Would you care to make a second offer?"

"That would be for me to kill your friend and to return to Iraq with the container and only your head in a bag." Sami was in no mood to make any new deal with Brian.

"You suck at negotiating. Has anyone ever told you that?" Brian continued to provoke Sami. I was getting nervous. I could see from my position that Sheriff Franks and his deputies were finally approaching on Main Street, but they might not arrive before Brian and Ben were gunned down. The sheriff's deputies were unlikely to survive their initial encounter with Sami's men if they arrived during a gunfight. "I will tell you what, I will give you the container in the spirit of international cooperation. The contents of this container belong to the Iraqi people, and you are the nearest Iraqi I see. You just need to agree to not try to take any part of me or Cooter Holland back to Iraq."

"I do not find this acceptable," Sami decided. "Both of you are criminals."

"Then consider this. This standoff will become a full-fledged bloodbath when Dudiyn Alekhin arrives and finds you meddling in his business. You, and your entourage, are about to take fire from two sides with no cover," Brian said with convincing detail.

"You are the ones who will be shot from two sides," Sami unexpectedly decided to continue negotiating. I admired his bravado. "Mister Alekhin is a family friend."

"Will Alekhin still consider you to be a friend when he learns your father sent you here to keep this container from him?" Brian argued.

"You will not live to tell him," Sami replied in a no less certain voice. I pulled my head from the scope and concentrated on what the two of them were saying.

"Are you prepared to stay and see who he decides to kill?" Brian challenged Sami. Brian was out of lies, time, and fresh ideas for how to stall.

Sami made his decision. "We will take this container from you and leave you to answer to Dudiyn. He will kill you himself when he thinks you have crossed him."

"He's due in just a minute, so you need to leave here right now," Brian tried to prod Sami.

"I must confirm what is inside," Sami unexpectedly declared.

"Get out of there," I told Brian over the phone.

Brian motioned for Ben to follow him as he turned towards the woods and began to run from the scene. The men with Sami laughed at the pair running away on foot. They no longer viewed the two Americans as a target or a threat. They were amused by Brian's belief he could put enough distance between himself and the container that Dudiyn Alekhin would not track him down.

I seethed silently as one of Sami's bodyguards approached my car. He tossed his AK-47 onto the passenger seat and sat on the driver's side and began adjusting the seat to his own height before he began looking for the key to start the engine. I was tempted to blow his head off but accepted that it would be better to surrender the car for a moment than to have to clean the man's brains off the leather upholstery. Brian must have kept the key with him when he began running.

Sami and his men approached the rear of the container. I was unable to see what was happening from my position, but I continued to monitor the Iraqis' activities as best I could.

Sheriff Rogers pulled off the road and parked beside the building I was still standing atop of. I was still watching Brian and Ben put distance between themselves and the container. I needed to get off the roof so he would drive me to the scene. His deputies waited to turn on their sirens and lights until they were already crossing the ballfield. Brian and Ben were caught in the open between the Iraqis and the deputies and wisely set their weapons on the ground and laid flat with their faces in the short grass of the playing field.

A blast of superheated air suddenly rolled over the top of the building where I was still lying on my mat. I could see heat ripples in the explosion that lit up the ballpark. The sound of the blast filled the summer air. This monstrous roar was mixed with the sound of nearby windows shattering and dozens of car alarms being triggered. The roof beneath me trembled for an instant and then the entire town fell silent but for the car alarms. I began to speak aloud to myself to be sure I had not lost my hearing as a fresh hell from the sound of the alarm in the building beneath me began calling for attention.

I hastily stored the rifle and bundled my gear into the backpack before I stood up and viewed the ravine beneath me. The steel-sided shipping container had ceased to exist. Ben's truck and my beloved coupe were heaps of burning metal. Sami's rental SUVs were intact, though the men standing beside them had fared poorly in the blast of superheated air.

The blast had somehow been focused to burst through the doors of the container rather than in the sort of widespread detonation one might expect from an IED. The sheriff's deputies had skidded to a stop short of the blast area and they all remained transfixed in their patrol cars.

I saw no sign of life or movement anywhere near the container. Whatever accelerant had been precisely rigged inside the container was meant to roar from the container's open doors like dragon's breath. The bomb involved a combination of accelerants which had immediately cremated Sami and his companions. The blast and flames must have ricocheted off the rock wall barely thirty feet behind the container and doubled back on the victims before rising to singe the leaves on the tree limbs hanging eighty feet above the ballpark and to ignite the fuel tanks in my coupe and Ben's truck. The ground behind the container was scorched bare and the rock bluff continued to burn from whatever the bomb maker used to murder whoever opened the container. It smelled and had acted like napalm, but the brilliant white material still cremating remains was likely something like thermite. Neither of these were easily obtained in the quantities used to make the bomb.

The flatbed trailer the container had been hauled here on lay flat on the ground, its tires melted and the flatbed itself blown nearly in two. I saw the shattered remains of a good-sized concrete culvert inside the container. The bomb maker must have used the thick, reinforced cylinder and a shaped charge to channel the explosion so the fireball would strike its unwitting targets in a precisely aimed blast. The bomb maker may not have anticipated his handiwork would detonate so close to a wall of stone.

I spotted Brian and Ben as they slowly retrieved their weapons and walked towards the blast zone. They had managed to put enough distance between themselves and the container to avoid being killed by the blast. I did not shout to them because I doubted either of them had recovered their hearing. Our phone connection had been lost.

Brian dusted himself off and turned towards me as he raised my carbine above his head.

"Wolverines!" he shouted at the top of his lungs and began laughing. Ben did not understand Brian's reference to one of our favorite movies from the 1980s.

I waved to Brian to acknowledge I was also still alive and unscratched by the blast. The two men approached the wreckage while Sheriff Franks' deputies retreated to Main Street to begin crowd control. Everyone in town was going to call the sheriff's office for an explanation of what they heard. I figured we had ten minutes before a crowd assembled on the rim of the ravine.

Ben paused beside the Ford Explorer. Its green paint was singed but the vehicle seemed otherwise unharmed. He leaned over and picked up the shattered rear-view mirror. He glanced up at me before he opened the SUV's driver's side door and tossed the mirror inside. This was the telling motion I had been waiting to see. Rangers and Special Forces members have an almost unconscious habit of collecting tokens from their firefights. I had no way to know Ben's military background, but he was no mere truck driver by trade.

Brian and Ben hurriedly stacked the bodies of the only unburned Iraqi gunmen into the back of Sami's Suburban and raced the damaged rental vehicles out of the park. Brian's unexpected departure was going to make me responsible for his eluding arrest and to be the guy who would have to explain what had transpired once SAC Rogers arrived on the scene.

Forty-Seven

Franks did his best to ignore the brief exchange I had with Brian when he stopped to return my carbine. The sheriff struggled with his sense of duty to not detain Brian and impound the vehicle and bodies, but he was too shell shocked to do anything but continue to cooperate in our charade. Some part of his barely functioning thought process knew that arresting Brian Hollis would most likely complicate his own life tenfold once the FBI arrived. He looked unhappy about having made the call to SAC Rogers, because he and a dozen agents would be arriving in the next few minutes.

The sheriff and I were standing beside the befuddled police chief's cruiser when Special Agent in Charge Rogers and Meghan Bridges arrived. Agents Bennett and Kinsey followed their boss's Chevy Suburban and the SWAT team he brought with him onto the playing field. The town's keeper of the peace was letting us know what he thought of our keeping him out of the loop about Sami Habib and Brian Hollis meeting in the middle of town, but he decided to leave when he saw the FBI marching towards us.

The local fire department had no choice but to watch the thermite continue to melt the wreckage of the container and to further cremate the victims of the blast. Their supply of the specialized materials for putting out such fires was too limited to waste on this. Using water to cool the smoldering mass would make it explode all over again. Their rebuffed efforts at doing their duty were unavoidably degrading the crime scene.

The rim of the ballpark was filled with gawkers who had ignored the late hour to get a look at the mess someone had made of their favorite ballpark. The sheriff's deputies were doing their best to keep everyone far enough back that they did not topple over the ledge in their quest for the best photograph.

Sheriff Franks was understandably upset by the damage to the town's best playing field, which he was going to have to both explain and take the blame for. This was not a positive position to be in during an election year. I offered advice on how to handle the situation, but all he gave in response was a shell-shocked nod of his head. I knew there was an anger building inside the lawman at having been drawn into whatever occurred here, which was far different than I led him to believe would occur.

"Where the hell is Brian Hollis?" Rogers bellowed at both of us as he strode towards us. Meghan looked appalled at the extent of the damage. She seemed to take very little comfort in knowing that the demolished container did not hold any of the antiquities she was chasing.

"Somewhere else," I calmly informed him. Sheriff Franks wisely chose to let me handle the FBI. He shared their anger.

"Okay then, where are Sami Habib and his men?" Rogers demanded in an even angrier tone.

"That is a far thornier question," I admitted and turned his attention towards the melted remains of the sturdy metal container. "Sami is somewhere in all of that."

"I don't need this making the news," Rogers let us know and glared at the peanut gallery above us. My hearing was not yet fully recovered, but it was clear that he was worried about this scene being captured in the 24-hour news cycle of someone like CNN. Neither Sheriff Franks nor I had noticed the presence of any television news crews among the concerned citizens standing overhead. "How do you suggest I inform the Director about what transpired here?"

"Sheriff Franks can report what happened here in either of two ways," I informed a stone-faced SAC Rogers. Sheriff Franks and I had discussed this thorny matter while we awaited the FBI's arrival. "The first is a simple explanation that will satisfy everyone's curiosity. The second explanation is a messy one that addresses the truth."

"Explain yourself," SAC Rogers snapped.

"Sheriff Franks can write this up as an encounter with one of one of those right-wing militias you keep warning him about," I suggested. "This could be the work of a bunch of militant crazies who chose to blow themselves up rather than be arrested."

"Bullshit. What is the honest explanation?" Rogers demanded. Lies are simpler stories to tell than the truth, but Rogers knew the truth would eventually rear its ugly head.

"Sami Habib, the eldest son of Iraq's corrupt Deputy Interior Minister, and multiple members of Iraq's secret police operating illegally within your jurisdiction, died when an incendiary device was detonated inside a shipping container which was originally intended to be opened in your presence."

"What!?" Rogers all but shouted as much in surprise as anger.

"Brian Hollis faked shipping a container from Iraq to lure Dudiyn Alekhin and Daniel Logan to a meeting where they could be ambushed. Apparently, this was meant to be a big part of that ambush. I was unaware of the IED within the container when I proposed using it to ensnare Sami Habib," I informed him. I was having a very hard time imagining Brian Hollis intended to set his own sister and an FBI Special Agent on fire to clear his name with the Iraqi government.

"Who built the bomb?" Rogers demanded.

"That no longer matters because Sami's death is a much larger problem to deal with than who wanted you dead," I said to refocus Rogers on the international incident confronting him.

"What am I supposed to tell anyone became of Sami Habib and the men with him if I go with your first option?" Rogers demanded. He was no fool and was open to any way of sweeping this under the rug before the FBI Director began asking pointed questions. "They cannot have simply disappeared."

"Sure, they could have. People disappear all the time. Does it look like there will be enough remains to identify who died in the blast? For all you know Sami Habib and his men decided to go to Las Vegas. What skeletal remains Sheriff Franks and I have been able to locate so far have turned to dust when the sheriff's deputies attempted to place them into evidence bags. The sheriff can give the ashes whatever names he chooses in his report," I suggested.

Rogers continued to point uselessly towards the decimated container and the blackened hillside but finally dropped his hand and took a deep breath.

"I was not a witness to Sami Habib's presence or to what transpired. I have no choice but to accept Sheriff's Franks's version of what happened here," Rogers sighed. He had found a way to put the responsibility for any lies on the sheriff. Not having to resign in disgrace had just become Harold Rogers's singular purpose in life. Making the sheriff and me responsible for explaining the explosion as being the work of some local militia gave him a way to avoid the FBI mounting its own investigation into the matter.

"I have never met Sami Habib, so I would not have recognized him on sight had I arrived before the explosion." Franks had already found his own escape route. I was going to need to find my own.

"If I were in your shoes, I believe I would prefer to decide that this is a local matter which has no relation to anything you have been investigating," I continued to pressure Rogers. Meghan bit her lower lip. She looked like she wanted to burst out in laughter at Rogers's dilemma. I was sure she would be laughing when she shared the story with a much-relieved Alexis over a bottle of wine.

"It is not impossible to imagine that Sami and his entourage really have decided to find an alternative to going home," Meghan suggested. "Perhaps they will surface to contact the State Department and seek asylum. I hear that Iraq is a very dangerous place to live."

"Enough with this nonsense. I still want answers, Holland, and I know you are hiding Brian Hollis from me. You are running out of time to produce him," Rogers scowled and waved his arm above his head to gather his agents before he stormed back to his vehicle. He opened his own door and slammed it shut before his driver could do so. The driver settled for opening the rear passenger door for Meghan.

"It sucks to be him," Franks chuckled. I looked at the sheriff with a grin on my face, but the truth is that I only wanted to get a good night's sleep and to be back in New Orleans in time for a plate of red beans and rice on Monday.

Sunday

June 27, 2010

Friends are just enemies

who don't have the guts to kill you.

-   Judy Tenuda

Forty-Eight

I called two rental car agencies at the airport in Kansas City, the only place that I found to rent one on a Sunday morning, and I commiserated with the Enterprise agent who apologized for their lack of SUVs in inventory. They were expecting two vehicles to be returned at any moment, but I accepted Dodge Charger rather than wait through eternity. Their vehicles were never coming back. The vehicles had likely already been torched as though taken in a random car theft and the bodies disposed of by Hank's men at D-Tech.

I also went online and ordered a bouquet of flowers for my hosts. I included a note thanking them for their hospitality and for allowing me my privacy. I was certain that they had already pieced together my involvement in the increased traffic which annoyed Carol on my arrival and the overnight spike in tourism at the ballpark which may have bothered her even more. I would need to make other arrangements if I ever found another reason to return to Lexington.

My welcome rolled out of town behind me. Sheriff Franks ordered one of his deputies to drive me to the rental car agency and to wait until my car was loaded and then to follow me east on Interstate 70 to make sure I cleared Lafayette County before he went on patrol.

I began debriefing myself as I rode to the airport. Every military operation has a debriefing to carefully analyze what transpired on the mission. These were little more than a review of how the long hours of meticulous pre-mission planning and simulations made a difference. It was a rare occasion that anything ever went as planned once bullets started flying.

A disturbing question came to mind as we approached the airport. It was going to be difficult to get a straight answer to what was suddenly bothering me.

"I hate to put you in this position, deputy, but I am not heading straight home," I apologized to Sheriff Frank's trusted deputy. "Let your boss know I had some things to finish tying up here and that I promise to find a route back to New Orleans that doesn't involve his jurisdiction."

"He's going to be mad," he warned me. I could see his real concern was that the sheriff would give him the earful the sheriff would want to give me.

"Not as mad as I am right now," I assured the confused deputy. He did not ask what was fueling my anger, and I was doing my best not to show the extent of the rage that had begun simmering under my skin for fear of traumatizing the young lawman.

He drove away without another word, and I left the airport barely able to drive within the speed limit. I took the Tiffany Springs exit from Interstate 29 moments later and drove to the address of the warehouse where Brian had intended to ambush Dudiyn Alekhin. The building was unexpectedly blocked by yellow crime scene tape and multiple local and federal vehicles.

I was about to back away when SAC Rogers stepped out of the warehouse and spotted me. He pointed and told me to stay where I was. I was not inclined to leave before I understood the crime scene, so I only acted as though I was going to be uncooperative. As far as I knew nobody had any reason to have shown up here the night before.

"What are you doing here, detective?" Rogers bellowed as he approached my rental car.

"Gawking, like everyone else," I said and walked towards Rogers. He lifted the crime scene tape as I ducked beneath it and followed him into the warehouse.

The focus of the investigation was the trunk of a late model Lincoln sedan. There was a body inside that I believed I could identify with very little trouble.

"Who's your stiff?" I asked Rogers as though I were clueless.

"Anthony Picarello," the FBI agent informed me and watched for any sign of recognition to cross my face. "He was known as Robbie. Guy got the name because he tried to rob a capo's card game when he was nineteen. They let him live but took his car, his wallet, and every stitch of his clothes. He was the 'robbie' and not the 'robber.' The name stuck and he has never made it any further up the ladder than gofer. Someone clipped him last night and left him here."

"Two rounds behind the left ear?" I asked.

"How'd you know that?" Rogers demanded.

I turned and parted my hair to show him the raw spot behind my own ear.

"It is Daniel Logan's calling card," I informed him. "The two of them must have been planning on killing you when you came to arrest Alekhin. It would make sense that someone from the local outfit would have tried to blow up as many people as possible. Killing you would have elevated Robbie within his own outfit, but it would also bring down the full resources of the Justice Department against that outfit. Logan may have been planning to use the reaction to the local outfit killing you to make his own move to take over from them. I ruined that plan, so he shot Robbie rather than risk him making this one of his stories."

"How can we prove Logan pulled the trigger?" Suddenly I was his colleague.

"You never will. Just be glad you are the one looking at Robbie this morning and someone isn't scraping your ashes off the floor," I told the special agent. He nodded grimly, but he was not satisfied that I had shared everything I knew.

"You promised to deliver Brian Hollis before you left town." Rogers had recovered his Special-Agent-in-Charge voice. He checked out the rental car decal on my car. "Are you thinking of skipping out on me?"

"No, I am as curious about what Brian Hollis has really been up to as you are," I assured him. "Give me two hours and we will be in Penn Valley Park."

"So, you know where he is," Rogers charged.

"I didn't until about an hour ago," I defended myself. "That was when I realized I have been played this entire time."

Forty-Nine

I called Sean and told him I was on my way to speak to Brian. Sean initially denied having any idea where Brian might be, but then gave his best performance yet when he tried to convince me that he and Brian 'just happened to be' having breakfast together. I let it slide and waited while he handed his cellphone to Brian, who immediately put the call on speaker phone. I imagined Peter and Hank were hovering close by.

"Hey, I am on my way back to New Orleans, but I wanted to see you one last time," I said to warm Brian to the idea of our meeting.

"You're already headed home?" Brian did his best to sound surprised. "Alexis and I wanted to treat you to a night on the town before you took off."

"Let's raincheck that," I said and got to the point. It did not miss my attention that the dinner invitation did not come from nor include our classmates. "I will come get you."

"How do you know where I am?" Brian asked. I liked that he sounded surprised.

"You have all been staying at Sean's club the whole time," I told him and hung up before he could question how I knew what I had just accused them of doing. It was the only rational explanation for such tight security on an empty clubhouse, and the three of them needed a place safe from Sami Habib and Daniel Logan.

Sean was standing outside the front gate with Brian when I pulled up in the rental sedan. Sean started to walk towards the car as though he was going to join us, but I rolled my window down and told him to stay put. Brian paused before he opened the door and buckled himself into the passenger seat.

"How are you doing this morning?" Brian asked to gauge my mood. I was unable to put any sort of friendly expression on my face while in the state of mind I was in after speaking with Special Agent Rogers.

"Better in some ways. Worse in even more," I told him as I backed out of the driveway and turned north on the nearby expressway. I watched the rear–view mirror for a chase car. It did not show up until we were six blocks from the club.

The nearly quarter mile distance proved to be important because it meant the men following us lost visual contact of my car when I made an abrupt right turn at the traffic light on 31st Street and then made an immediate turn to the left into Penn Valley Park. They would need a few minutes to backtrack and find us in the sizeable park.

"What's up, Cooter?" Brian asked when I finally parked and unlatched my seat belt. It was good that he was nervous about the situation, but I needed him to be frightened of me personally.

"I just want to go over a few things before I head home," I said and flashed a nasty thin smile. Brian nodded and hesitantly unlatched his own seatbelt.

I was parked on the west side of the circular drive around the monument to the Pioneer Mother. Brian was anxious as I began to silently lead him around the massive statue of a pair of heavily ladened horses with two men trudging on foot and a woman cradling an infant while riding sidesaddle between the two men. I have long wondered what sort of hardship pioneer families faced in whatever country they had immigrated from that made homesteading on America's barren and wind–swept plains seem like an improvement.

"You know what I like about Kansas City?" I asked Brian. It sounded off topic, but it was part of why I had brought him to this particular statue to discuss the past week.

"The barbecue?" he suggested. I had certainly enjoyed my fill. I still planned to have lunch at Gates and Sons before I left.

"No, it's the statues. Kansas City may have the only Boy Scout monument with a half–naked woman standing on it," I said but pointed towards the statue of a lone Indian scout a hundred yards in the distance. "These two statues are very impressive, but there is something wrong about both statues that most people probably never notice. All of us are inclined to accept what someone we trust says is true. That was my mistake in focusing my attention on finding you. The hidden ball in this shell game was never you or the container you hid. It was the reason why you took the container in the first place."

"I do not understand what you're trying to say," Brian stalled. I noticed the chase car had found us and was parked a dozen yards behind my car. The two male occupants could watch us talk, but they made no attempt to approach us.

"This statue was placed here in 1927," I began explaining. "In all that time, how many people do you suppose have realized that the statue faces to the east and not towards the west? Nobody seems to have realized that this simple error has made this statue into a tribute to human failure. The three adults in the statue would have come west with a covered wagon full of hope but they have given up and are headed back, broke and broken, with a kid in tow. Do you understand what I am saying?"

"Sort of," Brian glanced at the chase car rather than the statue. I had no idea what their signal was, but it would be very unfortunate if either of the two men left the vehicle. I intended to kill Brian before I took a shot at either of them.

"The statue of the Indian scout across the expressway faces west, but that was never where his biggest threat came from. He should be facing south, towards Westport, where the wagon trains full of white settlers passed through on their way to take his land," I elaborated.

"You didn't bring me here to discuss messed up statues," Brian finally spoke up.

"I brought you here to let you know I finally see things as they really are. Seeing the primary threat each adversary posed is what kept me alive in every firefight I was ever in. I have questions and a gun that won't trace back to me if I shoot you. You have answers and a decision to make," I told him. He started to laugh, but then saw my expression and understood I was absolutely prepared to murder him in cold blood.

"Jeez, Cooter, you have gone crazy," Brian tried to reason with me. "What sort of things do you think I kept from you?"

"Start with the truck driver from last night," I suggested. We would work forwards or backwards based on his answer. "He served, same as you and me."

Brian paused before he answered. He struggled to formulate a defense against what my response might be to his answer. "He was someone I had to use at the last minute. Robbie was supposed to drive the truck, but he dropped out of sight at the last minute."

"Robbie has dropped out of life," I informed him. "Daniel Logan clipped him after he and I met for lunch. I told Logan that the warehouse and your meeting were compromised, and Logan was probably convinced that Robbie had ratted him out. Who does your guy work for?"

"Does it matter at this point?" Brian stalled. He had a point, but I had a gun.

"The truth always matters," I said with an exasperated sigh. It really doesn't.

"He works for Hank," Brian confessed. "I knew you were going to figure that out sooner or later."

"And your story about the warehouse ambush?" I asked.

"All of that was true. The plan was to shoot both Alekhin and his attorney in the warehouse," Brian insisted.

"Why that warehouse?" I pressed. I held off mentioning what I had just seen.

"Because it needed to look like Alekhin died in a Mob hit. It would have worked if Alekhin and Logan had been killed in the warehouse Robbie had lined up," Brian explained.

"Was your plan to detonate that bomb in the warehouse?" I asked.

"Of course not," he immediately balked. "My sister and I were supposed to be standing right there."

"Along with half the local FBI office," I added. He nodded numbly. "If you didn't plant the bomb then who did?"

"Look, it's over now. Can't we just let it drop?"

"I couldn't now, even I wanted to. I am most upset that this is the second time you have pulled me into something that was entirely different than what you led me to believe it was," I heatedly pointed out. "I just want to know how much of the plan you laid out Friday night was even real."

"Most of it. I needed a fake container that I could use to lure Daniel Logan and Dudiyn Alekhin somewhere that I could kill them. I also needed a fall guy for their murders and pinning it on what is left of Civella's outfit by using a warehouse one of them owns would have satisfied the FBI that it was a gang war." Brian admitted. "But your telling Logan about the ambush meant we had to come up with a different plan."

I caught his use of the plural, but let it slide for the moment. I was sure that he was not talking about the two of us.

"So, were you looking for a way to kill the two of them before you decided to take the container?" I pressed him on the timing. One part of me was admiring the logic behind Brian's original plan. I began to focus on his motives.

"I needed to bait my trap," Brian said. "I knew Alekhin expected the caliphate to deliver the container to him. I took the container and called Logan to offer him a different deal."

"Can you stop saying 'I' when you really mean 'we', like you just said?" I asked irritably. "There were far too many moving parts to your plan for you to have acted alone. I think Peter and Hank roped you into their own plan, and that the three of you subsequently pulled me into the mess you created. You can stop acting like Peter and Hank had nothing to do with this."

"I'm not sure what you think they would have to do with it," Brian valiantly lied. "They wound up in a lot of trouble after I took the container."

"They lost some money. That is the only damage I can imagine that they would have suffered," I argued. "They have deep pockets, so they could afford to ride out the storm until you pulled off your assassination."

"What do you think they had to gain by my killing Alekhin or Logan?" Brian challenged me. I sensed he was trying to maneuver himself to be the one who was asking questions. He was obviously concerned that I may have figured out what he was doing his best to hide from my inquiry.

"You gave me a clue when you said gangsters operate the same way in every country when you told me about your father paying off Nick Civella. I think Peter and Hank have been paying protection money to Alekhin to minimize the number of attacks on Peter's convoys. Alekhin could keep anyone he was doing business with off their backs, or he could increase the attacks if it served his purpose. It was cheaper for Peter to pay the bribes than it was for Hank to have to keep replacing the men he lost in those attacks. Am I right?"

"You aren't far wrong," Brian grudgingly confirmed. "The truth is that Logan is the one who they have been paying. They hide the bribes as consulting fees. Anyway, Logan tipped off Peter that Sami was planning to hand the container over to the caliphate."

"How considerate of him," I mumbled sarcastically. Logan would have had a plan of his own.

"Not so much," Brian half-chuckled.

"Of course not," I sighed. My friends have had much less experience dealing with gangsters and warlords than I have. "So, you took the container and planned to deliver it when the heat died down?"

"We were not sure how involved Logan was in the plan to hijack the container. We knew his boss was working both sides, selling guns to the caliphate and black-market goods to Rashid. Peter and Hank were caught in a bind because they were directly responsible for the container. They would be in trouble with Rashid Habib if they refused to give the container to his son, and the Ruling Council would blame them for losing it if the caliphate hijacked it. The only solution was for me to take it."

"So, you did all of this on your own?" I asked skeptically.

"Most of it," he said rather proudly. "The container is still sitting on Peter's lot. I drove off with an empty container and paperwork claiming it was the one everyone is looking for."

"Nice stunt," I said with some admiration. "Why go to so much trouble?"

"We wanted to keep the container safe. If I got caught with the empty container then I just had to destroy the paperwork. It is parked in a garage about three miles from Peter's lot." Brian sat down on one of the benches, drained but happy to have shared his story. Except it was only half the story.

"How did you get from taking an empty container to trying to kill Dudiyn Alekhin and Daniel Logan at the airport?" I asked. "And how did the FBI get involved?"

"We miscalculated how much influence Logan had with the Ruling Council. He told the Interior Minister that all three of us were involved in the disappearance of the container, and then Interpol told the FBI about the phantom transfer Peter created in his own system to make it look like the container was being shipped to Baltimore. We only wanted to focus everyone's attention away from Iraq. The FBI decided I was a criminal mastermind when the non-existent container slipped through Customs. The plan changed to luring Alekhin and Logan here to kill them after the FBI made the container seem real by putting out the APB on me. We knew Alekhin had sources that would tell him the trailer was over here, and that I had it.

"I am sure Alekhin was displeased to find that his attorney was working against him. The Russian was happy with the way things were going and the Habibs were not going to get so much as a slap on the wrist had Sami allowed the caliphate to hijack the container. Logan misjudged how angry his boss would be. It must have forced Logan to move up his timetable for eliminating Alekhin," I suggested. I was in a free flow of thoughts now and reanalyzing everything I had been told on the fly. I had not expected Brian to be this forthcoming without my threatening him with injuries.

"Alekhin needed to be killed somewhere besides Iraq because Rashid Habib would launch a posse of agents to find who murdered his black-market supplier," Brian began to open up about the assassination plot.

"I think Rashid may be counting on Alekhin to negotiate with the caliphate to get his family back. You have supposedly had the container for over a month. The caliphate would have already killed the men and sold off the women they are ransoming if they did not anticipate an eventual payment," I continued to do my own analysis of the situation.

"This is why I wanted your help," Brian finally came clean. "You see the bigger picture and make better strategic decisions than I do."

"How does your sister fit into this?" I changed directions and ignored whatever Brian meant to accomplish by his gushing compliment.

"I never expected Alexis to get sucked into this. The FBI informed Peter that Interpol had informed them of the container slipping through their fingers in Baltimore, so Peter told them about our plan to use the container to assassinate Dudiyn Alekhin and Daniel Logan because he thought they might turn a blind eye to our doing something they cannot do legally. They were all in favor of luring Alekhin to the States, but they would not sanction murdering him. The FBI handed the case to the office in Kansas City, and they sent Alexis to New Orleansto get close to Logan so she could confirm Alekhin was going to show up," Brian began unspooling the conflicting plans he and the FBI had.

"Something went wrong. Why did you rope me into this?" I asked.

"The FBI put out an APB on me and cast me as the bad guy to help convince Alekhin that the container was being smuggled into the United States. We needed someone who could distract the FBI while we killed Logan and Alekhin like we planned to all along," Brian began to confess. "Arresting Alekhin was not going to shut down his criminal enterprise. He might have skipped bail, or he might have kept running things from prison. Daniel Logan is no less of a criminal than Alekhin and he would not hesitate to help Alekhin do either of those things. We knew we had to kill both of them."

"You might be surprised about Logan's loyalty," I countered. "Daniel Logan has been looking for a way to take Alekhin's place and he might have been willing to deliver Alekhin to your massacre or left him to rot in prison while he took the helm himself. That is my greatest fear. Daniel Logan makes Alekhin look like a pussycat. Dudiyn Alekhin has reached a point that he can order his men to get things done. Logan still likes to get his own hands dirty, like killing Robbie. It's why I know Logan shot me and that Alekhin did not hire an assassin to do his wet work."

"Daniel Logan really shot you?" Brian asked in what sounded like awe. I could not tell if he admired the attorney's audacity or that I had survived. "I thought that was a joke."

"Different story for a different time," I shook my head. I wanted to keep Brian talking for as long as I could. Sooner or later, the men in the car were going to decide we had been talking for too long and would attempt to intervene. "You wanted to make me part of a pre-meditated homicide conspiracy I had no idea existed. Is that why you called me?"

"That's a pretty harsh way to look at it," Brian complained, but he did not deny the accusation. "Our plan was taking too long, and Daniel Logan started acting like he thought something was wrong, which meant Alekhin might not come to the States. Alexis agreed to go to New Orleans to keep the plan alive. She approached you on her own. That had nothing to do with anything else but her."

"Good to know," I sighed. I tended to believe him about his sister's role.

"And that meeting Hank staged after I had breakfast with your sister, what was that all about?" I demanded. I felt the meeting had been nothing but a sideshow at the time.

"Peter and Hank thought telling you they were not involved might convince you to help me when I showed up," Brian told me. "I needed to look desperate."

"It was a convincing performance, but I don't believe Logan was in Kansas City to close your deal on the container. I think he knew Alekhin was not coming before I tried to dissuade him. Why do you think he was in town on Saturday?"

"Why do you?" Brian determinedly attempted to turn the table on me again.

"Because he had other business to handle, and he needed to deal with Robbie after I told him nobody was going to show up at the meeting. It must have been a business deal. Your turn." I was getting deep enough into his ruse that he might decide to begin stonewalling my interrogation.

"You are good at this, aren't you?" Brian asked in a bit of a daze. "Logan wanted to make a low-ball offer to buy Peter's trucking company. He thought Peter may have lost enough money that he would sell his Iraqi operations for pennies on the dollar."

"My next question should be how they met one another, but I think I know that one, too," I told him. "Your sister introduced Logan to Peter and Hank at one of Sean's clubs a few years ago. You have all been chummy for a while now, but Logan has been patiently waiting for a chance to get his hooks into each of you."

"You're right." Brian nodded his head. Brian was still answering my questions and confirming my conclusions, but he tried to not volunteer anything I did not specifically ask about. I glanced at his bodyguards to make sure this head nod was not a signal to come to his rescue.

"Where does Meghan fit into all of this?"

"She only wants to see the container delivered to the museum. She was not part of our plan and no one ever told her what was going on." This cleared Meghan if what he said was true. I wanted to believe that there was at least one other person involved in this charade who was as oblivious to the machinations behind the scenes as I had been.

"Well, she is going to get her wish," I said. "One last question. Who put the bomb in the container? Was it really Robbie or was that Hank's handiwork?"

"Robbie intended to, but Hank must have had one of his men build it," Brian said. "I honestly did not expect that to happen. I thought you would end up shooting Sami."

"When did Sami become your new target? You did everything you could to make me focus my plan on eliminating him as a threat." I saw no reason to admit that I had no qualms or regrets about Sami's demise.

"Sami Habib became a target after he threatened you and me with extradition," Brian readily admitted. "Killing him was supposed to distract his father long enough for us to get the container to the museum. Satisfied?"

"Hardly," I scoffed. His blithe response opened an entirely fresh can of worms. I needed only a couple of seconds to reach a conclusion on why Sami was targeted. "I was supposed to take the blame for his death, right?"

"What do you mean?" Brian asked rather than deny the serious accusation.

"You know the Iraqis will forgive the three of you once the container gets delivered to the museum, but you needed someone to blame for Sami's death. Who better than a guy whose head the Habib family has been after for years?" I said with increasing anger. "I think that killing Sami was your plan all along and it was why you pulled me into this."

"Do you really think we would do that to you?" Brian indignantly demanded.

"How did you put it when I asked if Peter and Hank would

hand you over to save themselves? You told me they would do it 'in a heartbeat' and I think you guys are no less willing to toss me to the wolves, if need be," I complained. "I was your perfect Oswald. Sorry to disappoint you, but being willing to die for you does not mean I am willing to get myself killed for you. It is more than a semantic difference."

"I am sorry you feel that way," Brian did his best to sound sincere.

"I am sure you are," I angrily agreed.

"What are you going to do about it?" Brian asked a little too defiantly.

"Whatever I have to," I promised with my practiced tone of menace. "My question is what are you going to tell the FBI?"

"Why would I tell them anything?" he wondered.

"Because you are about to be arrested," I casually informed him. "You did not seem all that surprised that Peter and Hank would hand you over to the Iraqis, and you guys have been pals all along since Wentworth. We haven't seen one another in years, so handing you over to the FBI shouldn't mess with our friendship."

Brian let forth with a string of expletives, but he did not try to run from the scene.

I had a solution to the problem of Daniel Logan, the only thing that the four of us genuinely had in common, that Brian was now poised to execute. This moment had always been my endgame. His leaving the scene last night was unexpected, but it also made me less guilty about using him as my Trojan horse into the FBI.

"Here's what we all need you to say when they question you," I began coaching him. Brian was still sputtering angrily, but he also listened to my instructions. "You need to place Daniel Logan at the heart of everything. He warned Peter about Sami, but taking the container was Logan's idea. He was the one who came up with the idea of making Alekhin believe the container was here, because he planned to kill him and blame it on the Kansas City outfit."

"Most of that is true," Brian pointed out. "But it would be nice not to be the only bad guy for a change."

"Logan blackmailed you into being the one to take the container by threatening Alexis' life. He knew about the two of you being brother and sister all along," I added details that Brian would need to make sure to give SAC Rogers.

"I can sell all of this," Brian said and calmed down. He realized that I was giving all three of my former classmates an escape route.

"Here is the most important part," I said. "It was Dan Logan's intention to kill Sami Habib from the start. He believed that his being Alekhin's attorney would make it look like he was following his client's orders to murder Sami. He wanted to create a wedge between Rashid Habib and Dudiyn Alekhin and position himself to take over in Iraq when Rashid moved against Alekhin."

"You know this is all a bunch of crap," Brian stopped me. "You are telling me to lie to the FBI. That is a major felony."

"Telling them what they don't want to hear is the crime they will prosecute you for," I countered. "You are handing Daniel Logan to Special Agent Rogers with a perfect bow wrapped around him. He gets to say that Russian gangsters were behind the theft of the container and Sami's death rather than three American businessmen, all of whom have vital government contracts in Iraq. It doesn't just sound better, it sells better when he sends his report to the State Department to present to the Iraqi Ruling Council. Rashid and Sami are allowed to look like they were victims of a conspiracy between Alekhin and the caliphate to extort money from the Habib family rather than very willing participants in a plot to hijack the container. The three of you become heroes for protecting the container all this time, and Daniel Logan has to convince the Mukhabarat that he is being framed rather than the FBI."

Agent Bennett arrived on the scene and parked his Crown Vic to box in Hank's men. Special Agent Rogers arrived seconds later with an additional half dozen agents and headed directly towards where we were standing.

"Brian Hollis, you are under arrest for the theft of cultural artifacts rightfully belonging to the government of Iraq and for conspiracy to murder Sami Habib," Rogers announced loud enough that his voice bounced off the nearby hospital building.

"You wanted answers. Don't blame me if you don't like most of them, but here you go," I told the Rogers as we watched two of his agents load a convincingly startled Brian Hollis into one of their SUVs and drive away.

"What do you mean by that?" Rogers demanded.

"Brian isn't your suspect," I let him know. "Dan Logan has been running this thing all along, and he is already on his way out of the country. Brian can tell you everything."

SAC Rogers gave me an angry look, and for a moment I thought he might arrest me as well. He relented once he grasped the opportunities for making his mishandling of everything look a lot better by shifting the blame from Brian to a known member of organized crime.

Dudiyn Alekhin would not make an appearance at the museum on Tuesday as I had suggested. I never believed there was any chance that he would do so even as I sold the idea to Daniel Logan over lunch. Alekhin would not want to get his name or face in the news. Logan, on the other hand, clearly saw the many things to be gained by returning the container and implicating Alekhin in the caliphate's plan to hijack the container. Alekhin was a known arms dealer and black marketeer. Arresting him would absolve the Habib family of any blame or suspicion and provide the Iraqis with an ideal defendant for their kangaroo court. This was going to outrage Alekhin and narrow his rage over losing the container to only Daniel Logan.

Wanting Logan dead might become the only thing that Alekhin and I would ever agree upon. It was my worth everything I had gone through to have found a way to eliminate the attorney who tried to kill me without pulling the trigger myself.

Fifty

My phone call disturbed Ralph Easter on his day off. Doing so stressed the urgent nature of my reaching out to him, but it also irritated Ralph immensely.

"What do you want that can't wait until tomorrow morning?" Ralph demanded. I heard feminine voices in the background. I thought I might have interrupted his brunch date. He softened his tone and asked how my trip had gone.

"Not so good," I informed him. "My car died."

"Your car died?" Ralph sounded properly saddened.

"Well, it was blown up is a more accurate way to describe the demise," I eased into what I called to discuss with him.

"Details to follow?" Ralph tried to joke.

"I need you to make a phone call or have someone else make a phone call if it is not the sort of thing you do. I still don't really know what your job is," I digressed. "Inform Rashid Habib that his oldest son is dead, and that there are no remains to repatriate. Sami died in a bomb blast last night and there was nothing to scoop up but charred teeth."

"That is going to send him through the roof. You know that, right?" Ralph said in an unamused voice. His Sunday was ruined.

"I know he is going to look for someone to blame," I assured him.

"And who should I tell him is responsible?" Ralph snapped. "If it is you then get this over with quick and shoot yourself. State cannot object to your extradition if you were at all involved in Sami Habib's death."

"I am not responsible for the bomb that killed Sami, nor for his death," I parsed my words. I was undeniably guilty of having placed him on the pathway to death. "Sami believed he had recovered the missing container. It was a fake and someone had booby trapped it to explode when the doors were opened. They used thermite to make sure there were no identifiable remains, and they packed the container with way more than they needed to. Sami was standing right behind the container when one of his men opened it up."

"My god," Ralph muttered. It was a disturbing image to describe. I could only imagine how it projected in Ralph's imagination.

"The FBI will have photographs and statements later today which will prove Daniel Logan's responsibility for Sami Habib's homicide. It is a small coincidence that Daniel Logan will arrive in Bagdad on Tuesday to take credit for recovering the container that Brian Hollis is in the process of telling the FBI that Daniel Logan blackmailed him into stealing," I told Ralph. I am only opposed to being lied to. I have no trouble lying to achieve my own ends. "SAC Rogers is about to understand that this is his best way to solve his problem prosecuting the murder in the States."

"That should take the heat off your classmates, and off the State Department to do something," Ralph said. I could hear the relief in his voice.

"The container will be delivered to the national museum on Tuesday morning, along with every other container the museum is presently storing on Peter Yoder's lot. I tipped Logan off to the delivery and I suspect he will want to be there to take credit for the container's safe return. He will probably spin some tale about negotiating for its safe return to the Iraqi Ruling Council and expect them to reward him very handsomely for his efforts."

"And you want him drawn and quartered instead," Ralph said. He could finally laugh at something I said.

"Nothing less," I candidly admitted. "While we are on the subject of meting out justice, I have a tip for you that may earn you some points with your boss. I started a rumor that the container will be coming to Baghdad out of Mosul. I am pretty sure the caliphate will take a run at it. SOCOM's intelligence guys should have no trouble spotting the ambush if they want to do a little interdiction."

"I will pass along both of those bits of news. Enjoy the rest of your day," Ralph promised, with a touch of joy in his voice before he hung up on me.

Tuesday

June 29, 2010

There is nothing better than a friend,

unless it is a friend with chocolate.

-   Linda Grayson

Fifty-One

Roux and I were enjoying a closing nightcap, my cocktail involved bourbon and Roux drank soda water, at Strada's bar late Tuesday evening when Ralph Easter came through the open double doors and took a seat next to me. Jason deposited a bottle of Heineken on the counter before Ralph had even sat down. I had spent the entire day watching the news in anticipation of reports about the safe return of a container filled with a fortune in recovered antiquities to the Iraqi National Museum. It was too much to hope for CNN to break into their normal broadcast with a story about an American attorney being arrested for the murder of an Iraqi bureaucrat's son.

"Quiet news day," I commented.

"Only on this side of the Atlantic," Ralph said and shook his head. "I only just now got to leave my office."

"Do tell," I begged him. He laughed at my eagerness.

"You were right. Logan showed up at the museum expecting to walk into a press conference. Rashid Habib personally took him into custody for murdering his son. The news came as quite a surprise to Logan, but Rashid expected him to try to deny any involvement. SOCOM also wiped thirty players off the caliphate's team. It is too early to tell if they killed anyone significant. Hellfire missiles tend to make a mess of things.

"Tough day for the bad guys," I smiled and tapped my highball glass against his beer bottle.

"Did you at least learn a lesson from this escapade?" Ralph asked rather pointedly. He had instructed me not to get involved, and I had ignored what proved to be very solid advice.

"Just that even a dog can shake hands," I replied and patted Roux's head. "It turns out I have three fewer friends than I thought I did a week ago."

"Sorry to hear that, but don't be too quick to write them off," Ralph said with what seemed like genuine empathy before he turned the conversation back to the topic at hand. "The FBI informed the Iraqis that Logan was behind the theft of the container just before he showed up with it. I doubt his claim that he was framed will work in their courts."

"The FBI SAC in Kansas City must have found a silver lining in the cloud I left him under. The whole thing went down in a rural county and the sheriff there has no idea what he was part of, so don't ruin his day by letting him know how badly he was used if you guys start thanking people," I requested.

"I do my best to avoid knowing the details about what you get yourself mixed up in myself," Ralph grumbled.

"I had to wait, but Logan will get what he is due for shooting me," I said.

"You needed to let that go," Ralph advised me. Everyone I knew had advised me to do the same thing, but none of them smiled this smugly when they did so. "I have a present for you."

"What for?" I asked him.

"Call it a peace offering," he suggested with a slight grin and slid the manila envelope he pulled from his jacket pocket across the bar to place it in front of me.

"Who from?" I muttered as I opened the lumpy envelope.

"Just say thank you," Ralph said and stood up.

I emptied the envelope on the bar top and immediately grabbed one of two shiny fobs bearing the Cadillac emblem. The paperwork was the automobile's registration.

"You're kidding me, right?" I refused to believe in my good fortune.

"This is one of those times it is best not to look a gift horse in the mouth. It turns out the Iraqis were offering a huge reward for the return of the container. We let them know you were instrumental in its safe return, and in delivering Daniel Logan to be punished for Sami's death," Ralph informed me.

"They bought me a new car?" I asked in no small wonder. These same people wanted to put me on trial barely a week earlier. My how times change.

"Not exactly," Ralph shrugged. "We suggested the Iraqis use the reward they were offering for the return of the trailer to ransom Rashid Habib's family. That bought you the closing of their investigation into your shenanigans with Tony."

"Then who bought the car?" I asked as I followed him to the valet stand.

"Logan is not the only one who feels guilty about how things turned out," he continued to refuse to give me a name, but this clue answered my question.

A freshly polished 2010 Cadillac XLR-V was parked at the curb. The sleek coupe was painted in a tone of black so dark that it almost disappeared in the shadows of the lower French Quarter. Even the light pouring through the plate glass windows of the restaurant could not properly illuminate the coupe. The top was down, and I could smell the new car odor of the black leather interior. My delight in having a new coupe made me forget for just a moment what it took to earn it. I still missed my original XLR, but my mourning period was officially over.

"Drive it in good health," Ralph said and patted my shoulder. "Just please don't drive this one into any more trouble, alright?"

"No promises on that," I laughed and paused to inspect the new model's menacing wire mesh grille that replaced the open slats on my trashed four-year-old XLR before I took a seat behind the wheel. The thick leather seats were as comfortable as I remembered the well-worn ones in what I was already thinking of as being my old car. Ralph and I shared a boyish grin when I pumped the gas pedal to hear the mighty supercharged V-8 NorthStar engine roar to life.

"You can give me a ride to the airport in the morning," Ralph suggested. "My presence is required in Washington D.C. Maybe I will get a new car, too."

"At least you aren't likely to get fired," I pointed out.

"It's Washington. Anything can happen," Ralph smiled ruefully. I wondered if he shared my fear that his handling of Sami's death and the return of the missing container might earn him a new posting.

"What time is your flight?" I gamely offered.

"I'll take a cab. You deserve to enjoy your new toy," Ralph said and shook my hand. He walked away rather than return to the bar with me.

I wanted to take the coupe for a spin but drove it only as far as our garage. I would not be able to enjoy it until I had the vehicle scoured for any tracking or other surveillance tech that Hank may have instructed D-Tech to install before Ralph delivered it to me. I was in no mood to forgive my classmates, but they were making a good first step in apologizing.

Cadillac Holland Mysteries

Blowback

Blue Garou

Can't Stop the Funk

Ghosts and Shadows

Parish the Thought

Everybody Pays

Shell Game

www.ingramcontent.com/pod-product-compliance
Lightning Source LLC
Chambersburg PA
CBHW061057100726
47911CB00012B/267